Praise for Irresistible Cozy Mysteries

FIVE FURRY FAMILIARS
"A fun read for those who enjoy tales of witches and magic."
—*Kirkus Reviews*

THREE TAINTED TEAS
"A kitchen witch reluctantly takes over as planner for a cursed wedding... This witchy tale is a hoot."
—*Kirkus Reviews*

ONE POISON PIE
"*One Poison Pie* deliciously blends charm and magic with a dash of mystery and a sprinkle of romance. Mia Malone is a zesty protagonist who relies on her wits to solve the crime, and the enchanting cast of characters that populate Magic Springs are a delight."
—Daryl Wood Gerber, Agatha Award winner and nationally best-selling author of the Cookbook Nook Mysteries and Fairy Garden Mysteries

"A witchy cooking cozy for fans of the supernatural and good eating."
—*Kirkus Reviews*

A FIELD GUIDE TO HOMICIDE
"The best entry in this character-driven series mixes a well-plotted mystery with a romance that rings true to life."
—*Kirkus Reviews*

"Informative as well as entertaining, *A Field Guide to Homicide* is the perfect book for cozy mystery lovers who entertain thoughts of writing novels themselves... This is, without a doubt, one of the best Cat Latimer novels to date."
—*Criminal Element*

"Cat is a great heroine with a lot of spirit that readers will enjoy solving the mystery (with)."
—*Parkersburg News & Sentinel*

SCONED TO DEATH
"The most intriguing aspect of this story is the writers' retreat itself. Although the writers themselves are not suspect, they add freshness and new relationships to the series. Fans of Lucy Arlington's 'Novel Idea' mysteries may want to enter the writing world from another angle."
—*Library Journal*

OF MURDER AND MEN
"A Colorado widow discovers that everything she knew about her husband's death is wrong… Interesting plot and quirky characters."
—*Kirkus Reviews*

A STORY TO KILL
"Well-crafted… Cat and crew prove to be engaging characters and Cahoon does a stellar job of keeping them—and the reader—guessing."
—*Mystery Scene*

"Lynn Cahoon has hit the golden trifecta—Murder, intrigue, and a really hot handyman. Better get your flashlight handy, *A Story to Kill* will keep you reading all night."
—Laura Bradford, author of the Amish Mysteries

TOURIST TRAP MYSTERIES
"Lynn Cahoon's popular Tourist Trap series is set all around the charming coastal town of South Cove, California, but the heroine Jill Gardner owns a delightful bookstore/coffee shop so a lot of the scenes take place there. This is one of my go-to cozy mystery series, bookish or not, and I'm always eager to get my hands on the next book!"
—*Hope By the Book*

"Murder, dirty politics, pirate lore, and a hot police detective: *Guidebook to Murder* has it all! A cozy lover's dream come true."
—Susan McBride, author of the Debutante Dropout Mysteries

"This was a good read and I love the author's style, which was warm and friendly… I can't wait to read the next book in this wonderfully appealing series."
—*Dru's Book Musings*

"I am happy to admit that some of my expectations were met while other aspects of the story exceeded my own imagination… This mystery novel was light, fun, and kept me thoroughly engaged. I only wish it was longer."
—*The Young Folks*

"*If the Shoe Kills* is entertaining and I would be happy to visit Jill and the residents of South Cove again."
—*MysteryPlease.com*

"In *If the Shoe Kills,* author Lynn Cahoon gave me exactly what I wanted. She crafted a well told small town murder that kept me guessing who the murderer was until the end. I will definitely have to take a trip back to South Cove and maybe even visit tales of Jill Gardner's past in the previous two Tourist Trap Mystery books. I do love a holiday mystery! And with this book, so will you."
—*ArtBooksCoffee.com*

"I would recommend *If the Shoe Kills* if you are looking for a well written cozy mystery."
—*Mysteries, Etc.*

"This novella is short and easily read in an hour or two with interesting angst and dynamics between mothers and daughters and mothers and sons… I enjoyed the first-person narrative."
—*Kings River Life Magazine* on *Mother's Day Mayhem*

Books by Lynn Cahoon

The Tourist Trap Mystery Series
Guidebook to Murder * Mission to Murder * If the Shoe Kills * Dressed to Kill * Killer Run * Murder on Wheels * Tea Cups and Carnage * Hospitality and Homicide * Killer Party * Memories and Murder * Murder in Waiting * Picture Perfect Frame * Wedding Bell Blues * A Vacation to Die For * Songs of Wine and Murder * Olive You to Death * Vows of Murder * Merry Murder Season
Novellas
Rockets' Dead Glare * A Deadly Brew * Santa Puppy * Corned Beef and Casualties * Mother's Day Mayhem * A Very Mummy Holiday * Murder in a Tourist Town

The Kitchen Witch Mystery Series
One Poison Pie * Two Wicked Desserts * Three Tainted Teas * Four Charming Spells * Five Furry Familiars * Six Stunning Sirens * Seven Secret Spellcasters
Novellas
Chili Cauldron Curse * Murder 101 * Have a Holly, Haunted Christmas * Two Christmas Mittens

The Cat Latimer Mystery Series
A Story to Kill * Fatality by Firelight * Of Murder and Men * Slay in Character * Sconed to Death * A Field Guide to Homicide

The Farm-to-Fork Mystery Series
Who Moved My Goat Cheese? * Killer Green Tomatoes * One Potato, Two Potato, Dead * Deep Fried Revenge * Killer Comfort Food * A Fatal Family Feast
Novellas
Have a Deadly New Year * Penned In * A Pumpkin Spice Killing * A Basketful of Murder

The Survivors' Book Club Mystery Series
Tuesday Night Survivors' Club * Secrets in the Stacks * Death in the Romance Aisle * Reading Between the Lies * Dying to Read

The Bainbridge Island Mystery Series
An Amateur Sleuth's Guide to Murder

MERRY MURDER SEASON

A Tourist Trap Mystery

Lynn Cahoon

LYRICAL UNDERGROUND
Kensington Publishing Corp.
www.kensingtonbooks.com

KENSINGTON BOOKS are published by
Kensington Publishing Corp.
900 Third Avenue, 26th Floor
New York, NY 10022

Copyright © 2025 Lynn Cahoon

All rights reserved. No part of this book may be reproduced in any form or by any means without the prior written consent of the Publisher, excepting brief quotes used in reviews.

Without limiting the author's and publisher's exclusive rights, any unauthorized use of this publication to train generative artificial intelligence (AI) technologies is expressly prohibited.

This book is a work of fiction. Names, characters, businesses, organizations, places, events, and incidents either are the product of the author's imagination or are used fictitiously. Any resemblance to actual persons, living or dead, events, or locales is entirely coincidental.

To the extent that the image or images on the cover of this book depict a person or persons, such person or persons are merely models, and are not intended to portray any character or characters featured in the book.

Special book excerpts or customized printings can also be created to fit specific needs. For details, write or phone the office of the Kensington Sales Manager: Kensington Publishing Corp., 900 Third Avenue, New York, NY 10022. Attn. Sales Department Phone: 1-800-221-2647.

The K with book logo Reg. U.S. Pat. & TM Off

First Electronic Edition: November 2025
ISBN: 978-1-5161-1176-3 (ebook)

First Print Edition: November 2025
ISBN: 978-1-5161-1177-0

The authorized representative in the EU for product safety and compliance
Is eucomply OU, Parnu mnt 139b-14, Apt 123
Tallinn, Berlin 11317, hello@eucompliancepartner.com

153060870

To the Browns, thank you for teaching me the reason for the season.

CHAPTER 1

As I watched the angry faces gathered around the tables in Coffee, Books, and More, my coffee shop and bookstore, I regretted signing a new ten-year contract to host and sponsor the business-to-business meetings here. Usually, the meetings went smoothly. Darla Taylor, owner of South Cove Winery, ran the meetings with an iron fist. Since it was the holidays, you would think that everyone would be in a festive mood. But there was no peace on earth, goodwill to men—I mean, personkind—feeling today.

No, Mayor Baylor had showed up to press the flesh because there was an election coming soon. The mayor typically only showed up around election time. He and his wife, Tina, didn't care about helping to run the huge Christmas craft bazaar scheduled in a few weeks or hiring enough elves for Santa's Village. The local power couple just wanted the votes to keep the smarmy Mayor Baylor in office. And the mayor had news for the group.

I'd broken the news last year that the mayor's office had planned to close Main Street for the holiday season, but, like all things that we don't want to deal with, people had already forgotten the warning. So, no one had petitioned the city council to rethink their idea.

No one except for one business that didn't even attend the monthly business-to-business meetings. Chip's Bar had asked for an exemption for motorcycles to use the street during the closure. With Diamond Lille's owner, Lille Stanley, voicing her support, the council's decision to grant the exception had been made back in August.

On Thanksgiving morning, only two days away, the barriers would go up, and cars and trucks would be banned from nine a.m. to midnight. Then the street would reopen to vehicles, allowing businesses to restock. Most of the businesses, like mine, had an alley behind our shops for deliveries anyway.

Darla banged the gavel on the lectern. "Folks, you knew this was coming. If it doesn't work, I'm sure the mayor and city council will be glad to discuss next year's plan."

Josh Thomas stood. "No one told us that there could be exceptions. My delivery truck needs to be loaded and unloaded in front of the store. What am I supposed to do? Unload in the dark?"

"There are streetlights…" Mayor Baylor interrupted what we all knew would be a long tirade from Josh. He was notorious for them, even when he was wrong. I thought this time, the antique dealer might just have a point. Instead of Josh continuing, another voice interrupted the mayor.

"And why are motorcycles allowed on the street? Those things are death traps. And they're so loud. If you're allowing motorcycles, you should just reverse the entire thing," Matty Leaven pointed out. She owned a jewelry store in town. Since she'd joined our business council, she always seemed to take Josh's side in discussions. "Maybe there needs to be new blood in City Hall. People who stand for the little guy."

Josh looked at Matty like she'd just won a Nobel Prize for standing with him. He wasn't used to someone agreeing with his ideas. Mandy, his wife, who came into my shop a lot for coffee, often laughed about Josh's infatuation with the jewelry designer. I thought he was playing with fire.

"Hold up, folks. This isn't about the upcoming election. We are a bipartisan group and our mandate doesn't allow electioneering during the meeting." Darla met my gaze and rolled her eyes. "Anyway, if we could get back on the subject, Main Street is closing. Any further comments can go to the mayor's office or any member of our city council. Their names and email addresses are on the city website. We'll talk more about the holiday festival next meeting, but Jill wanted to bring up our annual charity event. This year, we're partnering with Chip's Bar for a dart tournament to be held in the community center. The entry fee will be cash and a new toy, which will be donated to the California Central Coast Family Project for kids that won't be on Santa's delivery route this year. Jill, do you want to give us the details?"

I stood up, my list of talking points at the ready. None of them dealt with the closed road or the motorcycle exemption. I introduced myself, even though most of the people knew me. "Thanks, Darla. I'm Jill Gardner, I mean, Jill King. I own the coffee shop/bookstore you're sitting in and I'm your council liaison for the next ten years. Wow, that sounds like a long time. Anyway, I wanted to let you know that the dart tournament is also being sponsored by Coffee, Books, and More and is the brainchild of Chris Aquilla and Carrie Jones. It was at Carrie's suggestion that we started the book club last year."

I could see people starting to put their notes away. I was talking too much and needed to get to the point, quickly. Chris was digging in her bag, trying not to make eye contact with me for fear I'd ask her a question.

"Anyway, the fundraiser for CCCFP is this Friday night, sponsored by Chip's. The entry fee is ten dollars, and the bar is kicking in the money for the players' winnings so every dollar from entries goes to the charity. They're also kicking in fifty percent of that night's profits." I handed out flyers. "Please have these available for people to take. I believe Chris and Carrie have already stopped by your businesses to give you a stash, but just in case you've already handed those out, here's more. Both Greg and I are playing, and I hope to see the rest of you there as well."

"It's Thanksgiving weekend. We might have family at the house," a woman on my right side mumbled. She probably didn't think I'd heard, but I had.

"Bring them along! We have family in town as well. The more, the merrier." I pasted a smile on my face, hoping it didn't look as fake as it felt. Greg didn't want to go. He worried that the presence of law enforcement might dampen the celebratory mood. He also didn't want to go out when his family would be in town. I was hoping they'd tag along at least for the charity part of the night. The charity event hadn't been my idea, but I was supporting it like it had been. Besides, it was for the kids.

"Matt and I are coming too, but if you already have plans that night"— Darla looked pointedly at Marvin and Tina Baylor—"just drop a donation check off with Amy Newman-Cole at City Hall or before you leave here. We don't want any child to go without a Merry Christmas."

Josh glowered at Darla but didn't object. I knew that Mandy had already committed to coming on Friday night, so he couldn't say anything against the event. But I could tell he wanted to.

Darla ended the meeting and everyone scattered before Mayor Baylor could corner them. Tina had reached the exit first, blocking it and handing out *Baylor for Mayor* buttons as people left. I noticed that Matty Leaven snuck out while Tina was handing a button to another person. The girl was smart, that was for sure.

After everyone was gone, I moved tables back in order with the help of my barista on deck, Deek Kerr. He seemed quiet, distracted, and not his usual chatty self. Deek was a writer, so it wasn't unusual for him to be in his own world. I took his rag away when he'd cleaned the same spot for the last few minutes. "What's got you all up in your head? Plotting another book?"

He glanced toward the door. Everyone had left the coffee shop, and it was just the two of us. "I'm not thinking about a book. What do you think about Matty Leaven?"

"I don't know her very well. She seems to think like Josh a lot, though." I wiped the last table and went to the sink to rinse the rag. "Why?"

"I can't figure out her aura. It changes colors based on what she's saying. I don't think she agrees with Josh. I think she likes stirring up trouble." He poured himself a cup of coffee after following me to the coffee bar. "I'm probably just overanalyzing the situation."

"I don't like her at all," Tilly North, my newest barista, chimed in as she filled the treat display case. "She's nice to your face, then I overhear her saying mean things about people, like Josh and Mandy. She says awful things about Josh all the time to her friends while they're getting coffee. She's one of those people who thinks baristas or whoever is serving her are completely invisible. I worked with people like that when I was at the hospital. They think you can't hear them when they're talking right outside your room."

Tilly had been in a car accident and suffered a brain injury. She'd lost many of her long-term memories, like the fact that she and Toby Killian, another one of my baristas and one of Greg's deputies, had dated in high school. When she'd come to work for me, she'd been dating someone new. Now, that relationship was over, but Tilly had stayed in the area. She was a great addition to the bookstore team. And usually very perceptive about people.

"I'll watch her more carefully." I hoped that Josh wouldn't figure out that Matty was messing with him. He had enough self-esteem issues. He didn't need to know that Matty didn't like him. I poured myself a fresh cup of coffee. I had back-of-the-house tasks to do, namely accounting and scheduling, since Evie was in the city visiting her cousin, Sasha, and her daughter this week for the Thanksgiving holiday.

Toby had also dated Sasha. The boy sure did get around. It was a small town. We had connections all over the place.

"Just be careful around her, Jill." Deek was staring out the window again. "I have a feeling. And it's not good."

Now I was worried. Deek Kerr liked everyone. He could read auras, or at least he thought he could. Sometimes he told me things that, when I looked them up, didn't match the aura lore published on the internet. But when you're talking about magic and seeing things that aren't there, maybe the internet didn't have all the information. Deek was a good guy and he saw people clearly, which made him an excellent barista and bookseller.

I decided to change the subject. "Are you coming to Thanksgiving at the house? I haven't heard from either of you."

"Mom's out of town, so I thought I'd just hang at the house." Deek moved back behind the coffee bar. "I'll grab the boxes of books that need to be shelved."

"Deek Kerr, you stay right there." I didn't use my boss voice often but this was going to be one of those times. When he froze and turned to me, I continued. "There is no way you're not coming for dinner now that I know your mom's not going to be home. So what are you bringing?"

"Jill, it's your first family dinner since you've been married. You don't need strays hanging around." He blushed as he glanced over at Tilly, who now had her hands on her hips.

"Oh, so you don't think I should go, either?" she challenged him. "I don't appreciate being called a stray."

"I didn't say that." Deek stumbled over his words. Finally, he let his shoulders drop. "Look, I don't want you to invite me because I'm some loser who doesn't have family for Thanksgiving. Mom's just not into those traditions, so she's going on a cruise. I'm used to this."

"Which is why you're coming. My family isn't just those people who are related to Greg or me. You should know that by now. I won't have you sitting around the apartment eating ramen while we're having a turkey dinner. Besides, I think Harrold is bringing Lille, so I'll need some of my people to watch my back."

Lille Stanley, the owner of Diamond Lille's, was one of my Uncle Harrold's favorite people. Lille liked Greg and my Aunt Jackie too. She just hated me. Thanksgiving dinner should be fun. Not.

I'd say Lille would have Jim to chat with since he used to hate me too, but since he started dating Beth, he'd been more open to my presence. Besides, since Greg and I were married now, Greg's first wife Sherry was out of the picture.

"She hates you? How can anyone hate you?" Tilly's eyes widened. She was such a nice young woman, she didn't understand the concept. "Well, I'll be there to watch your back. I don't have the money to visit my folks now that they've moved to Tennessee. I don't want to be in the house all by myself. I love the holidays. Mom left me all the old Christmas decorations, so I've been working on getting the house looking like Santa's workshop for weeks."

"My mom never decorated," Deek admitted. "I hated the holidays growing up because we were always the one family who didn't have a tree or lights on the house."

"Well, Greg is going to get everyone to help string lights outside the house and we'll be decorating the tree after dinner. It's one of the King family traditions." I was looking forward to celebrating Thanksgiving this year. "Aunt Jackie and Harrold are leaving for a cruise on Friday. So you won't see her for two weeks if you don't come."

Deek stared at me. "I thought you wanted me to come."

"Stop it." I started laughing. "You love Aunt Jackie. I know you do."

"Did I tell you she updated my author questionnaire last week for people who want to schedule book events here? She thinks we should charge an event fee if they don't hit a certain amount of sales." Deek threw a clean towel over his shoulder as he talked.

I groaned. Aunt Jackie had been harping on that for a while. And she hated the Cove Connection book club. She thought that members should be required to buy the book from the store to participate. I didn't care where they bought or borrowed the book from, I just wanted people to be reading more. Besides, we worked closely with our local library on author events. "I'll talk to her. Just file away the changed copy and don't make any drastic movements. We're doing fine financially on author events overall. Some are just more popular than others. Everyone needs a shot in the arm every once in a while."

"Thanks. I'd rather not tell my newly published authors I don't think they're big enough to bother with." Deek nodded to the back door. "Am I excused? Those books aren't going to shelve themselves."

"Are you coming to Thanksgiving?" I stared him down.

He blinked first. "I'll bring focaccia bread. I've been working on my recipe."

Tilly watched him head to the back room. "He reads, he's cute, and he bakes? How on earth is he still single?"

From the look in Tilly's eyes, Deek might not be that way for long.

* * *

Greg came into the shop just before my shift ended at eleven. "Do you have time for lunch at Diamond Lille's?"

"I'd love to." I nodded to Deek. "You have the helm, good sir."

Deek laughed and pointed at Tilly. "This one thinks she's in charge. If I didn't know better, I would think I was still working with your aunt. Tilly loves the checklists."

Tilly playfully slapped his arm. "There's nothing wrong with a little organization now and then. With the sieve of my brain, writing things down is the only way I know I'll remember to do something. Oh, I forgot to tell you, I'm going to bring pumpkin cheesecake if that's okay."

I was a little thrown by the change of subject, but Tilly's mind just worked like that. And anything she thought came out of her mouth. Mostly. "Sounds great. I'll see you both on Thursday. Call if you need anything."

As Greg and I started down the street toward Diamond Lille's, he glanced back at the bookstore. "Are both of them coming to Thanksgiving?"

"Yes. Judith is going out of town. Toby, of course, will be there and Evie's already gone to see Sasha." I ticked off my staff members on my fingers as I listed them. "Anyone from City Hall?"

"Your friends Amy and Justin are heading to see his folks. Esmeralda is going to New Orleans to be with her family. And the rest of them are otherwise committed. I'd hoped that Tim and Dona might come and bring the baby, but they're going to her parents' place in Sacramento." He nodded to the antique store. "Josh and Mandy are going to her family's farm. He's not looking forward to it."

"He hates being around people." I knew there was more to the story, but at least Josh was trying to forgive Mandy's family for a few things that had happened before they were married.

"I should tell you that Jim and Beth are fighting. Mom called this morning to warn me." He checked the road, then we jaywalked across the street to the restaurant. It was good being married to the head detective, although jaywalking was about all Greg did to skirt the law. He was a rule follower.

"Oh no. What did he do now?" I liked Beth. Probably a lot more than I liked Greg's brother Jim.

"He's being a pill about her working once they're married. She's standing up for herself. Mom thinks it will blow over, but they may not want to go to this fundraiser thing on Friday. You know Jim and bars. Or she might want to go and he would want me to stay behind with him." He held the door open for me. "I might just offer to take Mom and them to dinner while you do this. I'll give you a check for the entrance fees we aren't paying."

"No way. You and your family are coming. I've already bought the toys to get us inside." I was going to say more, but then Lille walked up to seat us.

"Hi, Greg. I've got a booth just for you." She smiled at my husband, grabbed two menus, and walked us to the table. "Carrie will be right with you."

Then she disappeared without even looking at me.

Rolling my eyes, I slipped onto the red leather bench. I held up the menu to see what I'd read at least once a week for years. "Some things never change. I'm so glad she's coming for our family dinner on Thursday."

"Jill, I'm sure it will be fine. She was probably just—" Greg's phone rang. From the ringtone, I could tell it was his brother, Jim. "Look, I need to take this. I'll try to keep it short."

He walked out of the restaurant. I could see him pacing as he talked to his brother.

I had a bad feeling that Beth wasn't going to make it for dinner on Thursday.

CHAPTER 2

Once at home, I reviewed my plan for the holiday weekend. I'd taken Wednesday off to get ready for the big dinner. I needed to clean the house as well as start some of the food prep. According to Greg, Jim, Beth, and his mom should arrive later tonight. They had rented a house for the week down Highway One. Beth had told me she was spending as much time as possible on the beach between the time they landed at LAX to the time they climbed back on the plane. I wondered if Beth would end up living nearby with or without Greg's brother. The phone call had only been to update Greg on their flights.

First up, I wanted to make pies. I didn't need to make a lot, but I wanted to have leftovers after we packed everyone up on Thursday after the big meal. And there was nothing like pumpkin pie with whipped cream for breakfast.

Emma whined, staring at her leash. I already had the cookbook out on the kitchen table, waiting. "You want to go running?"

The joy in her bark was too much for me to tell her no. Besides, if I ran, I'd have more calories available for pie later. It had to work that way, right?

I went upstairs and changed from my work outfit to running clothes. Then I'd change into bum-around clothes when we got back. I just hoped we wouldn't get an invite for dinner tonight, which would mean another outfit for the day. Seriously, I wasn't that much of a girly girl.

Emma and I headed down to the beach. Esmeralda stood outside her house, packing a suitcase into her car. We crossed the street to see her. "Hey, I heard you were heading to New Orleans. We'll miss you at the table."

"I'm heading home to cornbread and oyster stuffing and pecan pie." Esmeralda closed her car door. "It's funny, you don't think about home until the holidays get close. Then all you can think about is the food. Nic's place will be filled between his sister's friends and strays and his own. That family tends to collect people, like you do."

"I don't…" I started thinking about Deek and Tilly coming to dinner. "Okay, I'll give you that one. But I can't deal with people being alone on Thanksgiving. Besides, we'll have way too much food."

"Well, I appreciate you taking care of my godson. I invited him to come with me, but he turned me down. I swear Rory never got the importance of holidays and home. When Deek finally does marry, he'll be living in that house on the corner that has way too many lights and a small town of inflatable cartoon characters on the lawn."

"I love that image of him." I laughed at the visual. "You're probably right. Anything you need me to do?"

"Deek's babysitting Precious and will be staying here, so I'm good." She leaned in to hug me. "Have a wonderful Thanksgiving, Mrs. King. I'll see you next week."

Then she froze, staring at me. Her hands gripped tighter on my arms.

"Esmeralda? You better get going if you're going to make your plane." I didn't like the look in her eyes. I'd seen that look before. Esmeralda was not only the town's primary dispatcher for the police and fire department, but she was also a fortune-teller or psychic. Maybe medium would be a better title. She'd found her talent in the streets of New Orleans as an orphan. Now, she saw clients in her home and had a strong business of repeat customers.

She also said I had a bit of the sight as well. A talent I'd never seen in myself.

The freaky thing was, Esmeralda's predictions were often right.

Her friend, Rory Kerr, Deek's mom, had her own fortune-telling shop in Bakerstown. And Deek saw auras. Most of my friends were normal. Esmeralda and Deek were just a little more on the woo-woo side of the scale.

She blinked several times, then dropped her hands to her sides. "Jill, I need to tell you something, so don't freak out."

"When do I ever freak out?" I asked. I didn't like where this was going.

"You're going to have to make a choice soon. It's going to be hard and you must make the right one." She bit her lip. "I hate it when the spirits don't give me what I need to make a clear statement. But if I get anything else, I'll call you. I promise."

A chill traveled down my bare arms and I didn't think it had been caused by the wind that whipped up at that moment. I heard Emma softly whine. "Tell me it's not Aunt Jackie."

Esmeralda took her keys out of her purse. "I'm sorry. I don't have any specifics—just this feeling. Please be careful over the next few days. I'll call when I get into New Orleans to check in."

I watched her drive away and wondered what the spirits had seen in my future. Emma nudged my leg and we headed down to the beach and our run. An activity that I hoped would clear my head of this nagging feeling Esmeralda had given me.

It could work.

* * *

Wednesday afternoon, the house sparkled, the laundry was almost done, and three pies sat on the counter, cooling. Emma had spent most of the sunny day outside sleeping on the back deck but now she stood at the screen door, smelling the baked goodness that filled the kitchen. There was nothing like baking a pie to make a house feel like a home.

Greg had gone to work this morning. I'd gotten a few calls from Tilly at the bookstore with questions. She hadn't wanted to bother Deek, who was writing before his afternoon shift. Besides, he wasn't upstairs in his apartment. I'd seen him walking down the street with his backpack and a duffel last night after he'd closed the shop. He was babysitting Esmeralda's cat and her ghost friends.

I'd been focused most of the day on clearing my to-do list. I had cleaned and changed the sheets in the guest bedroom, just in case. The in-laws, as I liked to call them, had arrived yesterday evening and had promptly invited us to dinner at the seafood restaurant on the highway for tonight. Which changed the timeline on my to-do list. But I'd gotten it all done.

Now I had a little time to read while I ran the good china through the dishwasher. Greg had power-washed both decks last weekend and several boxes of new outdoor lights sat on a table on the front deck.

Before collapsing on the couch, I let Emma inside and checked my list one more time. I was done. I pushed the pies away from the edge of the counter as I looked around my clean kitchen. The turkey thawed on the counter since it was still frozen after being in the fridge for two days.

My phone rang.

"Hi, Aunt Jackie." I sat down at the table, moving the book I'd been planning on reading closer. It could be a short call.

"I'm just checking in to see if there is anything you need me to do today." My aunt assumed I'd forgotten something. Sometimes she was right, so I let her go through her list.

"Floors, bathroom, kitchen, all cleaned," I said as she listed off all the areas that might need extra polish.

"What about the tree? Are you going fresh or artificial?"

"We've got a fake one this year. Greg and I agreed we'll have a real one on alternating years." I hadn't realized how stuck each of us had been in our traditions until we'd moved in together. And now that we were married, Greg voiced a stronger opinion about how we should decorate. He'd let me think I'd won the argument years ago until he was fully vested in the relationship. And he'd asked for me to buy whole milk instead of two percent. If these were the only compromises I needed to make, we'd be just fine.

"You don't have boxes in the living room, do you?" My aunt sounded horrified.

"No, they're still in the den. Don't worry so much. I've got it under control," I said as I glanced through my list one more time. My aunt made me second-guess myself.

"Okay, so you have appetizers to serve when people get there. And a pickle plate?"

"Chips, dips, bacon-wrapped water chestnuts, focaccia bread," I listed off. Then I realized what else she'd said. "What's a pickle plate?"

"Don't worry about it. I've made one and will bring it. It has pickles and olives. I'm bringing a crab dip and a few boxes of crackers as well. Are you serving wine with dinner? White and red?"

"Yes on the wine, but I only bought white," I said as I started writing things down for next year's list.

"I'll bring a couple of bottles of red." My aunt paused, then added, "Lille's bringing a date. So there will be one more person at the table."

"That's fine." I thought about the list of food I already had people bringing. "We should still have enough. Who's her date?"

"I have no idea." My aunt sniffed so loud I heard it over the phone. "I just hope he owns something besides worn out jeans and T-shirts to wear."

"We're not that fancy over here." I laughed as I imagined my aunt's look of horror. "Although I am dressing up for dinner tonight at SeaShore with

Greg's family. Seriously, who is Lille dating?" My aunt had to know since Lille would have told Harrold. And Harrold told Jackie everything.

"You'll find out tomorrow." My aunt always had the upper hand. "Go finish getting ready for the dinner. I'm sure there's something else on your list." Then she ended the call.

I glanced at the list and then at the book on the table. "Why, yes, Aunt Jackie, there is one last thing on my list. Reading until I have to get ready for dinner."

I grabbed the book and a cookie I'd brought home from the bookstore and headed to the couch with Emma in tow.

* * *

Thursday morning, I turned the alarm off and covered my head with a pillow, hoping to delay getting out of bed. For at least a day.

"We have people coming over. You need to get up," Greg's voice called from the doorway.

"Tell them I'm sick. Or the house burned down," I grumbled. I didn't want to go through another meal with Jim and Beth sniping at each other. My new mother-in-law, Amanda, had tried to mediate last night. Greg tried changing the subject. I just watched and ate. Two bread baskets. The crab dip appetizer. My fish entrée. Amanda had extended the suffering by ordering dessert and coffee for the table.

All the while Beth told stories about real women working while successfully raising children and managing a household—with a little help. Jim talked about men providing for their families by working, not doing laundry or changing diapers.

I was on Beth's side, but every time I said something, Jim and Greg glared at me. For different reasons, of course.

"I don't want to see anyone today. I did my share of peopling last night for the rest of the year," I said through the pillow. I felt Emma nudging my arm. Her nose was cold. "And we haven't even added Aunt Jackie and Lille to the mix yet. Thanksgiving dinner is going to be a disaster."

"No, it's not. I pulled Jim aside and threatened him with a night in jail if he didn't lighten up today. Mom's going to talk to Beth. All we need to do is feed nine people and then send them back to their corners. It will be fine." Greg always looked on the bright side. "Come on, get up and shower. I'll start breakfast."

"Ten. Ten people. Lille's bringing a date." I uncovered my head and climbed out of bed, hugging Emma before standing. I'd called my uncle for more information before we'd gone to dinner. "Dominic somebody."

"Dom Reedy. He's the head of the local motorcycle club. This will be interesting." Greg looked thoughtful.

"What? Is he a bad guy?" Now I was worried about my aunt. She never kept her mouth shut with anyone. If she angered the head of a motorcycle gang, I didn't know what would happen.

"There are rumors. But I've never arrested him for anything. So that's a plus." Greg grinned as I threw my body back down on the bed. "None of that. Get up and get ready. I'm making French toast and bacon. And we need to get the turkey in the oven soon. If we don't, we'll never get these people out of our house."

"As long as we're on the same page here." I stood and headed to the bathroom. Maybe my mood would improve if I washed away all of last night's bad energy. It was a new-age trick that Deek had taught me, but right now, I was willing to try anything.

What do you get when you mix a gangster, a cop, a grumpy aunt, a fighting couple, and the angst of a family holiday together?

I didn't know, but I was about to find out. And I didn't think it was a joke.

French toast and bacon soothed my ragged edges, as did a quick walk on the beach after the turkey had been stuffed and tucked into the oven. Greg stayed behind to make a salad while Emma and I met Beth on the beach.

I noticed dark circles shining under Beth's eyes as we took the stairs down to the beach. The waves were calm and the beach surprisingly empty, so I let Emma off her leash as we walked. After a few minutes of silence, I turned to my hopefully soon-to-be sister-in-law and said, "Okay, out with it. What's really going on? This can't be about working at the church office."

Beth's smile was tight. "You picked up on that. No, the job in question is one I've hoped for all my life. I've been offered a fellowship in Omaha's religious studies department. It's driving distance, and I'd only have to be at the university for three days to teach and I could do my research time then. I'd be writing my dissertation at home. And they'd pay me year-round." Beth's face filled with excitement as she talked. "And, if I do well, there's a chance at a full-time position, tenure track."

"That's wonderful. When do you start?" I knew Beth could do it. For her master's, she'd written a thesis that was now being considered for mainstream publication by several publishers. Her agent was hoping for a significant deal after it went to auction next month.

"And that's the problem. They want me to start at the first of the year. Jim's upset that it might interfere with the wedding this June. And he says I'll just quit after the wedding, anyway."

"He didn't say that." I knew Jim was conservative, but he knew who he'd fallen in love with. There was no way Beth wouldn't take this job and rock it.

"He did. Then he didn't know why I got mad at him. I told him last night I was taking the job and I was going to work after we got married." Beth picked up a shell and tucked it in her pocket.

"Good for you." I knew she'd win this argument. It was stupid to think she'd just stay home and, what, darn Jim's socks?

"I thought the matter was done, but then he opens his mouth again and gives me permission to work until the babies start coming." Beth rolled her eyes. "He. Gave. Me. Permission."

I didn't want to laugh, but it sounded like Jim. "I take it you're doing couples counseling before the wedding?"

"We can't agree on that either. He wants to use my current boss because he knows Reverend Black will side with him. I want to use an actual marriage counselor in town." She picked up another shell. "I feel like I'm choosing between being happily married and being a spinster with a house full of cats and a great job."

"He'll get past it." I wondered what Jim's first wife had done. Had she been the stay-at-home wife? They hadn't had time for kids before she died. "And cats aren't so bad."

"I'm not sure that's true." Beth turned around and we headed back to the parking lot. "Jim, not the cats. You're lucky Greg's more open-minded. Amanda is ready to throttle Jim."

"It should make our first King Thanksgiving pretty interesting though." I bumped her with my shoulder. "I'm so proud of you. The only thing that would make this better is if the offer was here in California, near me."

When we got back to the house, we had more visitors. The nice thing about a California Thanksgiving was that if the weather held, you could have everyone outside, enjoying the sun. Greg had people in lawn chairs in the backyard. Deek was running around getting people drinks. And Emma was lying on the deck, watching people invade her territory.

From my count, we were an hour away from serving dinner and we were only missing two people.

A motorcycle raced up the street and then parked in our driveway. Lille and Dominic had arrived. Greg met my gaze.

Now the party could start.

CHAPTER 3

Dominic had not been what I'd expected. He dressed in a black button-down with black jeans. His dark hair was pushed back away from a face that would make any woman swoon, with sparkling blue eyes and a dimple that showed in his five o'clock shadow when he smiled. He brought me flowers and asked me to call him Dom. He chatted with Aunt Jackie and Harrold about traveling in Italy and the best places to avoid the tourists. He talked about literature, including Shakespeare and the classics, with Deek and Tilly.

He was the perfect dinner guest.

Until, to Lille's and Jim's dismay, Dom took a strong interest in Beth's cult project. They talked long after the coffee and pie had been served. I'd pulled a chair close by, too, interested in the development of the book and what Beth had found since she'd last been in South Cove.

When dinner was over and most of the guests, including Dom and Lille, had left, Dom had charmed almost everyone in the house. Except, I noticed, Greg. He and Jim were hanging out on the side of the yard talking. Probably about Beth's unreasonable demands for an actual life after they were married. Lille had hung by Dom's side most of the day, except when he approached me to help get food on the table and later to clear the plates so we could stuff dessert into our already full bellies.

Deek was helping in the kitchen, filling the dishwasher while I tried to find room in the fridge for the leftovers. "Dom's not exactly what I expected. I've heard stories about Lille's boyfriend, but this guy is a dark romance hero just waiting to be redeemed by the virtuous heroine. I'm kind of in love with him too." He grinned at me. "In a totally non-sexual bromance way."

"He is different than what I expected," I said as I moved the olive jars to the back and pushed the plastic tub of mashed potatoes onto the shelf. Greg's family was coming for dinner tomorrow night before we went to Chip's Bar for the dart tournament. I glanced at Deek. "What are you doing for dinner tomorrow?"

"Probably grabbing some pizza from the winery before heading over to Chip's. I'm closing tomorrow, remember?" Deek handed me a storage bag he'd just put the leftover salad into. "I'll take some leftover pie if you want to get rid of it. I'm working tonight and tomorrow before I go in. Hopefully, it will be slow on my shift, since I'm on deadline for this book."

"I think the bookstore is in bad hands if it's ever just you and me." I tucked the salad into the veggie drawer and looked around the kitchen. The pumpkin pies and the rest of the turkey could go into Toby's fridge in his apartment. I looked around but he was already gone. "Where's Toby and Greg?"

"They had a call out." Deek took an empty pie plate and put three large slices of pie on it, then covered it with aluminum foil. "Something about a domestic dispute?"

"Great. Probably about dinner or the football game." I handed him a half-emptied tub of Cool Whip. "Take this. Are you sure you don't want some turkey?"

"If I get hungry, I'm just across the street. I'll let you know." He wiped his hands on a kitchen towel and looked around the kitchen. "And with that, I'm gone. It will give you some time to chat with the dude's family. Their auras are all kinds of messed up. Is there something going on?"

I didn't want to air Jim and Beth's dirty laundry, but again, Deek had seen the issue between them. Of course, the fact that they hadn't said one word to each other the entire afternoon might have been a clue as well. "I'm sure they'll work it out."

Deek shrugged. "If you say so. Sometimes we have to make choices for ourselves rather than for other people."

His words echoed the warning Esmeralda had given me earlier. Was this fight with Beth and Jim what she'd seen? I followed him out. "When was the last time you talked to your godmother?"

"Two weeks ago when she dropped off the key and a page of instructions on how to feed the cat." Deek paused at the door and the sun shone on his now blue dreadlocks. "Why?"

"Just wondering if she got into New Orleans okay." I tried to mask my question.

Deek shook his head as he left. "You're a horrible liar. Thanks for the grub and for inviting me. This was better than I'd expected."

I closed the door and turned to find Amanda staring at me, her arms folded. "Now what are we going to do to fix this rift between Jim and Beth?"

* * *

Beth and Amanda had gone Black Friday shopping first thing the next morning in Bakerstown. I'd begged off since Tilly was the only one at the shop and we had a "buy one coffee, get one free" sale for all the Black Friday shoppers. I knew Deek was writing, so I'd volunteered to do the shift. And, as Greg had reminded me, it kept me out of the Beth-Jim argument.

As we cleaned up the leftover dinner, Beth came into the kitchen and took the drying towel from Greg. "Go talk to your brother. I've told him I'm going to this fundraiser tomorrow night with or without him, so he might as well come."

Greg met my gaze.

"Don't even think about it. You're coming with me. Come hell or high water," I said.

"Yes, ma'am." He nodded his head and then grinned at Beth. "See, King men can be taught some manners."

"I'm beginning to think your brother is adopted," Beth deadpanned as she took a pan from me.

After Greg left the kitchen, I dumped the rest of the plates into the soapy water. "I'm sorry you guys are going through this. Especially on Thanksgiving."

"He thinks because it's Thanksgiving I will come to my senses and agree with him." Beth smiled sadly. "I guess I think that maybe the same miracle will happen on his side. Maybe we aren't the match I thought we were. Maybe the only thing he saw in me was my name. Funny he falls in love with two women named Elizabeth, isn't it?"

"Don't give up yet." I rinsed a plate and handed it to her. "Holding on for a miracle is always when the ending is the sweetest. He's got to realize we aren't living in the 1950s, right?"

Beth shook her head, setting the dried plate on the now clean table to put away later. "I'm afraid he's stuck there. He wants a life like it was with his first wife, but I'm not Elizabeth. Or I should say, I'm not that Elizabeth. I shouldn't be treated like I am."

I washed a few more dishes, letting the emotion in the room calm down a little. Then I turned to look at Beth. "Have you told him that?"

* * *

Saturday night, Chris Aquilla came to the house, and with Beth, the three of us walked into town early to get the community hall ready for the dart tournament. The town had set up a parking lot on a field near where the barrier closed off the road. A few cars were already parked there, but not many yet. Greg had promised that they would arrive right at seven with the toys I'd bought. Amanda had echoed his promise, but from the look on Jim's face, I wondered if I'd see any of them before the fundraiser ended. My new family might just be a no-show to the fundraiser. But I wasn't going to worry about that yet.

As we arrived at the bar, the owner, Chip Morgan, was outside, hanging lights and garland across the front windows. The adobe building had been built in 1922 and had an Old West façade, so adding modern lights and decorations made it look out of time and place. But I had to admit, the grumpy bar owner was trying. Chip liked things practical and useful. Red-and-green garland was neither. He stepped off the stepstool and plugged in the lights.

The community hall across the street had already been decorated outside as Santa's Workshop. We just needed to make sure the hall inside was ready.

"Oh, Chip, it looks magical." Chris squeezed his arm as we looked at the front of the bar that now radiated a tiny bit of seasonal joy. Along with the neon beer signs that flashed different colors.

Magical was one word to describe it. *Trailer trash holiday* was another. But who was I to judge? Like I'd told the group on Tuesday, it was for the children. And Chris seemed happy.

Chip grumped as she kissed his cheek, his face turning even more red than the flashing lights. I was beginning to worry about his health. "You better get set up and start taking people's money before they give it all to me for drinks."

Chris laughed and herded us all inside the bar. The bar was dark and the lack of seasonal decorations made the outside look positively cheerful. I watched Beth take a step backward as she took in the two men at the bar who, from the bottles in front of them, had been here a while. One tried to stand up and grinned at us.

"Wow, aren't you a sight for sore eyes?" He peered at us, his eyes narrowed. I wasn't sure he could see if there were three of us or six.

"Roger, sit down and wait for your wife to come get you." Chris turned us right, away from the bar and through a door. This room was bright. It must be Chip's office.

"We just need to pick up the registrations and the cashboxes and then we'll head across the street and get the hall open." Chris handed each of us a file and a cashbox. Then she hurried us out of the bar and across the street. Apparently, she didn't think Roger would listen. Or call his wife.

The hall had exploded with decorations. A tree twinkled in the corner, with toys already tucked underneath. A table was set up at the doorway with boxes behind it and three chairs. A line had already formed in the room, which held fifteen dart boards as well as high-top tables and chairs.

"Beth, do you want to help us check people in?" Chris asked as we made our way around the table. When Beth nodded, Chris smiled and pulled out a form. "Okay, what we need is their name, their donation, their toy, and their experience in darts. If they've played in a local league, they'll have a rating. I've got a sheet listing all the local players. Most people are honest, and it's a matter of pride with ratings. Some try to drop their ratings so they can get a better partner."

"I'm not sure I can do this." Beth's eyes widened as she looked at the form and the cashbox in front of her.

"You run a church office and just got your master's," I reminded her. "If you can't do this, no one can."

Beth nodded and Chris gently pushed her into a chair. "I'll help you with the first one. Troy? Come over here and we'll get you signed in."

I sat in the chair to the left and watched as Chris walked Beth through the process. Then I took the next person. By the time we'd gotten through the list, it was almost time to start and Greg, Jim, and Amanda hadn't shown up yet.

"I'm paying for Lille and me," a voice said as he set two boxes of LEGOs on the table. "I hope these are good."

The boxes of LEGOs were the expensive ones. There was a *Star Wars* one, and one that looked like a small village. I looked up into Dom's face. "They're great, thanks."

"I brought the guys from my club with me. So that should help raise money for the kids." He nodded behind him where a new line had formed.

Guys in leathers and jeans, most with a woman on their arm who held the toys. "Gunter, get up here and sign in. You and Trixy are next."

At the doorway, watching the Demon Dogs sign in, stood Greg and his brother. The gang was all here.

By the time we got everyone checked in and the pairings announced, I was worn out. Chris, on the other hand, was in her element. She had the first round announced and games started within minutes. She grinned at the overflowing boxes of toys behind us. "I think we did good. Who wants a drink?"

"I'd love a Coke," Beth said as she finished counting and straightening her money box. "I've got over six hundred dollars but I don't know what I started with."

"There was a hundred in small bills in each box. It's Chip's personal donation to the cause. I'll go get drinks, and you"—she handed Beth her cashbox—"can combine all the boxes and we'll announce the entry fee donation in a few minutes. I love it when we all work together."

Chris took my drink order—a hard cider—and left the registration table. I gave Beth my cashbox and she combined it with Chris's. Greg came up and handed me a bottle. "Oh, thanks. Chris just went to get me one."

"Not anymore. I caught her on the way there." He put a Coke in front of Beth. "Looks like you drew the short straw."

"I like counting money. I have to do it after every service, so I'm used to it." Beth glanced over to where Jim was already playing a game. He was partnered up with one of the club members. They looked like the odd couple. Jim was all clean-shaven, dressed in a polo shirt and docker shorts. His partner wore jeans and a T-shirt that barely covered his belly. "Lord, I hope that man can deal with Jim's narrow-mindedness for a few hours."

"Jim will be fine." Greg glanced at the pairings. "It looks like Beth has one of the best players in the league, as do you."

"I got a good player? Cool." My nerves went down a little. I hadn't played darts except for the occasional night out since college. "I hope I can hit the board."

"I think your partner will be fine. He's nationally rated and always gets lower players in open tournaments like this." Greg watched as Dom and Lille, who somehow got paired together, high-fived each other on the first board. "I'm not sure this was a great idea."

"What? We have probably a couple of grand to give to the charity and over three boxes of new toys. What could go wrong?" I said, not knowing I had just jinxed the entire night.

Greg shook his head. "The alcohol is just beginning to flow."

* * *

As usual, Greg's prediction was spot-on. We were down to six pairs still in the running for the win when the first fight broke out. Greg, who was still in it but not playing, let Toby handle getting the men out of the dart room. He looked over at me. "There's one."

I was watching my partner throw and ignored his comment. The way Dan could hit the board, I wasn't needed. Except for the lucky shot I got every other round, to our competition's dismay. We needed two more numbers closed and we would move onto the hill, which meant we hadn't lost a match yet. I was getting a top-notch lesson in darts.

Toby came back into the room and sat with us. Greg raised an eyebrow. "They both had sober rides home and agreed to leave rather than me putting them in the drunk tank, so I think that was a win."

"No one was hurt?" Greg sipped his soda. He might be off duty technically, but he knew he could be called in at any moment. South Cove was his town.

"Bruised egos. One guy made a pass at the other's girl. I think he forgot who he came with. His wife is mad as a hornet." Toby grinned as the next player grabbed his darts. "I think you're up, boss lady."

"I'm just delaying the inevitable," I said as I stood and went to the throwing line. Dan walked up to me. "What do you want me to get? Points or try to close the fifteens?"

"We always try to win the game, darling." Dan nodded to the board. "Just relax and aim at those fifteens. If you miss, I'll clean up."

I could hear the other team behind me, strategizing for their next turn. If I missed and they got a turn, they could add enough points that Dan wouldn't be able to win alone. I blocked out the voices. I needed to trust myself as much as my partner.

I aimed, and by the time I'd thrown all three darts, I'd closed the number and won the game.

Dan grabbed me and swung me around. "I knew you could do it."

Greg grinned as I came back to the table. "Nice darts."

"Thanks, but I think my partner just about had a heart attack," I teased as I finished my cider. We moved to another table to wait for our next game. Now I got to watch Greg and his partner play against Lille and Dom.

Lille wasn't happy and Dom, usually chatty, was silent. Something had happened between them since they'd signed in but I'd been too busy playing with Dan to notice. Chris was manning the board and had the next games already prepped to play. I walked over to talk to her.

"You're running this like a well-oiled machine." I smiled at her.

"Thanks, but you're winning, so of course you'd say that. I had a complaint that I was running the games too fast an hour ago. I think we should get out of here in just over an hour. I'm ready to go home. I forgot how tired I am of dealing with drunks."

"Did you used to work at a bar?" I didn't know Chris well.

She smiled as she watched the games. "You could say that. I was married to Chip, so I was free labor for ten years. It was fun the first few years, but it got tiring quickly. You don't have a home life. And Chip? Well, let's just say he's not the one-woman type."

"I'm sorry. You didn't have to come back for this." I wondered why she had.

"Carrie's a friend. I owe her. So I'm here." She nodded to the board where Greg was now playing. "Go on, your man's up. I hope it's a King versus King final."

The next fight was quieter than the first and happened right after Greg and his partner kicked Dom and Lille out of the tournament.

"You did that on purpose," Lille told Dom as she pulled on her coat. "I'm getting a little tired of your redemption tour. I prefer my men to have a spine."

She stormed out of the dart room and Dom turned back and saw me watching. "It was a good game," I lied. He'd been bad and Lille worse. The more he missed, the madder Lille got and the worse her darts got.

"Lille doesn't like my new life plan," Dom said, but he wasn't watching me. He was staring over my head. I turned to see Chip staring back at him with malice in his eyes. "And neither do a few of my former associates. Good night, Mrs. King. It was a pleasure getting to know you, and thank you for welcoming me to your home for dinner. I haven't had a family Thanksgiving in years."

He walked out and Chip started talking to him as soon as he got near. Or yelling at him. The only thing was, I couldn't hear what they were saying.

Someone had just turned up the jukebox, so all I could hear was Queen as the two men left the dart room.

There was something going on and I had no idea what it was.

* * *

The next morning, I got a call from Carrie. She and Chris had planned on meeting at the bar to pick up the toys and deliver them to the charity's office in Bakerstown. I was finishing off the last piece of pumpkin pie. I'd take Emma walking when Beth showed up, so I figured I had a little bit of room in my daily calorie requirements. Okay, maybe not, but whatever. It was the holidays.

"Hey, Carrie, are you already done? Did you take pictures for Darla? She said she'd put an article in next week's paper." I put more whipped cream on the pie.

"Where's Greg? He needs to get down here now. We're still in town, at the bar."

"Greg?" Chills went through my body. "What happened?"

"Chip. He's dead. Chris is freaking out." She paused. "Can you get someone here? I've already called Doc."

CHAPTER 4

After Greg talked to Carrie, he grabbed his badge and gun from the office. "I'll be back. Can you entertain Mom, Jim, and Beth?"

"I can't go with you," I said, more of a statement than a question. Of course, Greg didn't want me there and we had family in town. "I'll handle it. I guess it's too much to ask for Chip to have died when a keg fell or from a heart attack."

"It's never easy around here." Greg kissed my cheek. "I'm sure you'll hear it from the grapevine, so I'll just tell you what Carrie told me. Chip was in the back room where the safe is located. Chris put the cashbox from the tournament in there last night before she left. They'd already loaded up the toys from the community center. Then she went in to get the cashbox and found Chip tied up to a chair. With duct tape, according to Carrie. She's very good at giving a calm description of the scene. Must be her attachment to Doc."

He paused and looked around to make sure no one was listening. "He was used as a target for steel-tip dart practice for a bit, then appears to have been tortured. The killer left him to bleed out."

"Someone wanted something Chip had." I met Greg's look. "Dom's motorcycle gang was right there. I don't want to stereotype…"

"Then don't. I don't like the Demon Dogs much. There are way too many stories about them running drugs and other things that I don't want to even go into. But Dom was a perfect gentleman at dinner the other day. He charmed all the ladies, even with Lille glaring at him through the entire meal." He glanced at his watch. "Look, I've got to go. Take the group out for dinner for me. I'm pretty sure I won't be back until late."

I followed him out the door and, after closing it behind me, called out, "Don't leave me here with Jim and Beth fighting. I've never been good at conflict. And Jim hates me."

"He doesn't hate you. Just have fun. I'll be back as soon as I can. Maybe someone left their wallet on the floor or a note saying why they killed Chip and I'll have it tied up before dinner." He rubbed Emma's head. "Take care of your mom. I'll see you as soon as I can."

Emma and I watched as Greg got into his truck and backed out of the driveway. Across the street, Deek was walking into town. He raised a hand in greeting. He didn't have a long shift, and Sundays were usually dead, but he'd volunteered to open the shop today. I figured it might give him quiet time to write.

I waved, then went back into the house to face my assignment. Take care of the in-laws. Sometimes marriage was hard work.

Beth and Amanda were sitting around the kitchen table. I saw Jim sitting outside on the back porch. The table was covered with jars of red, green, blue, and silver paints, baubles, and sparkles. Beth grinned at me. "It's time to make this year's King family Christmas decorations. Last year we did door wreaths. We've brought paper reindeer to decorate. These will go lovely on the fireplace mantel. We might even find a red sleigh for them to pull."

Inwardly, I groaned. I was horrible at crafty things. I didn't have the talent to make something worth displaying. But this was a family activity. I couldn't say no. Maybe later, we could head to the beach and collect shells to put in the back of my Santa sleigh. I put on a smile and looked at Emma, who covered her eyes. "Where do we start?"

After a fun—for Amanda and Beth, torture for me—afternoon, we'd voted on having dinner at Diamond Lille's. The only full-service restaurant in town. It was homey and touristy at the same time and I loved their food. The only problem was the owner, Lille Stanley, hated me. And, after losing to Greg in the tournament, she hated all of us. Well, except Harrold. She adored Harrold. There was a story there, but I'd never heard it. Of course, it wasn't hard to adore my new uncle. He owned and ran the Train Station, a model train store. He had even built a model of South Cove in the middle of the store. All the kids made a beeline to his store as their first stop when they arrived in town.

He was Santa without the red suit.

As we were seated, I saw Carrie bringing us water. "Hey, how did the delivery go?"

"After a rough start"—Carrie smiled as she looked around the sparsely filled dining room—"we got the toys off to Santa. Greg said he'd let us know when we can take the money. It was a good thing that we counted before we put the money into the safe or we'd be trying to prove what we made. Thank goodness we got the bar's donation before we left last night. Chip said he wanted to sleep in, so he paid us out of the cash register. Oh, and Lille and Dom made a sizable donation as well."

"Well, it was a lovely and fun fundraiser," Beth commented. "And such a worthy cause."

Carrie blushed. "It was the book club's idea. The Cove Connection. We meet at Jill's store every Tuesday night. You should come when you're in town. I think you'd love it."

"That's a great idea." I turned to Beth. "I have the book at the house."

"I'm not sure Beth should..." Jim started, then stopped.

Whatever he was going to say about what Beth should or shouldn't do died on his lips when he saw the look Beth was giving him.

"I'd love to attend. Jill, I know you spend a lot of time at the store, but maybe you and Mom could come too? I'd love to read the same book as you guys. Maybe we could Zoom in for the meeting once we get home." Beth was all in.

I thought Beth's excitement about joining the group was mostly because Jim had tried to tell her no. One day, he might even learn.

* * *

Monday morning, Greg had been in the house and was gone before I'd even woken up. When I checked my messages, he'd texted the instructions for the day. His family, his plan, I guessed. I needed to pop in and make sure Aunt Jackie and Harrold didn't need me to do anything around their place since they were leaving first thing in the morning for a Caribbean cruise. Everyone, it seemed, was on a short winter vacation except for me. Well, and Greg. Now I felt guilty. At least I didn't have to work on a murder case.

I needed to get going fast. Amanda and Beth were being dropped off in a few minutes so Jim could spend the day golfing. I figured it was also a way to keep the couple separated for at least a few hours. Dinner had been tense.

I wouldn't want to marry the guy. I didn't know how Beth stood for his moods. My experience as a former divorce lawyer told me unless they figured this out soon, the marriage wouldn't last long. I'd heard too many stories about how a man changed after the wedding. I didn't know if they felt the societal pressure of caring for a family or a wife, but I'd seen laid-back guys turn into controlling freaks right after the honeymoon was over.

Maybe the credit card bills from the honeymoon caused the metamorphosis.

Either way, I wanted Beth and Jim to be happy. Whatever that looked like for them.

When Amanda and Beth came through the door, Amanda looked stressed. Beth had been crying. It didn't look like either one was ready to head out and do some touristing.

"Morning, family." I widened my smile when Beth grimaced at the term. "I still need to get Emma out on the beach. Who wants to go with me? We can just walk. The weather's perfect."

"I'll be doing enough walking through Solvang when we hit there. I'll stay and have some of that coffee I smell. I need something to eat if you don't mind. Don't worry, I can forage for myself. You girls go ahead." Amanda headed to the kitchen to make something for her breakfast.

I figured she wanted Beth to have someone to talk to who wasn't in the pro-Jim camp. Amanda loved Beth, but she also loved her son. "Sounds good." I grabbed Emma's leash that I had on the front table by the door and glanced down at Beth's shoes. They'd do. "Are you ready?"

"More than ready. I can't believe how centered I feel just from a small glimpse of the ocean as we drive past. You're so lucky to live here." Beth smiled and held the door open. "Amanda, we won't be long."

Amanda came out of the kitchen with a mug of coffee. "Take your time. I'm really into this book we'll be talking about on Tuesday."

I'd given Amanda my copy of *The Wishing Game* before they'd left last night. She'd gone out on the porch to read while we sat around the kitchen table, talking. Well, Beth and I talked. Jim had been on his phone the whole time.

As we walked down to the beach, Beth pointed to Esmeralda's house. "If your neighbor ever decides to sell, let me know. I might need three jobs to pay for the mortgage, but it would be worth it for ten minutes of beach time every day."

"You'll never leave Nebraska," I joked at her. Esmeralda's house looked different. Not sad or empty, but like it was adjusting to its new occupant. It somehow weirdly looked like a writer's home. Something Hemingway would have lived in. I had never seen that vision before. Usually, it looked like a fun house on Halloween. Not the scary ones, but the kid-friendly houses. "It is a lovely house, though. My barista, Deek, is staying there until Esmeralda gets back from New Orleans. Doesn't it look like a writer lives there?"

A smile crossed Beth's face. "It does. Maybe that's why I'm so drawn to it. My agent thinks that I might be hearing back from one or more of the publishers soon. She thinks the book might really sell. I've been working on a new final chapter. Something to make people want to buy another book from me."

"That would be awesome." I held up my hand for a high five. "So will that give you the money to get to this next level?"

"It won't hurt. And the admissions committee is excited about the book possibility. Seriously, they are more excited than…" She stopped talking.

"Than Jim?" I guessed.

Beth nodded. "I feel like it's a black-and-white choice. Even if I try to do both, I'll get this angry version of the man I love. Honestly, I'm not sure I can deal with him this way. And I'm not sure I want to give away this shot. It's the career I've been dreaming of."

"You shouldn't have to choose. If Jim can't see your potential, he's not worth dragging into your new life. I adore you and I'm hoping you'll be my sister-in-law, but if you and Jim don't get married, don't think you can get rid of me too. We'll be friends for life."

Beth hugged me tight. "You bet. Amanda said the same thing. I'm going to tell Jim I'm taking the assistantship starting in January. He's on the church board and I need to resign there anyway, so it won't be a secret. And if he can't see that *me* in his life anymore, that's his loss."

"The good thing is you'll have our support if you do it here. The bad news is you'll have to deal with him until you get back to Nebraska. You two aren't living together, are you? Do we need to fly up and help you move, in case this goes sideways?" The practical and logistic side of my brain clicked in.

"Nope, I still have my little house. Jim and I didn't want to live together until after the wedding. Maybe this is why the church doesn't support couples living together without a marriage certificate. In case we don't make it." Beth took her shoes off as soon as we hit the sand. "It's an interesting thought."

Since Greg and I had lived together for years before we got married, I doubted that was the thought process, but it would have made it easier for some of our fights to get out of hand. When Greg was involved in a case, sometimes I didn't see him for days. But at least I saw signs of his visits. He usually slept in the guest room to not wake me, but in the morning I'd find Emma downstairs, already fed and let out, and a pot of coffee waiting for me. And sometimes a note.

"I could go through my old case files from when I was a divorce attorney and see if there's a correlation between living together and divorcing later. Especially if there's a statement of religious affiliation in the file." Maybe this was an interesting idea.

Beth grinned. "Now I've got you stuck on a research bug. Maybe you should go back for your PhD. It might keep you from getting involved in Greg's investigations."

"Oh, if you solved Greg's problem with that, you'd be his favorite sister-in-law ever." We walked in silence for a few minutes. "Beth, do you think that Jim's overreacting because he lost his first wife?"

"I've considered that. She died in a car crash. He was at work and she'd gone to the store for groceries. A drunk driver hit her. The guy had been at the bar for hours and had left just after they cut him off. He was supposed to take a cab, but he had a hide-a-key on his truck. That he remembered. I had just started working at the church when it happened. Jim was devastated." Beth picked up a shell and then discarded it.

"It doesn't mean that you should change your life because he's scared though." I picked up the shell she'd just thrown away. "Just because something bad could happen doesn't mean you don't live your life. Bad things happen all the time. It's the world we live in."

"I'm afraid if he lost me, it would break him."

"He can't wrap you in bubble wrap." I tucked the almost perfect shell into my pocket. It would go into my flower bed. I added one shell to the bed every time I went to the beach. Seeing them there reminded me to take in the beauty around me. "And if he keeps trying, he's going to lose you anyway. You need to tell him that."

As we walked back to the house to drop off Emma and collect Amanda for our sightseeing adventure, I wondered if I'd just blown up Jim and Beth's engagement. But one thing kept nagging at me. Beth, like me, needed to be seen.

Greg had given up, mostly, trying to change me. He even used my natural curiosity as a way to gather safe information about the case. It wasn't his fault that the garden paths he sent me on sometimes turned out to be cliff-walking trails, so to speak. In exchange, I'd learned to tell him what I was doing. Even if I thought it might make him mad.

Honesty in not just words but thoughts was important to a relationship. That was one lesson I'd learned early.

Walking around Solvang later that afternoon, I was surprised to run into Darla Taylor and her boyfriend, Matt. She still didn't have a ring on her finger, but I thought it was coming sooner than she expected. Matt had his own demons, and as a guitar player for a traveling band, he was gone a lot.

"Enjoying the sunny day?" I hugged them.

"With everyone else in a three-state radius," Matt groused as he stared at the crowded sidewalk and streets.

"It's Black Friday weekend. What did you expect?" Darla squeezed him toward her. "I think sometimes he was raised by wolves."

"I was raised by wolves," he said as he kissed the top of her head. "That's why you love me. I'm a bad boy."

"I like my bad boys in my romance books," Beth admitted. She chuckled at Darla. "The real-life ones are too much work."

"Hey, I resent that remark," he joked. Then he pointed to the Dutch Girl Ice Cream Shoppe. "Who wants ice cream?"

"I do," Amanda said. She pulled out a notebook. "Everyone tell me your favorite flavor and we'll do scoops. But if you want a cone, let me know. I'll go with you, and you can help carry it back."

"We'll be here." Beth dumped her and Amanda's bags onto a bench and sat, lifting up her feet. "That woman can shop. It's like she has to make up for all the months she stayed home during chemo."

"I'm glad she had you." I sat down next to Beth and patted the bench next to me. "Sit and tell me what's been going on."

Darla laughed. "That's my line. I've got a column to write about crime in South Cove next week and your husband won't return my calls. I'm sure he's got the temp lying to me about him being in the office."

"He's been there or on the case since Sunday morning." I knew Greg did his best to avoid Darla's calls. As well as anyone from the press. "It's horrible what happened. What have you heard?"

"Just the rumors. Chip was killed by organized crime when he didn't pay his dues. He was sleeping with a bad guy's wife. Or my favorite, Santa did Chris a favor." Darla sighed after the last one. "I hear she's broken up about his death. She loved that guy for some reason. Did you know they got married three times? Then he'd cheat on her again and she'd find out and leave him. It was an unhealthy pattern between the two of them. But she still loved him."

"Love makes you think the bad things aren't all that bad," Beth said quietly.

"Well, owning a bar and being out at all times of the night isn't healthy for any relationship. The winery is bad enough and I don't get the hard drinkers like they do at Chip's place. I can't imagine what it would be like if Matt and I decided to have a normal family life." A tone of wistful ache filled Darla's words.

"If you have kids, you just bring them along. The winery is like having a restaurant. With music." I hoped my assessment was on target. Greg had said that the town troublemakers all hung at Chip's or headed into Bakerstown. He liked it best when they headed out of town. "I wonder what else was happening at Chip's Bar."

"You know that the Demon Dogs had to get permission to shoot in the tournament on Saturday, right? Chip had banned them from the bar last year. But Dominic, Lille's boyfriend, talked Chip into letting them in for the night." Darla was such a good source of information. Much of it she couldn't use in her columns since it wasn't a direct quote, but she always had the angles.

Her next words shocked me. "I also heard Dominic had been in prison for killing a guy a few years ago."

CHAPTER 5

The family and I, without Greg again, ate dinner in town, then Jim dropped me off at the house on their way back to the rental. With Greg still working, Emma and I headed out to the back porch with a notebook. Well, she went to chase rabbits out of her yard. I started writing down what I'd learned about Chip's death and the people who were at the tournament Saturday night.

Of course, it could have been unrelated to the fundraiser. Maybe Roger had sobered up and killed Chip because his wife had found out he was a drunken leech. But that was a long shot. Like Santa and his reindeer putting Chip on the nice list.

I hadn't known that Chris and Chip had been married, especially not three times. She had cared for him. That much was obvious from the kiss she'd given him when we found him decorating the outside of the bar. In all the years I'd lived in South Cove, the bar had always been the one building that was never decorated for the holidays. Not even with the town's regulations. Rumor was that Chip had something on not only the mayor but enough of the council to always get a special dispensation for staying sans holiday spirit. Maybe it was against his religion. But this year, he had taken the time to put up the lights and Chris had been joyful. They must have been in one of their "on" times.

As I pondered everything I knew about Chip, I started writing down possible suspects as his killer. Was Dom's reputation and the fact that he had been in prison before enough of a reason to write his name on the page? He was well-mannered. Easy to talk to. And he'd been a perfect dinner guest. Especially considering he led a dangerous motorcycle gang. At least, according to the rumors.

I was on the couch with a quart of vanilla ice cream when Greg came home. He put his gun away in the safe in the office, then came out and kissed me. "Reading or watching television?"

"I can do both." I looked up at him. We both knew that wasn't true. If I was reading, I'd get lost in the book. Or if something caught my eye on a show, I'd forget the book sitting on my lap. "Anyway, before you start laughing, what's going on with the investigation? Darla says that you're looking at Dom and his gang. Did he go to jail for killing someone before?"

"It's one theory. There are several. For the record, Dom never served time for a violent act. And I'm not talking to you about the murder." He sat on the back of the couch. "How was Solvang?"

"Well, Jim's grumpy, Beth's not talking, and your mom is chatty. So pretty stressful. We ran into Darla and Matt in town. He was shocked at the number of people out and about. I think he's pretty isolated out on the road." I pulled the lap blanket up around my legs.

"He has to be. It's rough when you're trying to stay sober and your job is playing in a rock band." Greg was in a men's group at the church with Matt. Of course, they both rarely attended the Saturday morning group due to work issues. They'd bonded and started having coffee anytime Matt was in town. "Either the band needs to blow up so he can make some serious dough and get out of there or he needs to settle down and just be the weekend band guy. He's getting tired of leaving Darla alone at the winery so much."

"That's sweet. I know she misses him. It's hard to be all on your own, especially running a business." I patted the couch. "Want some ice cream?"

"I'm not hungry but I need a shower and then I'm heading to bed. I'm wiped out." Greg kissed me, softer this time. "You're not alone too much, are you?"

"If I was, I'd figure it out. There's no way I'm going to make you question your job. You love it. Even on long days like today." I didn't want to be like Greg's first wife. Life wasn't all about one person. We each had the things we loved. Mine was reading and learning new things. Things I could do on my own. His was keeping South Cove safe for all. He had a little bit of the white knight syndrome in him. I pushed his blond hair away from his eyes. "Honestly, I'm good. And if I'm ever not, we can talk. Maybe I'll get another dog or a hamster. I'll be up in a few. I'm going to finish this chapter and let Emma out. I'll lock up and turn off the lights."

He smiled as he stood. "A girl after my own heart."

"I should hope so. You're stuck with me, remember? Forever and ever." I squeezed his hand before he left. I just hoped he'd feel the same way when he realized I was meddling in his case. He had to already know. Had he met me?

* * *

Tuesday morning, Greg was gone by the time I got downstairs. I wasn't scheduled to have a shift until Thursday when the in-laws left, but if Beth and Jim kept fighting, I might have to change that. One of the advantages of owning your own business. You decided when you worked.

Esmeralda was flying home today, so Deek would head back to his apartment over the store. Life was starting to return to normal after the Thanksgiving holiday. Or as normal as it got during the holiday season.

Emma and I went to the beach to run. There, I saw Deek walking toward us, so I let Emma off her leash and she ran to him. She only sidetracked once down to the shore to chase off some seagulls who were looking for breakfast. When I caught up to them, Deek had worshiped Emma enough that she wandered off again, sniffing for whatever goodies the beach had in store. Emma had her priorities.

Deek turned around so we could continue our walk. "How are things at the house? I saw Jim and Beth's auras were still a little tumultuous on Thanksgiving."

"Still in question." I didn't want to gossip about my in-laws but Deek was more than just my employee. The kid felt like family. "How was writing at Esmeralda's?"

"Surprisingly productive. The ghosts left me alone to do my work, although I felt their presence once I closed the laptop. I'm not sure I could live in a house like that." He picked up a shell, then threw it back into the ocean.

"Maybe the house is only like that because it's Esmeralda's. Beth and I were talking about it and she said it looked like a writer's cottage. She's in love with it. If she didn't have a great job opportunity in Nebraska, I think she'd be nagging Esmeralda to move back to New Orleans and sell the house to her."

Deek looked over toward where the house sat. We couldn't see it exactly since we were lower and the house was set back from the shore. "I'd always thought it would be a great place to live. The only bad thing is I'm not sure Esmeralda will ever sell it. Do you think her contacts would go with her if she moved?"

"You're asking questions way above my pay grade, but I think it would be a great house for you. Just don't tell Beth I said that." We walked for a few more minutes. "Did you know Chip?"

"I'd been in the bar before but the place wasn't my scene. A lot of hard drinkers hung out there. I'm a lightweight unless I'm trying to drown my sorrows due to another blown-up love affair. Then I can close a place down for a few days, at least." He winked at me. "Chip was a grump but he had a soft aura. I didn't understand how he could act so opposite from his true character. Chris, on the other hand, matches her aura exactly. Happy, trusting, and willing to give you the shirt off her back, especially for someone she loved, like Chip. She adored that man. And when they were on the outs, she worked at a bar in Bakerstown closer to her house. It was a much better situation for her, but she always returned to Chip and bartending here in South Cove."

We turned around then and started back toward the stairs and parking lot. "I just met Chris. She's part of Carrie's book club. I wonder if she'll be there tonight. Probably not. Losing even an ex-husband must be hard. Especially if you're still in love with him."

Deek agreed and then changed the subject. We talked about the author visits he had scheduled during the holiday season. "I told them it would be a crapshoot on how well attended these might be. If people were Christmas shopping, they might get a lot of sales. But if they were busy with holiday frivolity, they might be stuck chatting with me."

"Isn't that the way it is all the time though?" I called Emma over and hooked her leash to her collar. "Life goes on. Even when bad things happen. Are you working the late shift at the store?"

"Tilly's opening today, and then tomorrow Evie's back, so she's opening. Then you're back on Thursday, right?" He jogged up the stairs, waiting for us to follow.

"Unless I come back tomorrow," I joked. When he looked back at me, I smiled and added, "I'm just kidding, kind of. Anyway, Beth, Amanda, and I will all be at the book club tonight."

"Sounds good. I've got to go feed the cat and then switch out the sheets in the guest room before I move home. See you later."

We watched Deek run up the parking lot, then across the road and up the hill. Emma looked at me expectantly. "No, we'll let Uncle Deek do the running. We'll walk up the hill."

She huffed and I knew I hadn't lived up to her expectations. Even my dog was judgy.

Beth and Amanda parked at the house just before five. Beth hugged me as I came out to greet them. "We left the grump at the rental. He's watching golf or something stupid. Let's go to Lille's for dinner. Jim's ordering pizza delivery."

"Is he still mad about you joining the book club?" I waved them inside and went to let Emma out before we left.

"He's mad about everything," Amanda said as she sat down at the table. "I've tried to explain that women want to have a life outside of the home."

"That's not unreasonable." I sat down at the table. The door was open so Emma would come back when she was ready.

"Tell that to my son." Amanda patted Beth's hand. "Don't fret. Just stand your ground. He'll cave sooner or later."

"I'm not sure that's true," Beth said as she tapped her fingers on the book I'd lent her. "Anyway, I loved the book. Then I started on next week's book, *Memories of the Lost*. It feels like my life lately."

"I read anything by that author." I stood to close the door after Emma came in. "Anyway, I'm ready. Should we go get food? We probably shouldn't talk about the book until the club meeting or we'll have it analyzed and done."

"Tell us about the members. You said Carrie, the waitress, started the club?" Amanda stood and gathered her things while I locked up the house.

I'd been waiting for them, so there wasn't a lot to do. Greg knew I was going, but I put a note on the fridge, just in case he forgot. He had a lot on his mind right now. "Yes, she had the original idea for it a few months ago when I was looking for something to do with all my free time. I'd finished my degree and the wedding was over. So there wasn't much to deal with except the bookstore and whatever vacations Greg and I had coming up. But I've been surprised that my days are still full. Anyway, Carrie suggested the book club and I got it up and running. The Cove Connection is what the club's called. Cute, right?"

"I love it. I wish I had a bookstore near me. I have to go into Omaha to find an independent," Beth said. She sighed then. "And if Jim doesn't get his mind straight, I might just move there to a little condo and become an official single cat lady."

"It would serve him right and he'd be miserable without you." Amanda pulled Beth closer as they walked. "So you, Carrie, and this Chris? Who else attends?"

I was a little thrown by the quick change of subject, but I realized Amanda was trying to steer Beth away from talking about Jim or thinking of a future without him. "It varies. A lot of my staff show up. Some of the writers from Deek's groups may show up, depending on the book choice. We read a little bit of everything. I'll put you both on the club's newsletter list. Carrie writes it once a month and it lists out all the future books we have planned. That way if you want to get it from the library or listen to it on audio, you can."

Lille had a new girl working tonight, and from the look Lille gave me when she seated us, she thought it was my fault. She was probably taking Carrie's old shift on Tuesdays so Carrie could do the book club. Carrie had been trying to change up her hours since she moved in with Doc Ames, the local funeral director and county coroner. She said she was working on having a normal life for a while. But anything that changed any little thing in Lille's world was usually blamed on me. This time, she might be right.

"You can sit over here," she said as she threw the menus down. "Oh, and Dom told me to tell you thank you for inviting us to dinner. It was lovely."

She stomped off, jerking a thumb our way when she passed the new waitress. She had a name tag that said Janet, but I was sure that wasn't her name. Lille didn't buy new ones until the employee had been at the restaurant for more than a month. Sometimes longer. She had a lot of turnover.

"Well, she could curdle milk with that tone," Amanda said as she studied her menu. "I think it almost burned her tongue to say thank you."

"Lille and I have a complicated relationship." I knew what I was having. Fish-and-chips. I hadn't had it for over a week. Or at least since before Thanksgiving. "I'm not sure why, but she hates me. I thought maybe she was part of Team Sherry when I got here, but now I don't know."

"No one can hate you," Beth started, then laughed. "Except my betrothed and now this woman. You tend to bring out strong emotions in some people."

Not Janet brought us glasses of water and smiled. "What can I get for you all tonight?"

* * *

The book club was getting ready to start when the door opened and Dominic Reedy stepped in with another man. Each had a copy of the book we'd just read. They were both dressed in leather biker jackets, but Dominic wore a black button-down shirt. The other man had an old T-shirt with the words *Stay Wild* over a picture of a mountain. They both wore jeans and biker boots.

Dom smiled at us. "Are we late?"

"No, we haven't started yet." Carrie smiled and pointed to some chairs at the side. "Come on in."

I met Carrie's wide-eyed gaze with a shrug. "So, Dom, some of us know you, but who's your friend?"

"This is Gunter. He's our sergeant at arms for the club. He also thinks he's my bodyguard, so I told him if he was coming to the book club, he had to read the book and participate." Dom held up his copy. "Did anyone else think this was going to be a time travel book?"

As the evening progressed, Dom kept us laughing and Gunter had some insightful comments about the character development. Both men were a nice addition to the club. I watched Deek as he did the closing tasks. He was listening and watching the group closely. I wondered what his take on the new additions was, especially with their auras. Maybe like the bad boy heroes in the romance books that were so popular, these two men were just misunderstood.

Deek met my gaze then and shook his head. I hoped he was just reading the room and not my thoughts. But you never knew what you'd find in South Cove.

As we closed up, Dom paused to talk to me. "Thanks for coming tonight. We don't get a lot of men attending the club. At least men who aren't writing their own books."

"I want to start making an impression in town. I mean a better impression. Especially after what happened to Chip. I know I'm probably high on your husband's suspect list just because of my reputation and the fact the boys and I were playing in the tournament on Saturday night. I've talked to everyone in my club, one-on-one, and not one of them killed Chip. I'll give you my word on that." He and I walked over to where Gunter and Beth were chatting. "I haven't seen him so involved in something for a while."

"All these patches have a meaning. A loyalty or a place I've been. A group I belong to. It's like writing a journal of my life." Gunter held his jacket, pointing out different patches for Beth.

"So why does it look like some are gone? Did you lose them?" Beth asked.

Gunter and Dom shared a look. Gunter turned back and said, "We decided as a group to stop associating with the rougher side of bike culture. So some of the agreements and loyalty patches had to go. I'm sure there will be new patches soon to fill in the spaces."

Dom slapped a hand on Gunter's shoulder. "He's been a real asset during this change. We have to take off. I told Lille I'd meet her for coffee before we left town. I have to say, I'm excited about next week's book."

Carrie came and stood by me as the two men went to buy the next book from Deek before they left. She glanced up and asked, "Do they know the next one is a romance?"

"I guess. Dom said he was excited. Maybe he's going to give it to Lille after he reads it."

Carrie snorted a laugh. "I don't think Lille's ever even picked up a romance. She's more into horror."

"We'll have to do something in that genre during October for Halloween. Maybe Lille will join us then." I chuckled at the horrified look on Carrie's face. "I was kidding."

"Dom seems to assume that he's on Greg's suspect list. Is he?" Carrie asked, waving as the men left the store. "Doc says Chip bled out from all the cuts. He said it must have been torture. Whatever Chip knew, it took a long time for him to tell them. What could a small-town bar owner possibly know that anyone would want to know that bad?"

After not answering either question, since I didn't know the answers, I got ready to leave. As Amanda, Beth, and I walked back to the house to get their car, I wondered the same thing.

CHAPTER 6

Thursday was filled with already-planned family fun and frivolity. We were heading into Santa Barbara to go to the zoo and the beach, then we planned to have lunch at Amanda's and Beth's favorite Mexican restaurant. Amanda had fallen in love with the food when she visited Greg and Sherry, the first Mrs. King. Greg wasn't going to be able to go with us, so he called his brother and asked him to bring the family to Diamond Lille's for breakfast.

Greg was still at home when I got dressed, so I hurried down to have coffee with him and wait for the rest of the family to arrive.

"Good morning, dear wife. Sorry I've been absent so much." He held out a cup of coffee for me as I came down the stairs. "How did you sleep?"

"Who are you and what did you do with Greg?" I took the cup and had a long sip. Even though I worked the morning shift, it took a while for me to wake up and converse with anyone. It worked at the coffee shop since my early customers were usually a lot like me and just wanted some java to sip on while they drove into the city for work. I looked around for my dog. "Where's Emma?"

"Outside patrolling the yard. She's convinced a rabbit has been getting in somewhere. How was the book club?"

We sat at the table to talk. "Weird." I told him about Dom and Gunter attending.

"I don't understand what game he's playing here." Greg looked thoughtful as he sipped his coffee.

"Could he just want to go clean or whatever you call it? Maybe he's planning on marrying Lille and having little motorcycle-riding babies." I grinned at the image my words brought to mind.

Greg snorted and coffee went everywhere. He got up and got a dishrag to clean up the table. "That's a picture, that's all I can say. Anyway, he's right. He's on my suspect list, but no one's the top contender right now. Unless you count Chris."

It was my turn to choke on the coffee I'd just swallowed. "His ex-wife? Why on earth would you even look at that sweet woman?"

"It's usually the spouse. No one can drive you to homicide quicker than someone you love." He stood and refilled his cup. "Okay, so what else do you want to talk about that's not the murder?"

"Beth and Jim?"

Greg groaned as he refilled my cup. "Another lost cause. My brother is an idiot if he lets his pride get in the way of marrying that girl. I think she's the only one stupid enough to do it."

"Beth is far from stupid," I countered.

"If she still wants to marry my brother after his whole list of demands, I question that statement." He looked out the window. "And that subject is over because they're here. Did you take Toby off the bookstore work schedule?"

"No, but I need to. He doesn't have a shift until this weekend, but I'm thinking I won't get him back that quickly. Right?"

"I don't think he'll be back for at least another week. If not longer. Can you just slot him in when the murder is solved?" Greg looked out the window at the rental. "They're not getting out of the car. Why do I think the fight has already begun this morning?"

"Because you're a genius. Go open the door and wave. Maybe that will stop it." I finished my coffee and rinsed the cup. Emma was at the screen, waiting to be let inside. "You can't go with us. We're going to Diamond Lille's and you know she hates everyone. Especially dogs."

Greg chuckled. "You're going to give her a complex about Lille."

"Exactly my plan. She seemed a little chummy with my dog on Thanksgiving." I glanced at my watch for the weather. "I don't think I need a jacket, do you?"

"Changing the subject won't help you." He threw me my light jacket. "If you don't take it, you'll complain. Come on, it's time to hang with the family. I know you're on the hook all day with them and I appreciate you taking the time."

"It was supposed to be us, but I get it. You didn't kill Chip. So who *do* I blame for this?" I locked the kitchen door and headed out to meet the gang on the porch. Emma followed and I had to tell her she wasn't going with us. Again. Somehow, dogs have short memories.

At the diner, Carrie waved us over to her section. "Greg, I've got a bone to pick with you. Tell me you didn't question Dominic. Lille is going crazy. And when Lille's not happy, no one's happy."

"Sorry, but everyone who was at the bar after midnight is getting questioned. You and Doc went home before that, right after you got kicked out of the tournament. As did a lot of people." Greg sat down and opened the menu. "Can you bring us all coffee and orange juice?"

"And I've been dismissed." Carrie smiled at me. "Is your husband ordering for you?"

"I'll let him order the drinks." I glanced at the other three, who nodded. "Thanks, Carrie."

After she left the table, Greg groaned and set down the menu. "Sorry. I'll apologize to Carrie. Everyone just wants to know what happened to Chip but no one wants to talk about where they were that night. I'm just trying to eliminate suspects as quickly as possible. Instead, people are thinking I'm ready to throw anyone I talk to in the clink."

"I don't think anyone calls it the clink anymore, dear." Amanda patted Greg's shoulder. "They know you're doing the best you can."

"I hope so." Greg hugged his mother. "I'm glad you came for Thanksgiving. I know it was a long trip for you."

"We don't have jobs where they could call us back at any time." Beth studied her menu. "And besides, beach."

"I think that's the answer to any question," I teased. "Beach time always wins."

We got through breakfast without anyone else grilling Greg on what was happening with the investigation, including me. Beth and Jim had seemed to come to some sort of detente for now. As we walked back to the house, Beth pulled me aside.

"I have a favor to ask." Beth lowered her voice and slowed her pace. "Can I stay at your place for a couple of weeks?"

"Sure!" I loved hanging out with my soon-to-be sister-in-law. "When do you want to come back?"

"I'm not going home to Nebraska tomorrow. I need a week or so to make some decisions. Jim's doing the same. We've decided to take some time apart to figure out what's important. I need to get my application in for the teaching assistantship before the fifteenth, so I'll be at the library or tucked in the guest room writing most of the time." Beth didn't look at me while she was talking. Instead, she stared at Jim's back.

"Not a problem. In fact, you'll probably be doing me a favor since I won't be alone and getting myself into trouble while Greg's working on this investigation." I hugged her. "I hate why you're visiting, but I love having you."

Beth smiled at me. "You may feel differently in a week."

"No way that's happening." I nodded toward Greg. "I take it that's what the family is talking about up there."

"Amanda's not happy with Jim," Beth pointed out. "We'll be fine. I feel it. God wouldn't have brought the guy into my life just for my passion to be the reason we can't be together."

I wasn't quite sure that was the way things worked, but this was between Jim and Beth. I was just happy that she was going to be hanging out for a few more weeks. Especially since Greg sometimes got touchy about me running with Emma alone during investigations. Now, I'd have a partner in crime. So to speak.

"The guest room's all ready for you. I have to work tomorrow morning, but I'll be at the house until six." I smiled. "Emma will love having someone home while I'm gone."

"I'm riding to the airport with them and then bringing back the rental. We extended it so I'd have something to drive here. I'll park the car at your house and walk up to the bookstore if I get here before you get home from your shift. I can't tell you how much this means to me." She paused, then changed her wording. "To us."

Back home, Greg pulled me aside before he walked back into town and the station. "You're okay with Beth staying around?"

"I'm ecstatic about it. Having her here while you're busy will be fun. She's not as high maintenance as your mom." I laughed at the surprised look on his face. "All I meant was Beth has things to keep her busy. Your mom likes to play tourist and that's not as fun alone."

He kissed me. "I get that. Just don't say it in front of Mom. Have a fun day. Jim's promised to be on his best behavior. My prediction is he'll be begging her to come home with any conditions in less than a week."

I shrugged. "You King boys can be stubborn."

He laughed as he stepped off the front porch where we'd been talking. "You know it. See you soon, wife."

"See you soon, husband." I watched as he jogged up the hill and back into town. As he left, I said a prayer for his safety. I'd always thought it, but since we'd been married, it was something I spoke out of habit when he went to work. Just in case.

I stepped into the house, where the group was sitting at the table. "Where are we heading today, family?"

* * *

Luckily the day turned out nice. At least with the weather. Being the end of November, we never knew if we were going to get rain, but Amanda and Jim had a sunny day to send them back to Nebraska. Since Beth was staying, I didn't see the wistfulness in her like I usually did when she walked the beach. "You know even when you go back, you can still come and visit any time. Call it writing time."

Beth laughed as she picked up a shell to examine before throwing it back. "It's my happy place. If this offer from Omaha wasn't so good, I'd be hitting up colleges out here for my PhD work. I can't believe you get any work done with this just down the hill. I'd be hanging out here all day."

"That's exactly what I thought the first time I visited. I'd been stuck in my tiny office for so long, I'd forgotten that I lived in California. It was work, sleep, eat pizza or leftover pizza, then back to work. I'd promised myself when I moved to South Cove, I'd go down to the beach every day. That vow didn't last, but I still come here more days than not. I have a life now and not just the work." I had worked so hard to get my law degree and then burned myself out before my student loans were even paid off. "Being on the beach resets my brain."

Beth smiled and looked back where Amanda and Jim were quietly talking together. From what I could see, Amanda was doing the talking and Jim was staring at Beth. I hoped he'd figure out how to deal with Beth working once they got married. Because from what I saw, Beth wasn't backing down.

As we continued walking down the beach, a couple I recognized made their way toward us. Lille and Dom. I smiled, making sure it wasn't too big or not big enough. Lille was hard to judge sometimes. "Hey, it must be South Cove Day in Santa Barbara. Isn't it beautiful?"

Lille growled something I didn't hear, but Dom stopped in front of us and grinned. "South Cove people are the best. And it's the cult expert. I hoped I'd see you again before you left. I wanted to tell you again how much I enjoyed our conversation at Thanksgiving. I'm definitely buying your book when it comes out."

Beth blushed so hard I thought maybe she was dealing with heatstroke. "Well, I don't even have a publisher yet"—she swallowed—"but hopefully, soon."

"Good things happen to good people," Dom said. "I'm sure it's only a matter of time. Jill, nice to see you out and about. The book club was really fun. I didn't know we had one so close or I would have been there earlier. I love talking about books."

At this, Lille glared at him. "You talk to me all the time about books."

"Yeah, but you haven't read the ones we talk about." He pulled her into a hug. "You really should attend. Your waitress Carrie is there. Jill, you need to talk this one into coming to the book club."

I tried not to choke. Carrie would freak out if Lille came to book club. She saw enough of her boss on the days she worked. Lille met my gaze and glared. I finally stumbled out a compromise phrase. At least I hoped. "Some people like to explore books on their own, others like the group discussion. It's all good."

Jim and Amanda had caught up with us then, and after a round of greetings, we started back down the beach, but Lille grabbed my arm. I looked up at her.

"Tell Greg he's looking in the wrong places. Dom and his guys weren't involved in Chip's death." She had lowered her voice, but Dom heard her anyway.

"Lille, leave Jill be. I'm sure Greg is only doing his due diligence for the investigation." He lifted Lille's hand on my arm. "Besides, Jill isn't the one investigating."

"Ha," Lille spat out. "She's always sticking her nose in these things. If you want to know who killed Chip, you should talk to Chris about his backroom dealings. I'm sure she could give Greg a page of people who wanted Chip dead just because of the way he ran his drug business."

"Chip was dealing drugs?" I'd heard rumors that if you wanted something on the illegal side, Chip's Bar was the place to go, but I'd thought they were just rumors. Not everyone who owned a bar also dealt drugs. Especially those who wanted to keep owning a bar. From what I'd seen, most dealers started sampling the product and got themselves into money issues.

Dom sighed but nodded. "Our club was involved in those deals for years, but we stepped out after too many of our members lost themselves in the culture. I didn't want to lose any more of my brothers. I know we have a reputation, but it's something that I'm trying to fix. Anyway, when we stepped out, Chip stepped in and filled the void. I guess he saw it as a way to increase profits."

"Did you tell Greg this?"

He nodded. "Your husband knows everything I know. And, Lille, he's not going to arrest me for something I didn't do."

The look that passed between Lille and Dom made me think that there were at least a few things that Dom had done that he could be arrested for. Just not Chip's death.

"Anyway, I'll see you next Tuesday night for book club." He took Lille's arm and stepped away. "I'm looking forward to discussing this romance. Are all heroes bad boys?"

I didn't answer as they stepped away. I thought maybe it was a rhetorical question, especially coming from a real-life bad boy. I could see Lille's attraction. Not only was Dom drop-dead good-looking, he was intelligent. Add in his motorcycle and the possible danger he wore like a cape, and he was female catnip.

We'd walked for a few minutes away from Dom and Lille when Beth asked, "Do you think Dom could have killed that man?"

"Beth, it's none of our business. Greg is handling it." Jim stopped talking after Beth stared him down.

"I was asking Jill," Beth said as she turned back to me.

"I don't know, but I think it's interesting that he and Lille threw out an alternate suspect. I'll ask Greg about it the next time I see him. Although he probably won't answer me. He just takes the information I give him and then checks it out." I glanced at my watch. "Who's hungry?"

By the time they dropped me off at the house that evening, I was tired. Tired of playing go-between. Tired of the fighting. Tired of the snide comments. I wasn't sure Beth and Jim's relationship could withstand all this negative energy. Something needed to change and soon. But that wasn't my issue.

I wanted to throw Jim to the lions when we visited the zoo. As we stood there, watching the small pride, Jim gave us a lecture on the patriarchal system in the wild.

But if I killed Jim, Greg would have another murder to solve and I'd never see him. Besides, if I acted on my gut reaction, too many people would have witnessed the event.

As I thought about wanting to kill my brother-in-law and the flaws in my non-plan, I started thinking about Chip's death. The bar was usually busy on a Saturday night, but not as busy as it was the night he was killed. So either the killer knew about the dart tournament and wanted to take advantage of the chaos of all the extra people there, or he, or she, had been unaware of the event and thought the bar might be quiet since it was a holiday weekend.

Either answer had merit, but maybe one would clear Chris's name off the suspect list sooner rather than later.

I pulled out my notebook and started writing down scenarios as they came to mind. Maybe thinking like a killer was the key to solving this crime.

CHAPTER 7

Greg was still at home and in the kitchen the next day when I headed downstairs. He handed me a plate with a waffle with maple syrup and bacon on top.

"I heard you coming down the stairs. I figure I owe you one for shepherding around the family this week. Sorry about that." He went back and got the coffeepot and filled my cup as I sat down with my plate at the table. "Mom called last night and said Jim was being a complete butt."

"That's one way to describe it. Honestly, I'm not sure they are going to be able to get past this hurdle. Were you ever that mad at me?" I dug into the waffle, watching the melted butter mix with the syrup. Whatever I did to deserve this man, I needed to keep it up.

"A few times around investigations, but Bill helped me understand I wasn't mad, I was scared for you. So since real men don't show fear, I reacted with anger instead." He sat down and sipped his warmed-up coffee. He'd probably already eaten breakfast.

Sometimes, he'd leave my plate in the microwave with reheating instructions if he had to leave so he didn't wake me. I tell you, the guy's a keeper. "You talked to Pastor Bill about this?"

"We did pre-marriage counseling, remember? I told Jim he should talk to Bill about this but he says his pastor agrees with him. I think his pastor just doesn't want to lose his best church secretary ever."

"Huh." I thought about what he'd said about the counseling. I hadn't told Pastor Bill much about my feelings. I'd talked more about blending our lives together, especially our financial lives. Greg, on the other hand, had opened his heart to make sure he was seeing me clearly. Another reason my guy was perfect. At least until I got mad at him for not knowing where the laundry basket was when he got into the shower.

I decided to change the subject. "Beth should be here this afternoon. Are you sure you're okay with her being here?"

"I'm not going to be around much until I solve this murder. It will be nice for you to have someone to talk to and eat meals with. Just please don't talk her out of marrying my brother. I'm pretty sure she's the only person left on earth that's perfect for him. He just needs to realize that." Greg finished his coffee, then stood, putting the cup in the sink.

"I'm heading to Bakerstown to talk to the district attorney. I'm not sure why, but I think he wants me to put Dominic in jail sooner rather than later. With or without any evidence."

"Oh, speaking of Lille's bad boy, we saw him and her at the beach. He says he didn't do it and neither did his gang." I finished off my bacon.

"Okay, well, if he says so, I'll just take him off the list." Greg shook his head. "What was he thinking, talking to you about this?"

"Lille started it. I don't think you're on her good list right now. He just clarified that he was innocent and why." I pushed my plate away. At least I wouldn't be eating cookies at work all morning. Maybe just one or two. "She didn't seem happy with him at the dart tournament."

"Lille's never happy. Unless she's torturing one of her employees, or you." Greg kissed me and headed out the door. "I'll try to come home for dinner tonight. I'll text you if I'm not going to be here."

"That will work." I took my empty plate to the sink and rinsed off the maple syrup before I licked it off. I had to face facts. I had a sugar addiction. "Emma, you and I will have to put off our run until later. Maybe your Aunt Beth will come with us."

She thumped her tail three times, then lay down in her bed. She understood about half of what I said, and since I was dressed in my work uniform, a nice T-shirt, and a pair of jeans, she knew I was heading to work, not ready for a run. I rubbed her head and gave her a treat. Then I headed out to walk up the hill to work. I could have asked Greg for a ride since he'd just left, but I liked walking outside first thing in the morning. Especially after a big breakfast.

When I got to work, my regulars all greeted me like I'd been gone for weeks, instead of just a holiday. "So, how was the first married Thanksgiving?"

asked Candice, a lawyer who lived outside of South Cove and drove into the city most days. "My first turkey I cooked so long it about exploded into dust when we cut into it."

"The food was good." I grinned as I made her order. "The mix of people made it interesting."

"It's always that way at my house too." Candice stuffed a twenty into the shop's Christmas for Kids collection. I'd forgotten to take the jar home to give to Carrie. And from the way it looked, we would be helping several more kids when I finally took the money to the agency.

The next few hours went fast and I was just settling onto the couch with a mocha and a book when Evie came into the shop. I started to stand but then realized it wasn't a customer. "Hey, girl, how was the trip to the city? How are Sasha and Olivia?"

Evie poured herself a cup of coffee and then sat across from me. "That's what I wanted to talk to you about. Sasha's engaged. She swears this guy is the one. He's really sweet, has a great job. And Olivia adores him. Although she did ask about when she was coming to South Cove to see her Toby."

"Ouch, that had to hurt." I set the book down. "Does Toby know?"

Evie nodded. "Sasha met him for coffee about a week ago before she accepted Brick's ring. Can you imagine some mom naming her baby boy Brick?"

I'd heard worse names, but it was a little weird. I decided to avoid the question. "I wonder what she'd want for an engagement present. Is she having a party?"

"I don't think so. It's kind of low-key. But I bet she'd love a call or a FaceTime chat." Evie stood. "I've got some accounting to catch up on from being gone last week. If you need me, I'll be in the office."

I looked around the empty shop. "I think I'm good."

Evie laughed as she picked up her coffee cup. "Your aunt told me I should talk you into shortening this morning shift. She said you don't get enough customers after the commuter rush to make it worth staying open."

"There is no way I'm setting up a split shift for the morning. I'd be fine, but what happens when I'm off on vacation? Then someone has to work early, then come back for a later shift? It doesn't make sense for the employee." Sometimes my aunt looked at the business side without thinking about the human component. "Besides, it's my shift, I don't mind having some time to read some of these advance copies the publishers send. I still have my reviews to do for Deek's newsletter."

"Don't remind me. I'm behind on that too." She took another sip of coffee and headed to the back. "Thanks for being a great boss, Jill."

It warmed my heart when I heard things like that from the staff. I considered all of them friends. Tilly was my newest stray and she had fit in like she'd been on staff for years. Sasha had been one of my first employees. She'd been part of an employment program we'd participated in, and after the state-covered training time was over, I'd hired her on permanently. Then she went to school and now had a great job in the city working with computers. Or maybe she did accounting. Either way, she was a success. She and Toby had dated for years, and I'd thought it might turn into something, but neither one of them wanted to sacrifice their job to make the relationship work. For them, it was a location issue. Toby couldn't imagine leaving South Cove. Sasha couldn't imagine coming back. She didn't want to give up her job or her life in the city.

It reminded me of Beth and Jim's situation, except Jim didn't want Beth working at all. If Sasha had moved back to South Cove, she would have had to cobble together several jobs to make what she made in the city. And that would interfere with her time with her preschool daughter, Olivia.

Love was never easy.

When I got home, Beth's car was parked in the driveway. She was nowhere to be found. I had an idea where she was though, so I changed, and Emma and I went to the beach.

I found Beth sitting on a piece of driftwood, staring out into the ocean.

She waved as we approached, and I saw her wipe tears away from her face. When we got there, Emma greeted her like she hadn't seen Beth in forever. I unhooked her from her leash and she ran to the shoreline to play in the waves. My dog loves the beach almost as much as I do.

"Hey, I thought you were coming to the shop to get the key." I picked up a rock from the pile below us.

"I just got here, so I thought I'd wait here instead. I knew you'd come eventually." She watched Emma chase a seagull.

"Did Amanda and Jim get off okay?"

The only answer I got was a shrug.

"Okay, what did Jim do or say?"

She laughed and looked at me. "I'm kind of an open book, aren't I?"

"You wear your heart on your sleeve. It's not a bad thing." I saw a couple coming down the stairs and called Emma back to us. She ran fast, then sat in front of me, a big doggie grin on her face. I clicked the leash on and she lay down, watching the newcomers.

"I don't know if they got on their plane or not because he didn't even want me to go to the security line to say goodbye. He just pulled the car up to the curb and left it running. Then he got their luggage out and waited for his mom to say goodbye. He said he'd call me when they got in." She wiped tears away. "No hug, no kiss. No tearful goodbye. He's making me pay for asking for a little time to think."

"You can't give in. This is the opportunity of a lifetime." I realized what I'd said after it came out. "Sorry, I know, it's not my business. It's just such a good offer."

"The thing is, I agree with you. If I allow him to bully me out of this job, where do I draw the line? Number of kids? What color do we paint the kitchen? What books I can read? Is Jim thinking that a marriage means he makes all the decisions?"

I shook my head. "Sorry, I'm not a 'Jim whisperer.' Maybe you should ask Greg. I'm sure he's going to say Jim's an idiot. He tells me that all the time."

Beth laughed, which was what I'd hoped.

"Come on, let's walk and then go see what we have for lunch. We might have to run to that local seafood place you love and eat there." I stood and held out my hand. When she took it, I pulled her up to her feet. "No moping today. We're going to talk about what your life would look like in your new position. And we're going to eat. And maybe walk some more. Then make plans for the rest of the time you're here. What do you want to get done this week?"

As Beth mapped out her goal list for the upcoming week, we headed out to walk the beach. We were following the couple that had come down earlier, but the beach was straightforward. There wasn't much else we could do.

When the couple turned around and got close enough for me to recognize them, I stopped talking mid-sentence. We'd been discussing my work schedule, and I was about to tell Beth that we could visit the college library in the afternoons.

"Josh, where's Mandy?" I asked.

Josh Thomas was walking with the mean girl from the jewelry store. Matty. She narrowed her eyes when I said Mandy's name, and Josh turned beet red. He might not think this was a date, but Matty had other plans.

"She's at the farm. Her cousin's having a wedding shower this weekend, so she's helping to decorate. We were just walking and talking about the holiday programming for South Cove." Josh stammered a few times as he tried to explain.

"It's unfair for the motorcycles to be let onto Main Street. If the street is closed to traffic, then it should be closed to all traffic. Especially since that gang was probably involved in poor Chip's murder," Matty said, her eyes flashing her anger about the city's regulation.

"There's no evidence that any of the Demon Dogs killed Chip." I didn't understand why this woman was using lies and rumors to talk others into joining her lynch mob, but I didn't like it. "And if you don't like the council's ruling, maybe you should go to a meeting and tell them. I don't believe I've seen you at any of the city council meetings. No one came to complain about the street closing."

Now those angry green eyes were aimed at me. "I shouldn't have to tell the council. Isn't that your job?"

I laughed and shook my head. "Nope. Sorry. I bring the business group together to talk about marketing and ways to help each other. I told the group last year about the change and how to protest. But no one did anything."

"Well, that's beside the point." Matty started on another tirade, but I held up my hand, stopping her.

"Sorry, I only discuss business council issues during our monthly meetings. If you want something added to January's agenda, you can send an email to my council account. I'll add it and you can talk then." I turned to Josh. "I'm surprised you didn't tell her how to get something on the agenda, both for our group and the city council. You've followed the procedures enough."

"Whatever." Matty took off, then realized Josh wasn't following. "Are you coming?"

He shook his head. "Sorry, I need to talk to Jill about something. I'll see you at the next council meeting."

Her mouth dropped open, then she narrowed her gaze. "Maybe I'll just talk to Mandy then."

She turned away and stormed off the beach, sand flying.

"I bet she wishes she was on hard ground so she could stomp off," Beth observed.

I laughed, then turned to Josh. "Boy, you need to stay away from her. She's trouble. You love Mandy, right?"

"Of course I do," Josh sputtered. "This was just business."

"Maybe for you, but I think that woman would do anything to hurt someone else. You need to call Mandy and tell her you took a walk with Matty on the beach. Because that woman is telling her as soon as she can find Mandy's phone number. I don't think she'll be as truthful about what really happened. And the worst thing is, even if you are in love with her, all she wants is to cause trouble. She won't be there once she breaks up your marriage."

"Jill, it's not like that. Matty wouldn't do that," Josh defended her. "Besides, she knows I love Mandy."

Beth put her hand on his arm. "I know I'm an outsider, but I could see what she was doing. You need to talk to your wife. Now. She can't be blindsided by this. If you tell her before Matty does, she won't be wondering if you still love her. Take it from me, it's hard to rebuild that trust."

Josh's eyes widened. "You really don't think…"

"Yes, Josh, I do think Matty would torpedo your marriage just for fun." I squeezed his arm. "Call Mandy, now."

He met my eyes. We'd become friends as much as anyone besides Mandy could with Josh during a stressful situation a few months back. He knew I would do anything for him because I had. I had proven my loyalty. He nodded as he pulled his phone out of his pocket. "Sorry to hurry off, but I need to make a call."

Beth and I watched as he hurried toward the stairs, his phone to his ear.

"I hope he's calling his wife and not that other woman," Beth mumbled.

That thought hadn't occurred to me. I'd assumed that he would call Mandy, but it wasn't my decision either way. But it was interesting that Matty was trying to point a finger at Dom for Chip's killing. And if not Dom, one of his guys.

Josh wasn't the only one who needed to make a call. But first, we needed to finish our walk and plan out our week. I needed some time to do some research into Matty Leaven. As a jewelry store owner, she had high-end merchandise in her shop. I wondered where exactly she was sourcing those items from.

Okay, maybe I was being a little passive-aggressive. Just because I didn't like the woman didn't mean that she'd killed Chip. But at least it wasn't one of my favorite townsfolk that I was researching. It was one I didn't like.

And sometimes, my hunches played out. I needed to visit Mandy soon and make sure she was okay. Without divulging Josh's secret in case he hadn't told her.

CHAPTER 8

We'd decided to eat a late lunch at the seafood place today. If Greg came home for dinner, we'd do something simple like soup and sandwiches. If not, we might just split a quart of ice cream. Beth and I were soul sisters in our love of good food.

"Tonight, I'll get my notes together and make up a plan for the research I need to get done while I'm here. Then tomorrow, I'll pick you up at the shop and we can go to Bakerstown. You can use my car if you need to run around while I work. Or I could go in the morning without you," Beth said.

"No, I want to go." I had my own to-do list running through my head. I needed to talk to Doc Ames about Chip's death as well as see what I could find out about Chris. And drop off the donation jar money to the charity. "And I'll drive. I've got some stops I need to make anyway."

Beth's eyes twinkled. "You're not investigating, are you? Amanda told me about how you and she went to the New Hope open house together. Speaking of, is there any way to get on the property? Do you know the realtor who has the listing?"

"I might." I was interested in seeing the site of South Cove's first, and hopefully last, cult. "The last time I was there, we were only allowed in the meeting house. I'd love to see the other buildings. My friend, Amy Newman-Cole, is the city planner. She might know who's representing the estate."

The problem with the land was there were too many lawsuits attached to the property. Families of cult members who had lost everything when their loved one joined were trying to attach the property value to get at least some of the money back. I had a feeling that the land would be tied up in the courts for years.

"Well, I'll put that as a maybe, but I need pictures of the site to work off to finish this manuscript. I've had several interviews where they describe the compound, but they are remembering it differently. I wonder if it was their state of mind or if the cult kept them drugged to keep them compliant. Maybe Jim would want to study up on their techniques."

"You don't want that." I knew she was joking. "I've never seen you as a Stepford Wife type."

Beth giggled. "I think I'm the before Stepford version of a wife."

I had to agree there. I was the rebel wife as well. Especially since I planned my undercover investigation steps for the next day. Beth was watching me and I knew she was wondering what was going through my head. So I distracted her.

"I think I have some new cult books at the store. I've been watching for them in the new-release catalog for you. Do you want me to bring them home tomorrow?" The smile on her face told me I'd been successful.

Now to implement the real reason I wanted to drive tomorrow.

* * *

Darla arrived at the coffee shop right after my last commuter had bought her favorite Friday drink as well as a book to get her through the weekend. On Fridays, I always tucked a few copies of recent releases right on the counter as an impulse buy. I'd started doing this after watching several regulars try to scan the shelves while I was making their coffee orders. The first week, I'd sold more books that shift than I had in months. And the numbers kept growing as I figured out the different genres my customers read.

Today I'd sold fifteen books in less than two hours. It had been a good day. "Hey, what's going on? Do you need coffee, a book, or gossip?"

Darla picked up a shifter romance from the impulse-buy pile. "How about all three? Large coffee with one pump of caramel in a to-go cup and I'll buy you one as well."

"I get my coffee free, so no charge. Do you want to share a pumpkin spice muffin? Sadie said this was the last week she was doing fall flavors. She moves into Christmas flavors soon."

"Like what? Peppermint? I'm not a fan. But the pumpkin spice I could eat all year long." She handed me her card. "Did your in-laws leave yet? I thought I saw Beth at your house yesterday."

"She's staying around to do some research for her manuscript for a couple of weeks." I ran her card, then tucked the novel into a bag. Hopefully, Darla wouldn't see through Beth's cover story. "Let's sit over at the table. I'll grab the muffin and be right there."

When I arrived with the muffin and my coffee, Darla was reading the book she'd just bought. "I haven't read anything by that author before. Have you?"

Darla blushed as she tucked the book away. "I have the entire series. She's so good. The books are set in Eastern Tennessee by the Appalachian Trail. Right where you'd expect hot men in flannel shirts and jeans who shift into werewolves to live. And I mean they're all super hot."

"The stories or the werewolves?" I teased as I cut the muffin.

Darla snorted. "Both. Matt hates me reading them, so I binge when he's out of town. But he knows since I keep the books in my library on the 'keeper' shelves. He thinks I should read something more proper, like the books we read in high school. I don't judge the music he likes. He shouldn't judge my reading tastes. Hey, you need to ask her to come in for a signing. I bet a bunch of people would come for it."

"I'll tell Deek. He handles all of that now. I just come to the authors I want to hear talk. He's taken over so much of my marketing, it's not funny."

"You need to be careful about giving up everything. Your boy there is going to hit it big when his book takes off and he won't have to work."

I set down the knife. "I've taken care of that. I gave him access to a 401(k) and insurance benefits even if he works part-time. He can't leave me."

"Good plan. Speaking of employees leaving, did you hear about Sasha?" Darla glanced around to make sure no one had come into the store. "I'm happy for her, but poor Toby. How's he dealing with it?"

So the South Cove rumor mill had already gotten the news about our star-crossed couple's demise. "I don't know. I only found out yesterday and I haven't seen him since Thanksgiving."

Now that I thought about it, Toby had been slightly reserved at Thanksgiving. I thought it was all the people, but now, knowing that he and Sasha had already talked, I knew it was from the final breakup.

With that piece of gossip dying, Darla went back to the murder investigation. "Has Greg narrowed down a suspect? Tell me it was one of the motorcycle guys. Matt was teamed up with one at the dart tournament and they kept joking around about how Chip must be having a heart attack with the crew all there. I heard they got banned last year from the bar. I guess it happened after Chip asked for a motorcycle exemption from the no-vehicles list."

"I thought that was odd." I sipped my coffee, ignoring the original question. "I thought the dart tournament went well, didn't you?"

"You raised a lot of money. Carrie gave me an estimation but said you might have a total later."

I nodded toward the jar on the table. "We got a lot of cash contributions. Amy has some as well from people dropping off checks. And she went around and hit up the mayor and all the city council members for money if they weren't going to the actual tournament. I'm stopping by there this afternoon, then taking all that money to the charity. You could probably call them Monday for a total."

"I'll do that." Darla made a note on her phone. "You dodged the Greg question. Does that mean you don't know anything? Or are you hiding what you do know?"

I laughed, shaking my head. Darla knew me too well. "I probably know less than you do. I didn't even know that Chip and Chris were married three times."

"I heard it was going to be four. Chris told her best friend that they were driving to Las Vegas for New Year's to tie the knot. I feel so bad for her. I bet she is in his will. If he had anything. I have to admit, running a bar is profitable. Chip should have had a nest egg, unless he was doing drugs or gambling. Addictions can be a drain on businesses. Especially those like the bar that have a lot of cash flowing around." Darla leaned back, thinking. "I wonder if that might be a clue to finding the murderer. Rumor is he was tortured and then left to bleed out. That had to be scary."

I was right. Darla did know more than I did about the death. "Is Matt home for the holidays?"

"He was going to a New Year's Eve party to play, but he canceled after what happened to Chip. He said he wanted to be home with me. We're going to have a big bash at the winery for New Year's Eve. I was planning on being open anyway, but now I'll stay open until midnight. You and Greg should come." Darla finished off her coffee.

"I'd love to. Greg is a maybe. And we might have a third, Beth, depending on how long she stays." I glanced at my watch. Judith Dames would be here anytime to take over my shift. "Beth's coming with me to Bakerstown and I'm dropping her off at the library. I love book nerds."

"You girls are two of a kind." Darla stood and hugged me. "I'm heading over to the station to try to track down that man of yours and get him on the record for at least something I can use in my column this week. Stay safe. Call me if you need a sidekick when you're investigating. Or is that why Beth stayed?"

"Hey, you sound like I need babysitting. Besides, who said I was investigating?" I cleaned off our table as we were talking.

"Jill, you are always investigating. You can't help yourself." Darla held the door open for Judith as she came in for her shift. "It's in your blood."

Judith looked confused as she walked in to put her stuff behind the counter. After Darla left, she asked, "What's in your blood? Don't tell me you got food poisoning at Thanksgiving. People let food sit out too long."

"No, she was talking about my perceived need to investigate all of Greg's murder cases." I finished cleaning the table and grabbed the money jar. "Evie's in the back if you need help. I'm taking this to the nonprofit so they have time to use it for Christmas."

Judith was one of Deek's friends from his writing group. She loved books as much as the rest of us, but I had the feeling she worked just to fund her travel habit. She'd been full-time for a while, but now that she was back from Europe, she was doing short-day and two-day trips around the area. But she fit into the group well and even my aunt, who'd been less than positive about her hiring, had admitted she sold more books during her shifts than any of our other employees. Now that my aunt was retired, I didn't look at the details much. I looked more at the bottom line. Were we making money or not? If the answer was yes, I didn't worry about it. If not, then I'd have to dig into the specifics. I didn't want to do that.

Evie hurried out of the back room just before I left and shoved some cash into my hand. "Sorry, I forgot that Sasha and Olivia have been collecting for the kids too. She sent me home with this."

I set the jar down and opened the lid. I counted out the addition. "There's almost five hundred dollars here."

"Olivia can be very persuasive." Evie grinned. "That girl's going to be in sales, I swear."

"Or a politician," I suggested as I tucked the money inside the jar. "Tell Sasha thanks the next time you see her."

As I left the shop and headed to my house, I tucked the jar into my oversized tote. No need to announce I was carrying close to a few thousand dollars on me as I walked down the hill. South Cove was safe, but I wasn't stupid. Besides, Greg would have a cow if he found out. My husband was all about safety and not making yourself a target of random crime. So I locked my doors and walked in well-lit areas, staying aware of things happening around me. And I carried a container of mace.

I'd also grabbed a bag filled with cookies for Doc Ames. A girl can't go calling without a gift for the host, right?

Beth and Emma were sitting on the front porch waiting when I arrived. Beth was reading next week's book club book and Emma was watching ants on the ground in front of the deck. She didn't like bugs.

I unlocked the Jeep and put my bag in the back seat. "If you're ready, all I have to do is put Emma inside and grab a bottle of water."

"Sounds good. I wrote this morning and planned out my research for the afternoon. I may not get it all done today, but I have two weeks." Beth tucked her phone into her pocket. "Let me grab my tote."

We all went inside and got what we needed. Emma lay in her kitchen bed and stared alternately at me and her leash hanging by the door. "Sorry, I hope we're home early enough to walk tonight."

"We should be." Beth came downstairs with her purse and messenger bag. "Like I said, I'm pacing myself. I'm going to write in the mornings here at the house while you're working, then head into the library for the afternoon. You don't have to come with me every day, but I'm glad you're coming today."

"We'll set you up with a temporary pass so you can get in without any problem." I gave Emma a chewy and locked the back door. "Want a bottle of water?"

"Please. I drink so much more here than back home." Beth waited for me to hand her a bottle. "Thanks for coming today. I know you're probably tired of visitors after Thanksgiving."

"Beth, I love hanging out with you. Don't ever question that." I glanced around the kitchen and pulled out pork chops to put in the fridge. "I don't know if Greg will be home, but we can grill on the back deck."

"I'll make a pasta salad." Beth grinned. "I know how to make myself useful."

We settled into the Jeep and I turned on the music as we drove to Bakerstown. Beth watched the ocean as we drove by, then the hills when we were more inland. She didn't say much. I was lost in my own thoughts about who killed Chip and why. All signs pointed to either Dominic or someone in his gang, but I guess I was stereotyping him and the members. Just like everyone else.

The weird thing was the money was still there. And it wasn't hidden all that well according to Carrie.

I wondered where the bar's take for the night had been stashed and if that was gone. A question I could ask Greg casually. Or maybe someone else might know. I didn't want Greg to know I was looking into this until it was really necessary. Maybe he'd think I was just hanging with Beth.

And maybe pigs would fly.

"What did you say?" Beth looked over at me. She'd been staring out at the dry hills.

I hadn't thought I'd said anything aloud, but I was used to being alone, so I probably talked to myself all the time. "I was just thinking aloud, I guess. So have you talked to Jim?"

"Last night. He called to tell me he'd talked to our pastor and wanted to know if I wanted to do couples counseling. I told him I would, but I got to choose the counselor. Which made him mad. I know he wanted Les, that's our pastor, because he agrees with Jim. His wife has barely left the house if she's not doing an errand for him or the church since they were married. I'm not saying it's a bad life, just not the one I want." Beth stared out at the dry hills passing by. "Maybe I'm too old to be married. I'm set in my ways."

"One, you're not old. And two, I think Jim's the one digging his heels in on changing. You're doing something completely new for you. You'll be teaching, learning, and writing. I think Jim's worried you'll outgrow him."

When she didn't respond, I glanced over at her. "But I'm not in the relationship, you are. You need to do what's right for you."

Beth smiled at me. "Thank you for saying that. I've been so worried about what Jim wants that I've forgotten that this is my life too."

"Just tell him what you want. If he can't deal with that, he doesn't deserve you." I pulled into a parking spot near the library. "Let's go get you set up with a visitor card. Then I need to go make a stop. I'll be back around three if that's okay."

We made plans to meet on the reference floor. I'd find her in one of the little study pods. Then I left to deliver my packages. And hopefully, I'd come away from one of my stops with a little more intel.

CHAPTER 9

After getting Beth settled in her happy place, I went into town and the business district. The California Central Coast Family Project was housed in an older building next to the courthouse. They were the last stop for kids before they got sent to a foster family. The charity tried to replace some of what got left behind when they were taken away from their parents. The building also had family rooms where parents could have supervised time with their kids, based on the court order and the situation. This was one part of family law I didn't miss. I'd made the original suggestion to consider the group when Carrie was looking for a community project to support for the holidays. I still had friends in the legal field, even though most of them either thought I was crazy for giving up my law practice or felt envious that I stepped away.

Christmas music filled the cozy lobby as I walked inside. A desk sat in the waiting room and the woman working on a laptop looked up. "If it isn't our favorite bookseller. I didn't think I'd see you here. I thought you were delegating. What? Is the trip back in time too much? You should come back to family law. You were one of the best."

I'd hoped that the stop to the charity would be fast. Unfortunately, the woman greeting me knew me and my history too well. "Selma, what are you doing working? I thought you would be in Central America on your annual migration."

"I finished visiting all the Central American countries last year. I'm heading to Peru next week, so I told them I'd work the desk until I left on Monday. I should bring you back something as a reward for sponsoring this event. Are you guys in it for next year too? Nancy's already counting your donations into her budget." Selma Woods loved life. She traveled almost as much as Judith and still held a full-time job as a social worker. She'd helped with several of my more involved cases during my lawyer days. "I'm glad Angie just took a break or I would have missed seeing you. You look good. Happy."

"I'm great." I caught Selma up on my life, including the recent marriage. Then I handed her the jar of money. "I'm just the bookstore owner. The book club determines what agency they're going to support. But I'm sure they'll keep you guys in mind. We had a few late donations along with the money from the bookstore collection jar."

"Thanks. The women who brought the toys and cash a few days ago said there might be more coming in from South Cove, but I never expected this much." Selma handed the jar over to a young girl who'd come out of the back. "Please count this and then give Mrs. King a receipt. Come in and sit down for a bit while we wait for Katie to finish that."

"I really don't need a receipt," I tried to say, but she waved my words away and motioned me inside her office.

"Nancy wanted me to talk to you about the unfortunate incident that happened after the event. We try to stay away from events attached to drinking or gambling for just this reason." Selma looked embarrassed to be bringing up the issue.

"You've had murders happen during events?" I didn't like the way this was going one bit.

"No, I mean we've never had this kind of situation. She wanted me to ask if maybe next year the event could be sponsored by a different organization. Like maybe the local diner. Or a jewelry shop."

"I'm sure Chip's won't be sponsoring next year since the owner is dead, but sure, we'll be more discreet on who we let donate to the kids." I hoped I wasn't sounding as snarky as I felt.

Katie walked in and handed me the receipt. "With what Carrie brought in on Sunday, you guys are our largest donors this season. South Cove donated over twenty thousand dollars this year. That will be tough to match next year."

I stared at the receipt. When Carrie and I'd talked, she thought we could bring in about five from the tournament, if we were lucky. Where did the other thirteen thousand come from?

As I got into the Jeep and drove away from the charity, I called Greg. "Hey, something's up with the money."

"Our budget? Did I go over on food? I'm sorry. I ordered for the department the last two days, but Amy will reimburse us on the next check." He sounded distracted.

"No, not our budget." I explained how the donation exceeded our wildest dreams.

"What's the lady in charge's name again? I think I'm about to ruin her Christmas."

"You think it's why Chip was killed?"

"Not talking about that, but you probably should leave before I make my phone call. They might start to yell at you."

After putting my phone away, I drove off to Doc Ames's funeral home. I'd checked, and he didn't have any upcoming funerals, so hopefully he'd be doing paperwork in his office rather than down in his basement where he prepped the bodies for burial. I didn't want to even try to visit him there. Even if he didn't have a current customer, I had too good of an imagination to visit that room.

The front door was open, and as I wandered through the red velvet lobby with polished wood everything, I got a chill. I turned to see nothing, but I felt someone standing behind me. My imagination must be on overdrive. I knocked and opened the door. "Doc?"

"Come in, my dear. I've been expecting you." He stood and poured me a coffee. "I know it's late, but coffee goes so well with Sadie's cookies. Did you bring oatmeal? They're my favorite."

"I don't think you told me that before." I handed him the bag of cookies and took the offered cup. I hoped I'd be able to sleep tonight. "I think there's a few oatmeal in there. I'll make sure next time."

"Your husband is going to read me the riot act if I keep letting you pry information out of me with cookies." He grinned and held one up. "But it will be worth the beatdown for these."

I decided to get right to the punch. "So what do you know about Chip?"

"He drank too much, smoked too much, and would have been dead from lung cancer in six months. It was a horrible way to go, but someone just shortened his misery. He was walking to an early grave all on his own."

"Sad. I wonder if Chris knew."

"Chris was back in his life? Man, I thought she had said goodbye for good the last time when she caught him with that blonde from Bakerstown. He didn't understand the premise of monogamy."

"I'd heard they were on-again, off-again types." I was the opposite. I was a one-man woman until I said, "Enough." Then there was no looking back. Just ask my first husband.

Doc grabbed a second cookie. "He was flaky. Chris loved him since high school. I graduated the same year as Chip. Chris was a freshman when we were seniors. She fell hard and never gave up hope. True love, at least on her part. Chip, he liked the variety. But he had a soft spot for Chris."

I sipped my coffee. "Doc? Would Chris have killed him? Maybe a mercy killing?"

He shook his head. "One, I don't think she could have done it. Chris would have dragged him to doctors all over the country to save him. And two, she isn't strong enough to have put the steel-tip darts so far into his body. He was tortured. The killer wanted something and I don't know if they got it. Chip could be stubborn."

After leaving the funeral home, I thought about what Doc had said. The dart throwing had been playing with Chip. Making him hurt until he told them what they wanted to know. Then they'd started using the knives. Chip had bled out long after they'd left him tied up in that back room. Too tired and weak to even try to escape. I wondered if he'd hoped that someone would come looking for him. Chris was tucked in her bed at home, thinking he was home in his apartment above the bar. No one would have even been at the bar that morning except for Chris and Carrie, who were planning on taking the money and the toys to the charity. He could have been there until the bar reopened on Tuesday night.

It sounded like the killing had been planned. But by whom?

* * *

The next morning, Beth chatted about her research and a new source she'd found as we made breakfast. She was continuing the conversation she'd started while we made dinner last night. I went to bed as soon as the kitchen was cleaned.

I must have nodded or commented enough that she kept talking, but by the time dinner was over, I was bone tired. It must have been from working that morning.

"Thanks for letting me use your office. My apartment's so small that I've been using my dining room table. I feel like I've been upgraded." She refilled

Emma's water dish as we talked. "I want to turn the third bedroom in Jim's house into a den when we get married. If we get married."

"Don't give up on him yet. He really can't be that stupid to let a little thing like you working stop you two from being together. And if he does, he doesn't deserve you." I sat down with my bowl of oatmeal and fruit. Having Beth around was way healthier for me. I might just keep her here.

"You would think that he'd be used to me being independent and strong-willed. When Amanda was sick, he wanted to hire a nurse for her. I told him he was crazy and I'd do it. I took leave from the church and just worked on my degree back then. Huh, I'd forgotten, but Les wasn't happy when I did that either. I wonder if Les is pressuring Jim more than helping him discern our situation."

"Your pastor wouldn't do that, would he?" I didn't have a lot of experience with churches, well, at least those that weren't cults like the one that had moved into South Cove last year.

"Humans are fallible. I need to have a heart-to-heart with my spiritual advisor and see if his needs are messing with Jim's decision-making in this matter. Les is a good guy. He just doesn't like change." She smiled at me. "One more task on my to-do list. What's on your schedule today? Are you coming into Bakerstown with me?"

"I think I'll stay home. I need to run with Emma after work, then do some reading or maybe laundry. Or multi-task and do both." I also wanted to figure out how I could find out more about Chip without hanging out at his bar and talking to the long-term customers. Besides, I didn't think it would be open. Not for a while. If Chris was his heir, wouldn't she need a court order or something to start running it again? Maybe Amy would know. "When are you going to Bakerstown?"

"I'm going to head over early if you're not coming. Probably around nine or ten." She played with her spoon. "I'll be back to cook dinner. Maybe something creamy and baked. Anything you guys don't like?"

"We're pretty much open to anything." I stood and put my empty bowl into the sink. "Especially if I'm not cooking. You don't have to do that though."

"It helps me think. And I've got a lot on my mind between this manuscript, the new job, and, well, Jim. I might just bake all of your Christmas cookies before I leave."

"Knock yourself out." I grabbed my tote and said goodbye to my dog. "I'll see you sometime tonight. Call if you're going to be late. I worry."

"Yes, Mom." Beth grinned and shook her head. "I want to be part of a family again. What am I, crazy?"

"It's a possibility," I teased back as I headed outside. As I walked into town, I texted Amy to see if she could have lunch with me at Diamond Lille's. I didn't get an answer until I was almost at the shop. It was short but positive.

Sure. Noon?

All the businesses in town were bursting with holiday décor, ready for a busy holiday season Saturday. We'd had a sale at the bookstore last week for Black Friday and the sales for this week were just as high. People liked buying books for gifts. Especially since we had a huge local charm section where we had cookbooks, travel books, and even fiction that was set in our geographical area. I'd also ordered a few touristy items like South Cove pillows, jackets, T-shirts, and magnets. People loved magnets to put on their refrigerators.

This morning, I'd mostly sell coffee and paperbacks to the tourists staying at the bed-and-breakfasts scattered around the area. Holiday shopping traffic would pick up just as I was leaving. Which would make it Deek's problem. He loved working Saturdays. He was our one true extrovert in the bookseller group. The rest of us would rather just be there in case someone wanted to buy something. Deek reached out to everyone who walked into the store and had a high rate of success by talking to them about books. Books he loved, books they'd read, and what they were looking for. I'd watched his magic once, amazed at the way he brought even the most reluctant buyer to the register with at least one book, if not more, in their hands.

I thought it had a lot to do with the way he read people. Well, he'd say he read auras, but I knew his secret. He was a people watcher and could tell who was responding to his banter, changing it up when it wasn't working. He knew what people wanted most. To be seen. He saw everyone.

As I opened the bookstore, I was surprised to see the purple van of Sadie Michaels, my friend and owner of Pies on the Fly, pull up in front of the shop. "I didn't think we were getting a delivery today."

"Evie called in another one yesterday. She said they'd had a run on the snowman cookies, so I made you up a special batch of snowmen, snow angels, snowflakes, and even some pretty snow-covered cabins. Those are gingerbread. Since I had made the batter, you have gingerbread people as well. I went a little crazy." She glanced at her watch. "Come help me unload these before the parking police find me and gripe to the mayor."

"Hold on a sec." I hurried inside, then turned on the lights and tucked my tote behind the counter. As I came back out, I said, "The ban doesn't start until nine, and besides, I don't think Josh is open this early."

"I can handle Josh. It's that Matty Leaven. She's horrible. She complained that the choir practice was too loud last week. A church choir. She just thinks she is in control of everything and everyone."

"I'm not too fond of that woman either. She's not nice to Josh. I mean, he's an acquired taste, I get it, but don't be nice to his face, then laugh at him behind his back. It drives me crazy." I grabbed the two trays of cookies that Sadie handed me. "I have no respect for the woman."

"She's trouble with a capital T. I'm so glad I can say these things to you. If I said it to Bill, he would tell me I should turn the other cheek or see things from her side. But I could tell the choir thing didn't settle well with him either. He's just better at hiding his emotions." Sadie followed me in with four trays.

The discussion I'd had with Beth this morning came to mind. "Hey, would Bill ever tell his secretary not to take a better job? Or more specifically, tell her soon-to-be husband to tell her?"

"You're kidding, right? Bill is always without a secretary because he *finds* them better jobs. Church employees don't make a lot of money, so after they get the experience of working in an office, he makes it his mission to place them in a better-paying job. He sees it as his calling. Why?"

I told her about Beth's problem. I probably shouldn't have, since it wasn't my story to tell, but I trusted Sadie and I knew she wouldn't tell anyone else.

"If he's doing that, it's for his benefit, not God's." Sadie shook her head. She was in a class for spouses of members of the clergy. Her engagement ring sparkled on her left hand as she pushed her hair out of her eyes. "You tell her to stand her ground. God gives us talents for us to serve him, not hide them under a barrel."

"Maybe you guys could have coffee together some afternoon before she leaves?" I wanted Sadie and Beth to have some time to talk. I knew Sadie wouldn't lead her wrong.

"How about Wednesday? I have to be up for my women's meeting that afternoon. We could meet at three. Do you mind if we meet at Lille's? That way I can eat an early dinner while we talk and then crash before I have to be back up and baking."

"That's perfect. Thanks for making time for Beth." I hugged her. "And for all of these adorable cookies. I'll get them put away."

I'd meant to get them put away, but I started getting busy. I found myself selling off the baking tray sitting behind the counters as soon as the shoppers saw the cookies. I didn't think we would be as stocked up as Evie had hoped when she called in the extra order.

When Deek came in for work, he didn't say anything. He put on an apron, then took a tub out to the dining room to clean tables. When we finally had a breather, we were both putting cookies in the display case. "Good to see you." I grinned as I picked up a snow angel and broke off her wing to eat.

"I think we're going to be busy until New Year's," he said as he slid an empty tray under a full one.

"Not a bad problem to have." I glanced at my phone. I had lunch plans with Amy in ten minutes. "You good here?"

"I'm fine, but Jill, I think we need to talk about me taking some time off. I need to get a few things done." He picked up the cookie trays to put them in the back. "Before Christmas."

CHAPTER 10

Amy was already seated at our favorite booth at Diamond Lille's when I arrived. I'd wanted to stay and talk to Deek more, but he'd waved me off when customers came in. With Toby working overtime with Greg, I didn't have the room to lose Deek for any substantial time until after the year's end. Tilly was working full-time already and Judith was planning a trip around the end of the year. I couldn't even call on Aunt Jackie for a few shifts since she and Harrold had cruises scheduled almost nonstop this winter.

I couldn't put it off anymore. I needed to hire another person.

"You look miserable," Amy said as she pushed a menu toward me when I sat across from her. "Is it a fish-and-chips *and* milkshake day?"

I nodded and pushed the menu toward the edge of the counter. "Yes. I have to hire someone new for the shop."

"Isn't that a good thing?" Amy set her menu down on top of the one I'd pushed away. She was probably eating something healthy to make me look bad when I ordered. "I mean, your shop is busier than I've ever seen it. I've heard tourists chattering about how cute and well-stocked it is. Not to mention you serving Sadie's yummy treats."

"You're right, it is a good thing. I just don't like change. Or new people. It took me five years to hire my first employee and Aunt Jackie did that. Besides, I just hired Judith and Tilly." I leaned back into the booth. I didn't know anyone who needed a part-time job but maybe my baristas would. Well, except Beth, and as perfect as she would be as an employee, giving her a job here would just make Jim hate me even more. Besides, she had that university gig starting in January."

"Sounds like you're going to have to go out of your comfort zone. You depend too much on Deek. He's going to be busy once his book releases in May." Amy smiled at Carrie as she came over with two iced teas. "I think Jill needs something stronger today. Do you know anyone who needs a part-time job?"

Carrie's eyes brightened. "You're hiring?"

"Yeah, and probably soon." I took a long sip of tea. It didn't make me feel better. "Bring me the usual with a vanilla milkshake."

"Okay, what about you?" Carrie turned to Amy.

"Grilled chicken salad, vinaigrette on the side. And a slice of toasted wheat bread, please," Amy ordered, then focused on Carrie. "Are you looking for another job?"

She shook her head. "I wish. But the tips are good here and Lille's finally providing both health insurance and a 401(k). I just need my feet to hold on for a few more years. Or to win the lottery. But I might know someone who's looking. Let me talk to her."

"Okay, but I don't have a huge benefit package. We do have health insurance if they can work thirty hours a week." I guess I did have something to offer a new employee. "Have them stop by during my morning shift. I'll be working Tuesday through Saturday probably for a while."

Carrie nodded before she hurried away to get our order in. I turned to Amy. "Why not a burger?"

Amy shrugged and took a sip of her iced tea. Then she changed the subject. "So what did you want to talk about? Something about the case?"

"Oh yeah." I leaned forward. "Tell me about the business license for Chip's Bar. Is Chris a part owner? Will she be inheriting the business?"

"How would I know all that off the top of my head?" Amy asked as she looked around the busy diner. Then she leaned closer. "Unless Greg had just asked me to pull the file on the bar. You didn't hear this from me, but Chris isn't on the paperwork at all. The business was in Chip's name alone, until five years ago when another name was added as a partner."

"And?" I prodded. Amy always liked to draw out the surprise ending. She watched too much reality television. I was surprised she didn't get up and go to the bathroom before telling me.

"The new partner was Dominic Reedy." Amy leaned back, watching my reaction. When she saw my surprise, she nodded and continued, "I know.

But the problem is that Dominic has a felony. I guess he has a provisional license for his family bar because he's turning it into a restaurant. But Chip's doesn't serve food so he can't take over the liquor license. So with Chip dead, he owns a bar he can't open."

"And that bit of news is one more reason he wouldn't have killed Chip. He needs someone who can partner with him to run the bar." I shook my head. "This investigation is going nowhere. My best suspect is a former motorcycle gang leader who's also a super nice guy with an alibi and a business reason to need the victim alive. Besides, if I prove he did do it and he goes to jail, this might be my last meal at Diamond Lille's because she'll ban me and Greg. Well, maybe not Greg."

Carrie set the basket of Tiny's fish-and-chips in front of me along with my shake. Amy got her salad. I thought I'd won lunch wars, if there was such a thing. "Lille's not here today. She took a personal day. Dom's taking her out on the motorcycle up the highway. But I just heard what you said. And you're right. Dom has his demons but he seems like he's a changed man. He's good to Lille and that's something that should count in his favor. She's dated a lot of losers since I've worked here."

After Carrie left, Amy looked at me. "So what if you go on the premise that Dom didn't kill Chip? If that's true, who else would you be looking at?"

"Chris. She's the ex-wife. I thought she'd get the bar, but now, she doesn't even look like a good suspect. And, if you met her, you'd know in just a few minutes there would be no way she could have killed anyone. Maybe my Trixie Beldon skills are fading since I got married. Like how all those good television shows died after the two leads became a couple." I ate a French fry. Hot, crisp but not overdone, and soft in the middle. And just the right amount of seasoned salt. A perfect fry. Tiny, Lille's chef, was the best on the coast. At least in my opinion. Now that I knew she paid benefits, I knew why he'd stayed on in this little tourist town. He could have his own place but then he'd have to do management stuff. I could relate to hating the management stuff. "Besides, I like her."

"You like Dom too," Amy reminded me. "Anyway, I need to tell you about our Thanksgiving fiasco. Justin's brother-in-law set fire to the carport trying to deep fry the turkey."

The rest of the meal was spent with Amy telling stories about her in-laws and her Thanksgiving vacation. She and Justin had met during one of their surfing excursions. Now, they spent their time remodeling the house they'd bought after the wedding. Amy called it the Money Pit. She'd even teased that they should paint it green to highlight all the dollar bills they'd invested in the remodel.

She hadn't talked about surfing for a while.

"Where are you planning on going surfing next? Somewhere exotic?" I asked as we waited for Carrie to bring back our credit cards.

Amy sipped her tea. "We don't have one on the calendar yet."

"You always have a trip on the calendar," I responded. I was beginning to think something was going on with my friend. I knew remodeling could be stressful in a relationship. Greg and I were still talking about what to do with the backyard. He'd stopped redesigning the shed since it didn't look like Toby was moving out any time soon. "Are you two all right?"

Carrie came back with our cards and Amy quickly stuffed her card into her bag, signing the charge slip. "Justin and I are fine, but I've got to get back. The mayor is coming back this afternoon and I don't have the council agenda done yet. Thanks for suggesting lunch. I feel like I haven't seen you in ages."

We hugged and Amy hurried out of the diner. As I followed her, Carrie nodded toward the door. "I haven't seen her here in weeks. I'm glad you got her out of the office. She's working too much."

I thought maybe there was something else going on with my friend, but I didn't want to push. Jim and Beth, Amy and Justin, Dom and Lille. What was it with couples fighting around the holiday? If Greg and I fought, it was more likely due to me getting too involved in his case. Which I would be doing this time if I had a good suspect. Every time I thought I had found a clue, it turned out to be nothing.

I guess I'd just have to try harder.

I headed home to get Emma. The day wasn't turning out the way I'd planned, but a good run on the beach should clear my head. Then I'd clean the house. If I was still in a mixed mood, I'd sit on the back porch and read.

* * *

None of those things had helped, so I was happy to see Beth when she came home from the library. Usually, I enjoyed my alone time, but today, I felt anxious and off. Maybe I was getting sick.

Instead of reading, I'd sent an email to my staff, asking if they knew of anyone who wanted a part-time position. I'd gotten a text from Carrie saying that her lead hadn't panned out. Her friend had just taken on a new job. I thanked her and asked her to keep me in mind if she thought of anyone else. I'd found hiring a new staff member who fit into our little family was more about who you knew than throwing an ad into the paper. But if no one had any ideas soon, that was my next step.

Then I studied the upcoming schedule. Toby's hours needed to be covered for next week, so I moved Evie from my morning shifts to his. I made sure Tilly was full-time and then sent an email to Judith to see if she could cover the Saturday midday shift for a couple of weeks. Even with these moves, the hours weren't all covered.

Staffing was too tight. Especially for the holidays when people liked to take some time to celebrate, not just work.

Beth was making a salad in the kitchen as I seasoned the chicken to grill. "Why are you so grumpy? You haven't said two words since I've been back. Am I here too much? I could rent a room in Bakerstown for next week."

"What? No. I love having you here. I'm just trying to figure out staffing. I need to hire someone soon. Deek needs some time off and Toby's working with Greg. I might just have to do double shifts for a while. So you would be here alone anyway." I held up a finger. "Let me get these on the grill and then you can tell me about your day."

After I settled the chicken on the grill to cook, Beth came outside with two cups of hot cocoa. "It's peppermint. I found it in a coffee shop on campus. It's weird having something hot to drink when we're grilling dinner. But it is the season."

I took the cocoa and smiled at the whipped cream she'd added to the top. "California Christmas is a different thing. No snow, but then again, you don't have to drive in it. Did you get to the beach?"

"First thing this morning. I called Jim afterward. I think he's softening to my idea of doing couples' counseling with a secular counselor. He needs to realize that my demands aren't that unusual in a marriage." She curled her legs up underneath her. "I'm farther along in my research than I expected and should be done tomorrow. Maybe I could work for you for the rest of the time I'm here. I was a barista through college. You'd have to train me on the bookstore part and the register. But I'd work for room and board."

I felt my excitement rise as I considered her offer. "That would be amazing. I'd pay you. The room and board is free for keeping me company while Greg works twenty-four seven. And it would give me time to find someone permanent."

"Then put me in, coach. I could train with you tomorrow or Tuesday. But if you train me tomorrow, I could start working on Tuesday if you have a shift to cover."

"Evie is working in the morning. I'll text her and let her know that you're coming, then you can work with me Tuesday morning and cover a few shifts next week. This would be a big help."

"I'm here to serve." She smiled as she sipped her cocoa. "Now all I have to do is finish my Christmas shopping and mail off my Christmas cards on Monday. Yes, I brought them with me in case I had some downtime while Jim golfed. Do you want to come along?"

Since I hadn't started my shopping, I thought maybe that wouldn't be a horrible way to spend my day off. I stood to turn the chicken and realized I'd finally broken my bad mood. Or Beth had.

Jim had to marry this girl or I was going to have to adopt her as my long-lost sister. There was no way I was letting her leave my circle of family. I think Amanda would agree with me.

The next morning, Beth headed out to work with Evie while Emma and I went to the beach. I needed to make sure my bad mood didn't come back. I had scheduled a meeting with Deek on Tuesday morning to go over his schedule and extra duties. He'd taken on a lot over the years and I knew the work was weighing on him. He was just good at it all.

I started thinking about things I could move. Maybe Tilly would want to do the newsletter. Or Judith might want to take over planning the author events. As I ran, I thought maybe I should ask Deek first what he wanted to give up. I was acting like he was quitting, not just needing some time off.

But at least I wasn't feeling like I was drowning anymore. Beth coming on to take some shifts wasn't a permanent solution by any means, but it gave me some breathing room, without worrying about taking my entire crew underwater with me.

As I ran, my mind shifted to Dom and his partnership with Chip. If Chip had needed money to keep the bar running, maybe he'd borrowed from more people than just Dom. No, the killer tortured Chip to find something. The question was, what were they looking for?

For that answer, I needed to find out more about our local grumpy bartender. I needed to talk to Chris and maybe some of Chip's friends. If he had any.

When I got home, I started by Googling Chip's Bar. An older website popped up, probably set up by Chris years ago. It listed off the amenities of the bar. Cold long-neck bottles, mixed well drinks, authentic western décor, darts, and pool tables. It also had a dart schedule for a league that had ended in 1999. I'd bet that one of Chip and Chris's divorces must have happened at that time since the website hadn't been updated since.

I clicked on a tab that led to a page about the history of the building. It had been built in 1922 and used for years as a brothel as well as an undercover drinking establishment. At least until 1933 when the Eighteenth Amendment was repealed. Then it became known as the Time for Two until 1972 when Chip purchased the building and the bar. The article mentioned how he'd been in his twenties and had won money in Las Vegas to make the purchase.

Now, Dom owned it. Or at least owned the business. Who owned the building?

I started writing down what I knew and what I was guessing at. The building had a history of being used for under-the-table dealings. Maybe Chip was doing more than selling shots of Jack Daniels and draft beer. Dom and Lille seemed to think that was true. I needed to understand the history of the building and only one man in town knew more about South Cove than I did.

Josh Thomas.

If I was right, he'd be at his antique store right now, waiting for customers to wander in. Mandy, his wife, used Sundays to visit her family at the local farm. Family with whom Josh still harbored bad feelings. Mostly because they'd opposed the wedding. Josh could hold a grudge for years.

I changed out of my running clothes and into jeans and a T-shirt. If I timed my visit right, I could stop by the station and see Greg before going to the bookstore and picking up Beth. We'd head into Bakerstown and grab some lunch. And if she needed to visit the library, I'd do my research on the ownership of Chip's building.

Greg couldn't yell at me for hanging out at the library with his soon-to-be sister-in-law.

As long as he didn't know what I was looking for. And if I found something, I could just tell him I found it by accident.

Plausible deniability. Sometimes it even worked.

I had the timeline all worked out as I walked into town and entered Antiques by Thomas. Josh was reading a book at the counter. He smiled as he looked up, but then seeing it was me, he went back to reading.

"Hi, Josh." I hurried up to the counter.

"Whatever you want to tell me about Matty Leaven, you're too late. She told me you heard her talking on the phone about me. She was talking to her mother and telling her that I'm the only one who understands business around here." He didn't even look up at me.

"Josh, Matty wasn't talking to her mother when I overheard her." I paused, wondering what exactly I should say. I didn't want to hurt him but he needed to be warned. "She was walking with some friends. I don't think you should trust her. She doesn't have your best interest at heart. You know I've always been honest with you. Anyway, that's not why I'm here. I wanted to ask you what you know about the building across the street. The one where Chip had his bar."

This time, Josh closed the book and gave me his full attention. His curiosity about why I was asking about the bar overcame any warnings that Matty had given him. "The building was erected in 1922 and used as a brothel and speakeasy for years. People came from up and down the coast to frequent the establishment. Back then, South Cove wasn't much more than the brothel and the mission ruins. This side of the street wasn't even built. I bet you could see the ocean from Chip's front door."

I followed him as he walked over to a bookshelf full of California history books.

He pulled one out and handed it to me. "This is the most complete version of the origins of South Cove. I think your history professor had a hand in writing it. The one who died?"

I took the book from him. "Thanks, Josh. I appreciate your help."

"I know you're trying to find out who killed Chip. He wasn't the nicest person, but he didn't deserve to die that way." Josh handed me a second book. "This one's more recent but not as detailed in the research."

I nodded. "I'll get these back to you as soon as I can."

He walked back to the counter, but as I reached the door, he said, "I know you've always been on my side, Mrs. King. I appreciate the warning, and I will take it under advisement."

CHAPTER 11

Greg was in a meeting when I arrived at the police station, so I took a few minutes to catch up with Esmeralda. "How was the trip?"

"Interesting. I think Nic's sister is settling into her new life. Eddie reminds me a lot of you. She was planning a different life in Seattle, but things changed when she moved home."

"Like when I took out my retirement savings and bet it all on a bookstore in a tiny tourist town?" I laughed at the memory. "If I hadn't been so mad at my boss at the law firm for being passed on a promotion, I would still be there, locked in a tiny office and helping people navigate their divorces. And probably still living in that tiny condo."

"Your love of the beach would have led you out of there eventually. The fates work in mysterious ways." She moved a piece of paper into a file. "Your sister-in-law, Beth, caught me at the beach yesterday. She's a bright soul. I enjoyed talking with her."

"She's here doing research for her book." I didn't know what Beth had shared with Esmeralda, but it wasn't my place to talk about Beth's relationship.

"If you say so," Esmeralda responded, clearly sensing there was more to the story. "Anyway, Deek did a nice job watching my house. The spirits were pleased. He's getting ready to start his new journey. I'm going to miss having him around."

"You think he's leaving permanently?" I was prepared to have Deek around less, not gone. But Esmeralda was his godmother. If he'd told her he was leaving, it was probably true.

"Don't be so upset. The boy has to go find his calling. He'll come home." Esmeralda glanced at the phone. "Sorry, I've got to take this call. I'm dispatching this morning while the team meets on the investigation."

The phone wasn't ringing, but I didn't mention that fact. "Well, I'll see you soon. Maybe we could do a girls' night before Beth leaves?"

"That would be lovely. Just let me know when and where." Esmeralda nodded as the phone lit up and rang. "South Cove Police Department, may I help you?"

I shook my head as I walked out of the station and headed toward the bookstore. My friend was always a step ahead of everyone and everything. She credited the spirits. I thought she was just good at watching people. But that phone thing was weird.

Evie was behind the counter, helping a customer with a book purchase, and Beth was clearing tables in the front. She looked up as I came in, then glanced at the cat clock on the wall. "I can't believe it's already that time. The morning flew by. I've missed working with people. I mean, I have a few people come in during the day at the church office, but it was always the same people."

"I'm glad you're enjoying yourself. I feel bad having you work on your vacation." I waved at Evie, who gave me a thumbs-up. Apparently, the morning had gone well. We didn't stay open all day, but we had enough morning traffic that it was worthwhile staying open until one. "Evie, can I steal her away? Or do you need her for the next hour?"

"You're kidding, right? I got so much done today." Evie came over and handed me a travel cup filled with coffee. She always added a pump of salted caramel when I came on Sunday as my "treat." "Beth handled the coffee shop and bookstore while I worked on payroll. I know she lives in Nebraska, but can we keep her? You said we were looking for another part-timer."

Beth laughed as she took the bin of dirty dishes back around the counter. "Sorry, girl, I've got a job starting in January. This just keeps my mind working while I'm doing other things. I'm dying to get to the library this afternoon."

"Deek says the same thing when he's stuck in a story. He starts cleaning the shop and rearranging the bookshelves. Then you lose him to his laptop for hours." Evie shrugged. "Must be a writer thing. I avoid cleaning at all costs. Especially when I'm working out a problem in my head. Do you want a coffee to go?"

Beth grabbed a travel mug, stepping over to the coffee machine. "Please, let me. Are you sure you're okay with me leaving?"

"It's been fun working with you." Evie glanced at the display case. "I've got all our treats out in the display case, but I think it will last until Sadie's delivery tomorrow morning."

"We've been selling a lot of cookies." I scanned the limited offerings in the case. "Beth, you'll meet Sadie tomorrow morning. She's the one you're having coffee with on Wednesday. She's engaged to the local minister. I thought you might have some things in common."

Beth rolled her eyes as she took off her apron. "Thanks. It will be nice to compare notes. I know Jim isn't clergy, but he's on the board of deacons, and until we started dating, he mostly focused on church business. Now, I need to teach him how to have a life too."

I wondered if that was even possible. Jim was determined. And focused. And single-minded. When he made his mind up, he tended to stick to his decision. But I was hopeful. "We still have to walk back home to get the Jeep."

"I'll drive. I don't want that rental just sitting there," Beth said as we walked outside. She looked at my tote. "That looks heavy. You didn't pick up books at the bookstore. Did you mean to leave some?"

"No, I got these from Josh Thomas." I pointed out his store as we walked by. "He loaned me a few on South Cove history. I thought researching the building might give me a clue as to why Chip was killed."

"Tell me the building held pirate treasure." Beth sounded hopeful.

Laughing, we crossed the street before the barricades keeping traffic off. "I don't think so. But maybe something from the golden age of flappers and bootleggers. The building wasn't built until 1922."

"So that's why you want to go with me to the library. To research South Cove history." She glanced backward at the station. "Does Greg know?"

"I stopped by to chat with him, but he was in a meeting. Besides, I'm going to a college library. How much trouble can I even get in?" I ran up the porch stairs to the house. "I'm going to let Emma out for a few minutes and drop these books off. Do you want to change?"

"I need my laptop and backpack, and yes, I'll change into jeans and a shirt that doesn't smell like coffee and sugar. Although, it's not such a bad perfume."

It took us less than ten minutes to get ready and on the road. Beth had the windows down and the soft rock station music blaring as she drove. I just leaned back and enjoyed the ride. As well as thought about the world when Chip's building was built. It could have nothing to do with why he was killed, but I had to wonder, what were the killers looking for? Did the building hold its own secrets? If it was a well-known legend, I'd find something about it in the library. And if not, well, that was one more thing that didn't explain Chip's death.

An investigator I'd heard talking at one of Deek's author events said it was all about clearing away the invalid answers and reasonings first. Then you could see what was left. Sometimes I think I cleared away too much stuff. Like taking Dom and Chris off the suspect list because I liked them both as people.

Could I feel good about or like someone who had killed someone else? I guess that was a question I needed to ask myself. Maybe I was being fooled by Dom's in-your-face honesty. But he'd been so engaging at Thanksgiving. Not just with me, but also with Beth.

I looked over at her, wondering what she thought of the motorcycle club leader.

Beth turned down the music without looking at me. "I can feel you staring. What do you want to ask me? Did Evie tell you I did a bad job at the bookstore? If so, don't feel like you have to let me continue. I can take bad news."

"You did an amazing job at the bookstore. Like Evie said, if you lived here, you'd be already on the full-time payroll. If you wanted a job, that is." I glanced around to see where we were. I'd been daydreaming for a while and we were almost at the library. "Tell me what you thought of Dominic Reedy. When you met him at Thanksgiving dinner."

Beth rolled up the windows and slowed the car a little. "He's interesting. He's focused on what you say. I can see why Lille is attracted to him. He's intelligent. He truly listens, which sometimes is rare in a man. Clearly, he's done his research in cults, which made him a good source of local gossip about C-scam—or New Hope. He said he had a relative who joined a cult a few years ago and went deep. And another friend who knew someone who joined New Hope and gave the leadership their life savings. When it blew up last year, the guy had to go live with his mom for a few months. He's still convinced that the government killed Kane and blamed it on church leadership. But he has a job again and is learning to adjust to real life."

"That must have been hard for him. Watching someone go so deep into the fantasy they built." I paused, thinking about what Beth had shared. "Did he say anything more about the relative? I wonder how close they were and if it affected his decision to join the motorcycle club. You hear about people joining gangs for the family connection."

"Funny, I was wondering about that too. I asked him if he thought being part of his motorcycle club was the same thing as joining a cult." Beth took the exit to the college and slowed the car even more.

"You didn't." I was shocked at Beth's forwardness. I wasn't sure I could have asked him that.

"He blinked a couple of times, then he laughed." Beth parked the car in a visitor spot. "He said he'd never thought of it that way, but to an outsider, he could see how it looked like a cult. Then he shrugged and said, 'We have rules that others might not see as normal and we tend to be insular, but the club doesn't expect you to turn over your life or all your money. We even stopped killing people who wanted to leave years ago.'"

"Oh, my goodness, he said that?" I could feel my pulse start to race.

"He was kidding, sort of, but I do think he's changed things in his group. He doesn't want to be on the wrong side of the law anymore." Beth paused before opening her car door. "He did say he lost several members for going soft. He didn't want that life anymore. He just wanted to hang with his friends."

"A reformed motorcycle gang. I guess it could happen. Greg still thinks they're dangerous." I climbed out of the car and wondered if there was anything on the club I'd find in the library.

"Jim was furious with me for even talking with him. That's one of the reasons I stayed." She locked the car and then looked at my shocked face. "Oh, not because I wanted to talk to Dom or had any interest in him. Lille made it very clear he was her property. I don't want Jim telling me who I can talk with and when. He needs to learn I'm a person, not his possession."

"I think Lille needs to learn that as well about Dom." I adjusted my backpack. "Should we go play student?"

"Dom has to deal with that problem, not me." Beth joined me on the sidewalk. "See, this is why I love spending time with you. You get me."

"Two of a kind." I thought of Amanda's comment. "The King boys have excellent taste in women."

* * *

By the time we'd left the library and headed to dinner at a seafood restaurant in Bakerstown, I'd found nothing on Dom's motorcycle club, but several articles about his crimes and convictions. They were all ten plus years old and the angry young man in the pictures looked nothing like the calm, centered Dom who I'd met. I'd made copies, but I still didn't think Dom should be high or even on Greg's suspect list.

The stories about Chip's building were more interesting. There had been a death in the building much like the one that befell Chip, but it had been in 1970, just before he'd bought the building and opened his bar. The man had been tied to a chair, stabbed several times, then left to bleed out. The bar was closed down due to the owner being arrested for drug charges. And this bartender wasn't found for days. Until his girlfriend came looking.

The similarities were too close. They'd never found the killer in that murder. And the reason for the torture had never been released to the press. I wonder if Greg had the cold case files in his building. Would he let me research that, just in case solving it might help solve the new killing?

It was a long shot, but I could ask.

The bar and building had passed from owner to owner, with a few years of being held in trust for the state. No one had owned the building for long. And that fact, with the murder, had given the place a bit of notoriety. It was called the Bar of Death by a few newspapers.

I'd sent several articles to my email to read and had printed several others so I could read them later and highlight passages. With these articles and Josh's books he'd loaned me, I might be able to create a timeline of any oddities for the building. Maybe they would paint a picture that would lead me to a better answer. For both of the victims who'd died in the building.

"Did you know that there are more than ten thousand cults in the US, and California isn't the state with the most?" Beth asked as we drove to the restaurant. "I'm thinking of starting my book with a what you think you know about cults quiz, then I'll blow up the stereotypes. For example, if you go by a ratio per number of people who live there, the District of Columbia has a higher percentage, over fifteen percent, than any other state."

"Seriously, DC? I would have guessed California."

Beth nodded. "I know. Me too, until I started researching. Nevada is the state with the largest percentage, besides DC. And New Mexico is next. California is third."

"What other questions would you ask? Age of participants?"

Beth went on to explain her idea, and not for the first time, I knew she needed to take this job with the university. She had a way of providing information to others that stuck. She'd be an excellent instructor. I'd read part of her thesis, and even though it was academic, it was interesting. If she just tweaked it for the everyday reader, she'd have a winner on her hands.

As we walked into the restaurant, her phone rang. She glanced at the display and put it back in her purse.

Then after we'd ordered, it rang again. This time, after checking the caller ID, she turned it off. She saw me watching and shrugged. "It's Jim. He's called every hour since he got out of church. I'll call him back this evening when we're back at the house."

"Maybe it's important."

She shrugged. "He knows how to text. He wants me to come home. On his terms. I keep telling him the frequency of the question does not change the answer. I told him I was staying until Monday after next, and that's what I'm doing. Unless you kick me out."

"Then who will I have to keep me company while Greg works the case? I'm thinking about calling you to come visit every time he's involved in a big case." I studied my menu. Beth and I got along a lot better than I'd ever expected. Especially since Jim, her betrothed, had never liked me.

"I know you're kidding, but that warms my heart." Beth grabbed my hand. "I've never had a sister before, and no matter what happens with Jim, you're always going to be my sister."

"I feel the same way. What are you thinking about getting? I'm torn between the seafood pasta and the scallops." I squeezed her hand back and turned my attention to the menu.

"I'm going to ask about the specials, then I'll probably go with the pasta. It's Sunday. You should celebrate the day."

Greg called as we were on our way back home. "So where are you two?"

"Driving back from Bakerstown. We spent the afternoon at the library and just finished dinner. Don't tell me you're already home." I glanced over at Beth.

"Okay, I won't tell you. Don't worry, I'm only here for a few minutes before I head to Bakerstown. The county commissioners want a report on the murder and if it affects the holiday tourist season. They want me to tell them it's fine to have the annual parade next week." He sighed so loud I could hear it over the phone. "The fact that I'm in the middle of an active investigation is weighing on their minds. Especially after someone leaked that Dominic and his boys were at the dart tournament that night."

"Sorry, I would have liked to see you. Maybe you'll still be home when we get there."

He chuckled. "Maybe. I've fed Emma, so don't let her con you out of another can of food. And tell Beth that Jim's looking for her. He says he hasn't been able to reach her."

"Like I said, we were in the library, then at dinner," I repeated our schedule. "Oh, and she's taking a few shifts at the bookstore since you have Toby busy."

"I'm just the messenger. But please ask her to call. I'm afraid if she doesn't, he'll get on a plane tonight to make sure she's okay." He paused for a minute. "I love you, Mrs. King. Tell me you weren't investigating my murder case."

"I won't lie to you. And I love you back," I responded. I could see the ocean now in the distance. "We're about thirty minutes out."

"I'll wait. I can call Jim and let him know Beth's alive while I wait. You know he's going to blame you."

It was my turn to sigh. "He always does."

CHAPTER 12

Monday morning, Beth and I were sitting at the kitchen table talking about our plans for the day when a knock sounded on the door. I went to answer, checking the window first before opening the door. Greg worried about being so close to the highway, so he frowned on me opening the door blindly. I thought it was overkill.

Carrie and Chris stood on my porch.

"Hey, guys, come on in. We're just digging into a coffee cake that Beth made this morning. Save me from myself." I held the door open, and Emma came to greet our new arrivals.

"I don't want to be any trouble," Chris started, but Carrie took her arm and led her into the house.

Carrie paused in the living room. "What a beautiful home. And your dog is so friendly."

"Thanks, Emma loves people." I closed the door and pointed the way to the kitchen. "How do you take your coffee?"

After we got settled and Beth had cut generous pieces of the coffee cake for our visitors, I saw Carrie nudge Chris with her elbow. But instead of talking, she took a long sip of her coffee.

Carrie sighed and shook her head. "Sorry to barge in on you. Especially on your day off, but Chris wanted to tell you something. Well, she wanted to tell Greg, but she's concerned about how he'll take the news."

"Chris? What's going on?" I felt my body tense, but I stayed leaning back, looking more comfortable than I felt. I didn't want to scare her any more than she already was.

"Greg will throw me into jail if I tell him this. I don't think I'd do good in jail. Chip went to jail once when we were young. He was a bit of a partier before he got sober and, well, drinking never worked in his favor." Chris stared at her coffee. "I hated visiting him there. I thought everyone was watching me."

"Chris, Greg's not going to throw you in jail. Unless you killed Chip." I paused, trying to gauge what Chris might be trying to tell us. "Did you kill him?"

"Oh, heavens no. We were going to get married again. We were in a good place. I promise." She started crying and Beth ran to get the tissue box from the bathroom. "He did love me. I know what people say, but he'd changed."

Carrie rolled her eyes and pushed the box closer when Beth set it on the table. "Just tell them what you told me."

"I think this was a mistake." Chris was sobbing now.

"Chris, it's fine. You're safe here. What's going on?" Beth rubbed the woman's shoulder as she talked.

"Chip was involved in something bad. Something illegal. He had been before, but he swore to me it was over. Then, as I was cleaning out his office, I found a notebook hidden in his desk. One of the drawers has a false bottom. He used to store money and, well, pictures in there. Pictures I'd rather not have anyone else look at. We were just playing around, but the pictures would be embarrassing." She stopped talking and started nibbling at the coffee cake. Her face was bright red. "Of course, I was a lot younger and a lot stupider when I let him take them."

"Okay." I didn't think some racy pictures had Chris so freaked out. "What did you find in the notebook?"

She dug into her purse, pulling out what must have been the notebook she'd found. "He kept a journal. Some of the pages are people who had a bar tab and owed him money. He'd get paid, then he'd let them run a tab again." She opened the book and looked for a page. "Then there was this. I don't know what it means, but it looks like Chip was holding on to something for someone. Several someones."

I took the book and scanned the page. I turned back and found a bar tab page to compare. It listed the person's name, the date of the tab, and a running total. It also showed dates where they'd been asked to pay and the result. Some just had cut-off written at the bottom, but most had a paid-in-full note, and then a new tab had been started, usually just a few days after the other bill had been paid.

The page Chris had pointed out had a lot of the same details. But it was all in code. Initials versus names. Drop-off date, storage fee, and initials for the other person. The description of the items just said parcel or four parcels with dates they were picked up. From what I could see, the "storage fee" was always paid in advance for a certain period. Then a set of initials ended the line. This was more of a tracking than a running charge page. I flipped through several more and found two more pages like this. There were probably more. It reminded me of when my mom used to do layaway for my new school clothes.

I met Chris's gaze. "Did Chip ever say anything about the building having a safe or a hidden room?"

Chris shook her head. "No, and I thought I knew everything about the building. We always talked about turning the top floor into hotel rooms with a prohibition-age feel. Maybe even a brothel room. People pay big bucks for experience stays. We just needed to save enough money for the remodel. We had plans for the future."

Carrie pulled Chris into a hug as she fell apart again. I flipped through the journal. Maybe Greg would know more about what was going on. All I knew was that Chip was hiding something for someone. Which was next to nothing.

But could that have been what got him killed? What was he storing? At least it was a clue. "Can I give this to Greg?"

Chris nodded as Carrie helped her stand. Coffee klatch was over.

"Chris wanted to get this to you as soon as she found it," Carrie said as she gathered Chris's things. "She wants Greg to find out who did this to Chip."

"Could you not mention the pictures? I'll turn over the money, but I'm going to burn the pictures as soon as I get home." Chris grabbed my arm as Carrie walked her to the front door.

"Chris, I must tell him, but he will be discreet. Just don't burn them until you talk to Greg." I followed them to the front door. If I were her, I would have burned them as soon as I found the photos. But then, I would never have let anyone take compromising shots. Probably not even when I was young and stupid.

After they left, I returned to the kitchen, where Beth was still flipping through the journal. "I guess we need to walk into town today and deliver that to Greg."

Beth closed the book and started cleaning off the table. "I'm always amazed at how different my life is compared to other people. Then I am truly grateful that I don't have to deal with those issues. What was Chris thinking? If Chip hadn't kept his word and kept the pictures to himself, it could have turned out bad for her. I can't even think of all the problems she could have had. Being embarrassed when she told us about them would have only been the beginning."

"She was young. And in love. People do strange things when they think they are in love."

Beth shook her head. "Maybe, but I'm glad I didn't fall in love until I was older. Even now, with our problems, I'm wondering if joining our lives will be worth it. But our issues won't haunt me for years later."

We decided to wander through the Castle even though Beth had visited when she'd come for our wedding. She wanted to take the second, longer tour. Since I'd never taken anything but the first tour, I was excited to go along. Then we would grab some lunch and end our day, weather permitting, reading on the beach. Greg had said he'd be home for dinner. Especially since both Beth and I would be at the book club meeting tomorrow night.

I grabbed Emma's leash to take her with us on our walk to town. Greg didn't mind if she was in the station. In fact, I was pretty sure that when we left Emma with Toby when we went on vacation, she spent most of her day there with her guardian. I gently placed the journal in a plastic bag and then tucked it in my purse. Hopefully, this would be the clue that Greg was looking for. And Beth could attest that this clue had come to me. I hadn't gone looking for it.

Unlike the research I'd done on the building that clearly stated that it had a secret room where the money and bootlegged booze were hidden from the authorities. I'd send him those articles later tonight.

As we strolled up the hill, I was surprised that more decorations had been put out in yards and on the houses-turned-businesses that lined the street. The parking lot was nearly full and people were walking into town, excitedly chatting about what they were buying for gifts.

"I wonder if we should be open seven days a week during the holiday season," I murmured as a group of women who were clearly together went into the first business after the parking lot.

"Sometimes everyone needs a break. You might get more sales, sure, but even God rested once a week," Beth responded to my musing. "Or did you expect an answer? I can keep my mouth shut if you need some quiet."

"Never. Soon you'll be off teaching undergrads and I'll be walking by myself with no one to talk to at all." I thought about what she'd said. "I always wonder how much is enough. Greg and I are doing good. The house is paid for, so our salaries pay our living costs and give us money to travel and play. We're even putting money away into retirement funds. So is me opening another day serving my pocketbook or just my need to be busy?"

Beth grabbed my elbow and steered us around a group of octogenarians who were slowing down our progress. She let go when we were around the group and then laughed at my reaction. "Sorry, I'm around Amanda too much," she said. "That woman wouldn't pass someone unless her pants were on fire."

"Okay, fine, you've caught me. I'm also wondering what my life would look like without meaningful work. Jim wants me to what, stay home and clean? Or worse, get hooked on soap operas? I need to work to keep my mind active."

"I'm supposed to tell you to call him, by the way. Greg's worried he'll waste his money coming out to see if you're okay." I didn't meet Beth's gaze. "Don't kill the messenger."

"I'll call him while you go in to see Greg. I can watch Emma for you."

I shrugged as we passed by the almost empty motorcycle parking lot set up in front of Chip's Bar. There were several three-wheelers and an older couple climbed off their bikes and smiled at us as we walked by. Chip and Lille's insistence on an exemption to the town driving ban for motorcycles was at least being used, if not by the types they'd set it up for. "I'm not your babysitter. I'm just passing on a message."

Beth changed the subject. "I don't understand why there's a separate parking lot for motorcycles. Especially one past the barriers blocking off the street." She waved at the woman, who was now taking off her helmet.

"I'm not sure about the reasoning, but the mayor and council were already on the edge of being tarred and feathered by the business community. This exception almost pushed them over the edge." Emma got stuck on a scent near an art gallery and I paused to let her explore. Which put the slow group in front of us again. Beth rolled her eyes as she took in the street, which had been filled with people.

"I guess having the street closed makes the foot traffic easier." She stepped over to the jewelry shop window.

It was Matty Leaven's shop, and according to her signs, she didn't open until ten. The place looked closed down. She took the jewelry out of the windows at night, not wanting someone to be tempted to break in and see what they could grab.

"I guess if the baubles are out of sight, no one's tempted?" Beth walked back to where Emma was now waiting for us to continue our walk. She stopped and picked up a patch from the lawn and held it up to me. "One of the Demon Dogs has lost their tag. Will they kick them out for not being properly decorated?"

I giggled at the idea. "We can stop by Diamond Lille's on the way back and drop it off with her. She can give it to Dom."

"Men and their associations. Jim's just as bad with the church group he goes to. They have breakfast together once a week, I think mostly to grumble about their wives. I bet these guys spend their weekends riding their motorcycles on the coastal road. I'd do it all the time if I rode a bike. And lived here," she added, a wistful tone to her voice.

I looked over at her, but I didn't have time to dig into that emotion. We'd arrived at the station and Greg was just coming out. He smiled in surprise as he turned away from heading to the parking lot to join us. "Hey, what's going on?"

"We have a gift for you." I pulled the journal out of my tote. I explained our early morning visit from Carrie and Chris and what she thought the journal meant. "She also has some personal items that she kept. We can talk about those later, but I asked her not to burn them."

He looked up from the journal. "Personal items. Like pictures?"

"How did you know? Or was that a guess?" My face felt hot.

"Honey, let's just say if it's something the surviving member of the couple wants to burn, it's usually letters or pictures. I was heading into Bakerstown, but I'll swing by Chris's house first. Thanks for bringing this." He knelt and rubbed Emma's head, bringing her into a hug. "And were you guarding the humans as they walked the journal to me?"

"She was too busy sniffing all the smells to be a good guard dog." Beth teased her and gave her a rub.

Greg noticed the patch in her hand. "Don't tell me you're buying a bike and joining our motorcycle club. Jim will kill me."

"No, I found this in front of that jewelry store. I didn't even get a good look at the pretty things. They'd put everything up for the night," Beth admitted. She handed him the patch. "It would look good on my pink puffer though, don't you think?"

"The jewelry store is being cautious now. Of course, it's an example of closing the barn door after the cow got out." When he saw our confused look, he added, "They had a break-in on Thanksgiving. A lot of their high-end stuff was targeted."

I felt blindsided. "I hadn't heard about that. Why weren't you called out?"

"I was called out. Toby and I went for a few minutes, but then the Bakerstown guys showed up and handled it. I was off for the weekend, as was all of my staff. The mayor was upset at the extra cost, but the council approved it. When I got back to work, we had the murder to deal with. I thought I told you this. It's one of the reasons I've basically been sleeping at the station." He rubbed his chin where a five-o'clock shadow was showing through. "I'm running home for a shower and shave before heading out. I came in early to do paperwork."

"Oh, Deek thought he heard it was a domestic disturbance." I realized I hadn't followed up when Greg came back so early. I'd been lost in the whole Thanksgiving holiday thing.

Beth's phone rang. She looked at the caller ID and sighed. "It's Jim. I needed to call him anyway. I'll be over on that bench."

As she walked away, Greg looked at the patch. Then he held it up on his police shirt. "We should get new city patches for our uniforms. What do you think?"

"I think you need more sleep. Are you sure you want to drive to Bakerstown alone?" I rubbed his arm and Emma leaned against his leg. She missed him when he was on a case. And I worried.

"I'll be fine after a shower. Did you guys leave me any breakfast?" He tucked the patch into his pocket.

"Beth baked." I hugged him. "I'll wait for her to be off the phone. Do you want to take Emma with you? She's been missing you."

"I can do that, but I've got to go now. Thanks for bringing this up and for the patch. I can't believe the Bakerstown guys missed seeing this. Of course, it could have been lost after the break-in, but it gives me a reason to chat with Dom again." He took Emma's leash.

"Great, another reason for Lille to hate me." I hadn't thought about it being a clue to a crime when Beth found the patch. I watched Greg and Emma jog down the street toward home. Even without a full eight hours of sleep, Greg had more energy than I did. Especially in the morning. I sank onto a bench, waiting for Beth to finish her call. From the tone of her voice, I didn't think it was going well. But I tried not to focus on the words.

A lady came up and stood in front of me. "You run the bookstore, don't you?"

I stood up and smiled. "Yes, I'm Jill King."

"I came over last night but your store was already closed. Now the sign says you're closed on Mondays too? When are you open?" The woman glared at me. "I only brought one book with me thinking that you'd be open. Especially with the holidays coming up."

"I'll be open at six tomorrow." I tried not to remind the woman that the store wasn't open twenty-four seven. That we had lives too.

"In the morning?" Her eyes widened. "Does anyone come in that early?"

"Yes, a lot of people stop in for coffee on their way to work. The store will be open until nine at night, but we have book club tomorrow at seven. You may want to come." I tried not to laugh as I told her about the book we were reading and she shook her head.

"I'm not much for people. I just like books. I'll be over sometime tomorrow. But not at six." She walked away, still grumbling about my early open hours.

Beth walked up next to me and watched the woman leave. "Someone you know?"

"Nope. A customer dissatisfied with the hours the store is open. I guess she's staying at one of the bed-and-breakfasts in town." I tried to push the nagging feeling that I should be open on Mondays out of my head. I couldn't be all things to all people. Even as much as I tried.

"Jill, the store hours are fine. You have a good mix of people working for you. Don't stress about it." Beth turned off her phone. "Jim wasn't happy when I told him I was working at the bookstore. He said if I had time for that, I should just come home to my real job."

"I'm thinking he was talking about the one at the church?" I nodded toward the other end of Main Street. "Have you seen the whole town yet? I'd love to check out all the holiday decorations."

"I need the walk to burn off some of this annoyance. Why can't he just love me as I am?"

I thought about her comment, and as we came up on the winery, I finally responded, "I think he loves who he thinks you are. Jim did the same thing to me. I was a home-wrecker in his eyes and he couldn't get past that, even though Greg and Sherry were divorced before we started dating. He needs to understand that people grow and develop. Maybe he's scared that you'll outgrow him. Which is pretty insightful on his part since I think you already have. But don't tell him that. Love is love."

Beth giggled. "You are so bad. But I think you're right. When I call him tonight, I'll just tell him what I'm doing. And I'm scheduling a counseling appointment. He can be there, or we're done. I'm willing to see him as the head of our family, but he needs to see me as a helpmate, not an employee."

"You'll still talk to Sadie on Wednesday, right?" I didn't want to be the only voice in Beth's head. Sadie would be able to understand Jim's side much better than I could. I would have dumped him the first time he told me I couldn't do or be something.

Beth nodded. "Don't worry about it. I'm getting good counsel from all sides. I'll make an informed decision."

That was what I was worried about. But it wasn't my place to say. We headed home to get the car so we could start our day.

CHAPTER 13

Tuesday morning around ten, the woman who'd complained about the store hours came into the bookstore. She nodded a greeting, then went right to the stacks. When she finally came out with five books, I offered her a coffee or treat to go with them.

"Coffee, please. My sister-in-law is dragging me to more tourist spots and I'll need to be awake. I told her that we weren't going anywhere until I visited your shop. Sorry I was a little grumpy yesterday. Being with her all week is going to be a challenge. But when she suggested the trip, I thought we'd be hanging out at the beach, reading. Instead, she stops at every historical sign and has a whole list of places we need to visit here. She's already talking about doing the Amish area in Pennsylvania next year. I think I'm going to have to get a job to have an excuse not to go." The woman pulled out her credit card. And then picked up a flyer that listed our open hours. "I'm sure I'll be back. Thresa goes to her room right after dinner and I'm more of a night owl."

"Where are you staying?" I grabbed a couple of cookies and put them into a bag. When she narrowed her eyes, I shook my head. "On the house."

"South Cove Bed and Breakfast. The couple who run it are nice. He's the one who told me about the bookstore."

"Bill and Mary have a great library if you run out of reading material and we're closed. Mary loves sharing her books with guests."

"Huh, I didn't think of that. Of course, I saw the library, but I assumed it was off-limits. I don't loan my books out at all. Sometimes I weed through and put books in the little library down the street from me, but I never let someone borrow one of my keepers."

I rang up her purchases and handed her back her card and the receipt. "I have a hard time letting books on my keeper shelf go as well. But I have lots of room at home. Not an actual library, but my den has several full bookshelves. Thank you for coming in and not giving up on us."

She blushed a bit. "I did buy a couple of ebooks yesterday, but I love reading print. Holding the book lets people know I'm busy and they leave me alone."

"Catherine, come on. We're going to be late for our first tour." A blond woman came into the store and stood by the treat display case. "Ooh, those look good."

Catherine rolled her eyes. She handed her sister-in-law the cookies I'd packed up. "Here you go, Thresa. Thank the nice lady for the cookies she gave us."

"People here are so sweet. Especially that Mary and Bill where we're staying." Thresa smiled at me. "Catherine has been dying to get inside this shop since we got here."

Catherine grabbed her sister-in-law by the arm and headed toward the door.

"Bye, thanks for the cookies," Thresa called over her shoulder.

As they left, Judith came inside. She had a key to the back door, but I noticed she always came in the front if we were open. She walked around the counter and washed her hands before putting on an apron. "Those two look like trouble."

"Oh, I'm sure it's going to be an interesting week for the two of them. First trip together." As I thought about my most recent customers, I wondered if Beth would be up for a girl's trip one of these days before they started having kids. I'd have to schedule it around her school year, but I'd always wanted to see Belize and the Mayan ruins. Beth might like that.

I'd call her, but she was at the library working this morning. I was going to miss her. We'd talked about doing at least one FaceTime coffee hour a week when she went back to Nebraska. We were going for an early dinner at Lille's and the book club later tonight, so I'd bring up the subject then.

I finished up my end-of-shift tasks. Now that Evie was doing the general manager role, she was a stickler for checking the sheets. And she had no problem reminding me, the owner and her boss, that I was slacking. I loved her for it.

The morning shift had been busier than usual, and as I walked down the street toward home, I thought the afternoon might be even busier. I texted Judith and let her know if she needed help to reach out to me. I was meeting with Deek after book club tonight to talk about what time he needed off. Evie had sent me two names of people looking for part-time work. I told her to have them come into the store during my shifts this week. I might just hire both of them if I liked them. Having Beth take some of Toby's shifts had helped, but we were still short. Especially on weeks like this when everyone and their dogs were shopping.

I did my usual daily routine when I got home. Run with Emma. Start laundry or fold what I washed and dried yesterday. But when all that was done, I still had time before we needed to leave for the book club. Beth still wasn't home.

I made a shopping list for Christmas. I know, I was late. I needed to decide on what I was getting my out-of-town friends and family. And we hadn't started Christmas cards yet. I went to the office and searched the closet until I found the cards I'd bought on sale last year. Then I opened my desktop and looked for the file with the addresses. I always said I was going to change this file over to a label-maker format. And today, I had time. I looked up a template and updated the list I'd added to last year. I had to search in my Google history for the business addresses of some friends whose home addresses I didn't have.

The first listing in my search history was Zillow. I opened the folder and saw someone had been on the computer, looking up houses under $500,000 in the area. Was Greg looking for a new house for us? Or was Beth checking out her options? Both had been working in the office recently. I finished my label project. Now that the address file was set up, I just needed the actual labels. I'd run to Bakerstown tomorrow to the office supply store.

Then I went back to Zillow and looked at the houses. The ones highlighted were definitely Beth's vibe, as they were near the college and mostly condos. Greg would rather sleep in a tent than move closer to town.

"Hi, honey, I'm home," Beth's voice called out from the front door.

I jerked and closed the computer down. I hoped I'd saved my label file, but it was too late to check now. "I'm in the den. I'll be right out."

Beth came in and dropped her laptop bag on the shelf behind the desk. "What are you working on? Bookstore stuff?"

"Christmas card stuff. I haven't even started." I stood and walked out of the room, leaving the boxes of cards on the desk.

Beth picked up a box. It was a Christmas beach scene with a star shining over the water. "These are beautiful. Maybe I'll buy next year's cards before I leave town."

"There's a card shop in town but I could snag you some after Christmas that would be a lot cheaper." I headed to the back door to lock it. "We better get going if we want to stop there before the book club."

"Let me run up and change and I'll be ready." Beth placed the box of cards back on the desk and closed the den door. I kept my sofa pillows in there if I was going to be gone for a while and leave Emma home, so we always kept the door shut if we weren't in there working.

I let Emma outside and checked my backpack for my wallet, my planner, and the book we were talking about. I'd told Beth about my meeting after the club, and she said she'd wait and walk back with me. When she came downstairs, I let Emma in and locked the door behind her. Then I grabbed my bag. "Let's go. I'm starving."

At Diamond Lille's, we were halfway through dinner when Dominic Reedy approached our table. "Are you two heading to the book club after this?"

"Yes, we are." I glanced around to make sure Lille wasn't watching.

"I'll be there as soon as I eat. I got caught at work late." He smiled but made no effort to move.

I wasn't going to ask him to join us. Lille would have a coronary. And ban me from the diner for life. I turned back to my dinner but Beth wasn't so cautious.

"Where do you work?" she asked, adding a smile to her question.

Man, Lille and Jim were going to be mad if this went anywhere.

"I run my family's bar down on the highway. We've been in business for over fifty years now. My grandpa started it when he moved here from Pennsylvania with my grandmother. Then my father ran it. Now, I'm trying to turn it into a bar and grill. It has a bit of a reputation as a biker bar from when my dad ran the place. Lille's helping me." He cocked his head. "I thought you'd be back on the plains by now. Nebraska, right?"

"I stayed over to do some final research on my book and Jill and Greg have been nice enough to let me crash at their house." There was the smile again. "I'm surprised you remember."

"You're kidding, right? You're one of the most interesting people I've met in a long time. I've always had an interest in cults. My sister joined one when I was still in high school. She died a few years later. They told her she needed to not eat to prove her love for their god. But she was diabetic. They said their god would heal her. He didn't." He raised a hand to wave at someone behind us.

I could feel Lille's cold stare on my back but I didn't turn around. If I ignored it, maybe she wouldn't blame me.

"I better go. Tiny's made me a special burger we're thinking of adding to the menu at my place. Looks like it's ready. See you later." And with that, he left the table.

"He's so interesting. Did you know his family was affected by a cult like that? He didn't mention it before." Beth went back to her meatloaf as she talked.

"I didn't know that. But really, all I know about him is he's dating Lille. The woman who owns the diner." I tried to stress the word, dating.

"They're so cute together. They must be bonding over their love of food. I'm not sure Jim and I have anything we can bond over together. He doesn't read. He doesn't like cooking. And if I mention going to a show or a museum, he tells me he has a game or a race he has to watch. And this is while we're still dating. What's it going to be like when we're married and he doesn't have to be on his best behavior?" Beth snuck another glance at Lille and Dom. Then she focused on eating. "Is Amanda Zooming in for the book club tonight?"

"I think so. Deek's handling the meeting link." I should have asked if he needed help, but he probably would have laughed at me. I wasn't the most technically savvy person. That's why I hired people who were smarter than me. At least in that area.

As we finished our dinner, I was glad that the subject of Dom had dropped off the table. Maybe she was just interested in his personal cult story. I didn't want to be responsible for bringing them together if she dumped Jim and Lille dumped Dom.

I was overthinking the interaction. At least I hoped I was.

Besides, Beth would be back in Nebraska next Monday and I wouldn't have to worry that my almost sister-in-law had gotten me thrown out of my favorite eating establishment. I guess I could eat at Dom's new bar and grill if that happened. And Beth would be around more.

We walked over to the bookstore and helped Carrie set up chairs. Deek already had a monitor set up in the bookstore's seating area. We moved chairs around the couch and the fireplace that I never used. But it was a pretty focal point for the book gatherings we held in the bookstore.

As we settled in for the book club, I started to relax a little. Dom was focused on the book and didn't make eye contact with Beth or me. I wondered if Lille had said something. Instead, he chatted with the guy who had attended last week's meeting with him. Gunter was Dom's "bodyguard" and he'd read the book.

When Deek brought up the topic of suggestions on what to read next month, Gunter was the first one to raise his hand. He suggested they read one of the Lincoln Lawyer books by Michael Connelly. "It's kind of a hero's journey with a flawed protagonist."

I stared at him, but Deek nodded as he went over to the shelf behind him and pulled the books from the shelves. "The first one is kind of old, but we should start there, so if some of us like the books, we can see the character growth. Great suggestion. Anyone else?"

Mandy Thomas raised her hand. "What about the Harry Dresden books? We always say we're going to read something in the urban fantasy genre, but it always gets left off for women's fiction or thrillers."

Josh looked horrified and countered his wife's suggestion.

"We haven't read a California history book yet."

"That's because this isn't a college history class, honey." She patted his leg. "Besides, you need some variety in your reading choices. Did you know that before we joined the group Josh hadn't read anything but history and nonfiction in years?"

I tried to hide my smile but it broke out anyway. Mandy was good for my friend. He was stuck in his ways and his new wife was transforming not only the clothes he wore but his connection with the world.

"Besides, you suggesting we read history is like me suggesting we read fruit and garden how-to manuals. Not everyone wants to always be thinking about their jobs." She leaned over and kissed him.

Deek's face was red at the show of affection between the couple as he came back with the first book in the urban fantasy series Mandy had suggested. "We have two more slots, even with taking a week off for Christmas."

Dom raised his hand. "If nonfiction isn't banned, maybe our last week could be a book on goal setting for the next year. I've been meaning to make a business plan for the bar, but I keep putting it off. Lille said annual goal setting changed her financial outlook at the diner in less than a year."

A lot of our group ran small businesses in town and I noticed a lot of head nodding at Dom's suggestion.

So of course, Deek had the perfect book. And when someone else suggested a holiday feel-good book, our monthly schedule was set.

Deek ended the club and he and I went to the back room to have our talk. I paused by Beth before leaving. "I'll be out in probably thirty minutes. Do you want the house keys, or do you want to wait?"

"I grabbed the second set you gave me last week. If I get bored, I'll head home. Or I might find something to read while I wait." She patted me on the shoulder. "I'm an adult, Jill. I know how to find my way to your house."

"If you get home before me, can you let out Emma? She's good, usually, but she still can have an accident," I called over my shoulder as Deek poked his head out of the back to see where I was. "See you after or at home."

I should have asked her to wait for me.

CHAPTER 14

Deek was flipping pages in his planner as I sat down. I glanced at the planner and then asked, "Do I need to open the computer and get these dates on the staff calendar? Or can you do that after we talk?"

He looked up and blinked. "You don't even know what I'm going to ask for."

I shrugged and pulled out the notebook I'd brought along with me to the book club since I knew this meeting was going to happen. "I don't care what dates you need off. I don't want to lose you here. One, you're an amazing renter and I'd have to find someone new to move into your apartment. And two, with Evie, you guys handle more of the bookstore tasks than I've ever done. So what days do you need off? Also, what do I need to take off your plate so you won't look this stressed all the time? Lately, you look like you're going to have a stroke most days I see you."

He sighed and leaned back. "You don't know how hard it was to even bring up cutting my hours a little. I've got a new manuscript to write and now edits on the second book. And they've scheduled me a week's worth of in-person events for March. Not to mention blogs to write and video interviews."

"Have you scheduled a release party here yet? I would like to host it on release day if you're not already booked." I smiled as his eyes widened. "Don't tell me you didn't expect it."

We planned out his schedule for this next week while Beth was here and Toby wasn't. Then we booked out the next three months. He'd told me he would figure out what he needed to pass on, but if I left it to him, he probably wouldn't stop doing anything, so I made a couple of suggestions. Like asking Judith to take over the author events. "After we put yours on the books, that is."

"I like talking to other authors," he grumbled.

"Okay, then how about one of the writer groups and maybe the book club?" The look on his face was priceless. "You could still come, of course, but you won't have to be in charge of ordering books or handling the discussion."

"That might work," he admitted as he looked at his schedule. "Right now, I'm in the bookstore almost every day for one thing or another. If I just had a few empty days, I think I could do more writing."

"Okay, then it's settled. I'll talk to Judith tomorrow, and if she doesn't want all three, I'll ask Tilly if she can do one. If you think of anything else you're willing to give up, like the newsletter, let me know." I finished my to-do list and closed the notebook. As I put it away I asked, "You don't have any friends who need a part-time job, do you?"

"I've been thinking about that. It's too bad we can't keep Beth around. She's amazing already without much training." He closed his planner and went over to check the lock on the back door. "I'll go ask Evie if she needs me to make a bank drop. I know she needs to get home to Homer."

Homer was Evie's spoiled Pomeranian. "I've told her to bring him on evening shifts."

"She said he's not feeling well after the Thanksgiving trip, so she left him home. I think Olivia fed him too many treats while she was dressing him up in her doll clothes and having tea parties." He held the door open for me, and when we walked out, just Evie was left finishing up the closing task sheet.

The store looked empty.

"Did Beth already leave?" I grabbed my jacket and slipped it on.

"She said she was walking home." Evie glanced at the doorway. "She left with Dom and Gunter."

That didn't mean anything. Dom's and Gunter's bikes were parked at Lille's. I'd seen them when we'd left the diner. "Oh, okay."

"She's all right." Evie saw my hesitation, then added, "Right? Should I have asked her to stay and wait for you?"

"Beth is an adult and knows where she's sleeping." I repeated her words to me and smiled, but inside, I was worried. I just didn't need my staff to see it.

"Okay, well, then I'm out of here." Evie handed the bank deposit to Deek. "If you still want to drop it at the night drop."

"I can do that." Deek turned to me. "Unless I should walk you home."

"I know where I'm sleeping tonight as well. I'm fine. I'll talk to you all tomorrow. Remember, we're looking for one or two new baristas who will fit into this crazy crew." I paused at the front door. "Don't let me down. I know you two know more people than I do."

As I passed by the antique store, Mandy and Josh were sitting outside at a table she'd had him set up a few months ago. Mandy called to me, "Hey, Jill, want to grab a glass of wine with us? We're heading down to the winery for a few minutes."

"Thanks for the invitation but I'm worn out and I've got the early shift tomorrow, but have fun." I smiled as I walked away. The look on Josh's face told me he didn't want to go to the winery but had been outvoted. Mandy had two votes to his one. Especially if it was regarding a social activity.

Walking home meant running into almost everyone in South Cove who wasn't already inside watching television, reading, or sleeping. Or at the winery. We lived in a safe town. Especially if you read the mayor's marketing ads. Unless you asked Chip.

I hurried home. There were two motorcycles still in Diamond Lille's parking lot. From a quick glance through the windows, I spied Gunter, sitting alone at a booth. Dom was probably in the back with Lille talking about the book club.

I relaxed a little on my last stretch home. The sky was clear tonight and I could hear the waves on the beach. A full moon lit my path to the house, adding to the streetlights that the council had finally installed last year. The beach parking lot was also lit up, but there weren't any cars there. At least none that I could see from the top of the hill.

When I reached the house, I heard voices coming from the front porch. Emma greeted me at the gate, and when I opened it, I saw Beth and Dom sitting on the steps, talking.

"Jill, that was quick. I should have waited for you." Beth stood as I approached the porch.

Dom nodded his head in greeting. "If you need any more information, I can see what my mom has of my dad's old papers. He was obsessed until the cult leader was imprisoned and for years afterward."

"Thanks for talking to me about your family's experience. I think people don't realize how easy it is to be swayed by these groups. Especially when you're young." Beth waved as he left the yard and headed back into town to gather his bike and Gunter. She looked at me. "Don't look at me that way. We were just talking about his sister."

"Beth, you're not from here, and Dom, well, he's been in trouble before. I just want you to be safe." I called Emma inside just as Beth's phone rang.

"Just like clockwork. He's been calling every fifteen minutes since I left the bookstore. He needs to get a life." She answered the call and asked, "Is Amanda okay?"

From the response to the answer, I assumed she was and Jim was just pushing Beth's buttons. "I told you I'd call after the book club. I didn't tell you I'd call the minute I left the bookstore. You need to stop this."

I watched as Beth climbed the stairs to her room. I turned on the television and plugged in the electric kettle to heat water for herbal tea. Then I turned the television on to a cooking show and grabbed my laptop to email Judith.

I'd be here to talk if Beth came back downstairs. If not, I was going to talk to Greg and tell him to call Jim and tell him to back off or Beth might just be in our guest room for a lot longer than we'd expected.

I finished my email, then put the laptop away and cuddled on the couch with Emma. I wasn't going to think about Dom and his connection to Beth. At least not today. She had enough people questioning every step she took. She didn't need a friend to do it too.

* * *

Beth had come downstairs after talking to Jim, and we'd drunk tea and watched two episodes of a cooking show until she caught me sleeping through the final judgment.

The next morning, Greg was up and downstairs when I came down. I glanced around. "Is Beth still asleep?"

"As far as I know. Why?" He set his phone down and focused on me.

I poured a cup of coffee. "Jim's driving her crazy and, I'm afraid, away from him. You need to tell him to cool it."

Greg drank some coffee. "Have you ever tried to tell Jim anything? I'll call him today and mention that he's driving his fiancée over the edge but I can't promise it will do anything. He loves her and he's scared."

"But not scared enough to give her what she needs?" I held up my hand. "Not my circus, not my rodeo, but if he drives Beth away? I'll never forgive him. Having Amanda and Beth around is the best part of hosting your family. I don't think I could deal with a new girlfriend. Especially if she's as dull as he wants Beth to be."

"Elizabeth, Jim's first wife, wasn't dull. She was bright, funny, and sharp. She just wanted a family and to be a full-time wife and mother. She made the best cookies. Sherry hated her." He smiled at the memory. "I think you would have liked her."

"If you say so." I drank more coffee and watched Greg. "So how's your investigation going? Lille says Dom didn't do it, and the more I see of him around town and at book club, the more I agree with her."

"So if someone talks your book language, they probably won't kill anyone?" He chuckled. "Should I ask to see every suspect's home library?"

"I don't think it would hurt. At worst, you'll get to know them a little better." I shrugged. "Why do they have libraries in prison? Kane Matthews wasn't a great guy but he had a great library. There has to be a correlation."

"I'll have Esmeralda dig up any relevant studies." He glanced at his watch. "So the talk with Deek went well after the book club?"

"He's just freaking out about this first release. He wants everything to be perfect. With Beth here this week, she can fill in for Toby and maybe I'll have someone hired later today. Evie is sending a couple of friends over to interview. Judith is working the afternoon shift and has sent me her free days to add her to the schedule." I stood and grabbed two cookies out of the jar that Beth had filled with the cookies she'd baked yesterday morning. I put one on a napkin and handed it to Greg. "Be sure to tell Jim that if he doesn't get his act together, I'm more than willing to find room for Beth here. She'd have to talk Bakerstown University into giving her the same deal Omaha is giving her, but I bet there would be somewhere close that would match or exceed what they're offering. And I'd have a part-time barista and partner in crime."

"You mean that figuratively, right? The partner in crime thing. Because if the two of you are investigating my case, I'll put her on the plane to Nebraska today." Greg took a bite of the cookie. "Well, maybe I'll put an ankle monitor on one of you and keep Beth around. These cookies are amazing."

"I know!"

Footsteps on the stairs made us look up. Beth was standing there laughing at us. "I love both of you so much, but I've got to go back. At least by January. Maybe if Jim freezes a little, his heart will warm up and grow."

"Like that Christmas cartoon. But I don't think the green monster froze. I think he was overcome by love." I held up what was left of the cookie. "Like

I am for your baking. You could work with Sadie here too. It's not just the bookstore, but I'd have to fight her for you."

Beth came and filled a cup of coffee and refilled both Greg's and mine. "I'd love to stay another week and talk to Dom more about his sister, but I think Jim would explode and that would make Amanda sad."

"What about Dom's sister?" Greg asked, keeping his tone bland.

"She was killed by a cult because they wouldn't let her eat. She was diabetic. So she went off her medications as an act of faith, in their words, and they started starving her. They told her that God would save her if she was worthy." Beth pulled another cookie out of the bin. "My God knows I'm his child, so how couldn't I be worthy!"

"You have an excellent take on the whole idea of self-confidence." I loved having Beth around. She was always positive.

"I didn't realize Dom's sister was in a cult. Who told you that?" Greg was being nonchalant, but I could tell he was curious. "And when did it happen?"

"Dom told me. He walked me home last night from the book club but I think he first mentioned it while we were having dinner and he stopped by our table. I'm always interested in the firsthand family stories around cults. They tell you a lot more than the written accounts do. It must have been twenty years ago now, don't you think, Jill? I was planning on running to the library to see if I could find some information before I meet with Sadie this afternoon. Then I'm helping Deek with the evening shift. So I'll be home late, Dad."

I snickered as Greg shook his head and added, "I swear, you two are going to give me a heart attack."

"Dom said he was in high school. I got the impression she was a little older, but not much. He's changing up the bar he runs into a bar and grill. I guess Lille's been helping him with the menu and stuff." I wanted to change the subject. As I talked, I didn't meet Greg's eyes. I might not have been investigating, but I'd found out a lot about one of his prime suspects. And my observations were making Dom look less and less guilty. Then there was the thing about Dom walking Beth home. I lowered my voice. "I told you that Jim needs to get his act together."

Beth laughed just as she took a sip of coffee. She set the cup down and grabbed a dish towel to wipe the coffee off the table. "Please don't think I'm interested that way in Dom. He's a subject matter expert. Nothing more. If Jim and I don't work, I may never date again. I'm finding that I don't like people telling me what I can and can't do."

"And on that note, I'm heading to work. Thanks for the cookies, Beth. Be careful walking home tonight. If you want an escort, stop by the station and I or one of the guys will be glad to walk you home. Like I have to tell my dear wife often, a murderer is running loose, so be vigilant."

"You just tell me not to take Emma running and Toby comes to walk me home," I corrected his wording.

"I haven't done either one this time, have I? But I kind of expected you'd have company last night." He looked pointedly at Beth. "I won't tell you what to do, but if anything happened to you on my watch, Jim would never forgive me. So please, be careful."

We watched as Greg left the house. Emma stood and walked him to the door. I called her back to the kitchen and rubbed her head. "You're going to be on your own today, girl, until I get back from work."

Beth sipped her coffee. "I'm going to miss all of you when I go home. It's stupid that we live so far apart. Maybe after I graduate, we can convince Amanda to move down here. Once I have my degree, nothing is tying Jim and me to Nebraska except his mom."

I didn't want to get my hopes up, but I sent an invisible positivity bubble up in the air to the granter of impossible dreams. As I stood to go to work, I said, "That would be amazing."

As I was walking out to the sidewalk, a voice called, "Wait up."

I turned and saw Esmeralda crossing the street. "You're going in early."

"Greg has a meeting with the Bakerstown chief and the county district attorney. I want to make sure everything's set and keep him from having to dispatch until nine when Toby comes in. I have a feeling it's going to be a busy morning." She pulled a woolen shawl around her shoulders. Its red color contrasted nicely with her blue pants and dress shirt.

I didn't respond right away, but then I asked, "You have a feeling? Or the spirits told you?"

Esmeralda paused at the entrance to Diamond Lille's, where she was probably picking up food for Greg's meeting. "Is there a difference? Be careful today, Jill."

As I walked the rest of the way into town, I realized that both Greg and Esmeralda had ended conversations this morning the same way. Be careful.

I looked around before crossing the street. The dark empty windows of Chip's Bar gave me a chill.

Be careful.

I unlocked the door to the bookstore and turned on all the lights, letting the smell of coffee and sugar chase the scaries away. Time to focus on work and not killers.

CHAPTER 15

About nine that morning, after the coffee rush had ended, I was working on next week's schedule when a young man in a suit and tie walked in the door. He looked like a lawyer who lived on the bluff overlooking the ocean and came in every day for a large coffee and two cookies. He said it was just enough to get him through the commute. He was one of our audiobook customers from the store Deek had set up on our website. Now, several people bought audio for their drive to work after seeing the new release on the shelves when they were buying coffee. I would have, but my walk wasn't long enough to get involved in the book.

He walked up to me where I sat on the couch with my laptop and held out his hand. "I'm Andrew Walsh and I'd like to apply for the barista job."

"Good morning, Andrew. Let's do your interview now. I need someone soon." I set my computer down. "Did someone refer you?"

"Evie. She's my mom's best friend. Of course, I don't expect any special favors from that." The kid's face flushed down to the collar of his white shirt. His hair was bright red. I knew they liked to call it ginger, but he looked more like a carrot top. "I'm in school in Bakerstown and studying English Lit as my major. I'd like to focus on libraries in the future. I think they're dying out."

"Do you now?" I took the piece of paper he handed me. "What work experience do you have?"

"I worked summers at the Shake Shack in Bakerstown, but I'd like a more professional position where I could expand my knowledge of current literature and buying trends. My boss, Caryn Moss, said all you had to do was call her and she'd give me a good reference." He squirmed a little. "Well, she said great, but I don't like to brag. It was all about making and serving shakes there."

"Great customer service is what I need here as well. I'll give her a call. So can you start today?"

His eyes widened. "Of course. I go to school on Tuesdays and Thursdays, but other than that, I'm free. And I could work nights after five."

"Okay, Andrew. Let's start now. Do you have something besides that suit to work in? I'd hate to have you stain it." I paused as I stood. "I'll go get the hiring paperwork while you go change. Or do you live in Bakerstown?"

"No, I live with my mom about five miles away. I can be back in about ten minutes. Should I wear something specific?" Andrew stood with me and followed me to the counter.

"Closed-toe shoes, a full T-shirt—no sleeveless shirts—and long shorts or jeans. No short shorts. We're probably a little more formal than the Shake Shack." I paused and looked at him. He seemed smart. His resume was clean and showed he'd made honors in high school. As long as the reference cleared, and I thought it would since Evie sent him, he'd do just fine. "Do you go by Andrew or Drew?"

He rolled his eyes. "My mom calls me Drew, but I go by Andrew. I have since I started writing my name."

After Andrew left, I went to get the folder of employee paperwork I'd had Evie set aside. She'd already processed the paperwork for Beth. Two more folders lay on her desk. Just in case. I had a feeling I was going to be able to use both of them.

When Andrew came back, he wore jeans, tennis shoes, and a Have a Happy Day T-shirt with a yellow-and-black smiley face right out of the seventies. "You look perfect," I said as I handed him the file. "Fill out this. I've set you up with hours this week. You'll be training with a lot of different employees, but if you have a conflict with any of those days, just let me know."

I stayed a little later on my shift than I'd expected, getting Andrew set up, so when I ran into Beth coming into town as I was leaving, I wasn't surprised. "How did the research go?"

"Great. There was a lot of material to back up Dom's memories. Sometimes that isn't the case. Especially since he was so young when she died. A lot of similarities with the Matthews group, especially the fact that they started in Idaho and the local community ran them out of town. So they settled in a little town near Bakerstown. They hung out at the university to find converts."

Beth had paused in front of the Train Station, Uncle Harrold's shop. His son was running it now, with Harrold popping in now and then between cruises. I waved at Christopher as he watched us through the window.

"Do you need to stay longer with this new information?"

She shook a finger at me. "You're trying to get me in trouble with Jim. My agent loves the new information. I'm going to send her new pages tomorrow morning, once I review what I wrote today."

I glanced backward toward the bookstore. "If you don't have time to work the store, I can take you off the schedule."

"Don't you dare. Besides, Deek and I are going to talk about what to expect during the publishing process. I know his experience won't totally match mine, especially when you look at possible sales potential, but I really want his take on working with our agent. Sometimes I feel like I'm asking for too much." She glanced at her watch. "I've got to run. I'll eat at the diner before I go into the bookstore, so don't worry about me."

"And just like that, I'm on my own again," I teased. "This empty nest syndrome is hard to deal with at times."

"I'm sure you have tons of things to do." Beth looked around. "Besides, Greg kind of scared me when he threatened us with ankle monitors. He really doesn't like you messing with his investigations, does he?"

"He just worries." I adjusted my tote. "Oh, and Andrew should still be there when you get to the bookstore. Deek's going to train him in closing since you're there tonight."

"Andrew?" Beth grinned. "Don't tell me you already hired someone. Is he nice?"

"He is nice. Let me know what you think of him tonight when you get home. I don't want to miss anything."

"Okay, I guess I better hurry. I'm meeting Sadie in five minutes." Beth hugged me. "Thanks for setting this up. Maybe talking to someone who's actually dating a pastor will help me understand Jim a little better. Or at least she can give me scripture to throw back at him when he becomes too clingy."

"I live to serve." I headed down the street and toward home. Matty Leaven's store was still closed. Had the thief taken too much stock for her to reopen? Or was she on vacation? Whatever it was, at least she wasn't here making a fool out of Josh. Or getting Mandy riled up. I thought Mandy could take Matty if it became a fistfight. Mandy loved Josh and she wouldn't put up with anyone messing with his head like that.

At least I hoped so. Maybe I should finish reading those books he gave me and make my notes so I could take the books back and talk to him. Because if I didn't bring the books, he'd probably worry me to death about why I hadn't brought them.

First up, running Emma. Then I'd dig into the history of South Cove and the building that had housed Chip's Bar. Hopefully something would add to the storyline, because as of now, my only theory was that a roving steel-tip dart player had wanted Chip to tell him something.

It didn't sound probable. Not even in a B-movie plot.

* * *

It was almost dark when I finished reading the parts of the books that dealt with Chip's Bar building. One of them even had pictures of the inside of the bar when it was first built. I wondered if the library had more pictures and maybe a blueprint. In my notebook, I wrote down a theory and what I'd need to prove it. If the building had a secret room, Chip might have had something in there that someone else wanted.

I texted Chris to see if she could get me in the building sometime.

Surprisingly, I got a text back saying that she was going in tonight to access the work that needed to be done to reopen. She wanted to put a plan together and present it to Dom before he decided to sell the building and recoup his investment.

Greg had called earlier. He was in Bakerstown having dinner with the police chief there. Alanzo? I'd met him once when he'd wanted to talk to me about my old history professor and to tell me to stay out of his investigation.

I swear, these guys were like a broken record. No one even asked what evidence I'd found until I had pinpointed a killer. But to both Alanzo's and Greg's defense, most of the time I just had hunches.

Like the idea of a secret room.

I grabbed a tape measure and Emma's leash. At least I could pretend like I was just going on an evening stroll. I tucked the notebook and a couple of pens into my tote and we headed back outside. Emma glanced toward the beach, wondering why we'd be running twice today, but when I turned toward town, she quickly fell into place. Maybe she thought we were going to get Greg or even Beth.

No matter what my dog thought, just the size of her would deter anyone from messing with me.

I saw a few bikes in Lille's parking lot. I didn't know an Indian from a Harley, but I knew these bikes were large and made for distance driving. There weren't any three-wheelers or dirt bikes in the lot.

A flicker of light caught my eye as I turned to see a man leaning against a bike. The light from the flame added to the streetlamps and the moonlight to confirm it was Gunter sitting and watching as I walked past. I wondered if Dom was in the diner with Lille. He probably felt safe there, but if I was going to have a bodyguard, he'd be with me all the time. I waved and kept walking. I thought I saw his head tilt in greeting, or it could have been a shadow.

Emma had seen the guy, but didn't growl. Was that a sign that Gunter was one of the good guys?

The sky was dark when I got to the bar. The streetlamps shone on the front sidewalk and I saw Chris sitting on a bench, smoking. Not a lot of people I knew smoked, so to see two in less than five minutes was unusual. Chris's cigarette smelled different. Hers were menthols and had a touch of mint. I only got a whiff of sulfur when Gunter had lit his with a match.

Chris quickly put it out on the concrete with her foot, then picked up the butt and put it in her jeans pocket. "Thanks for coming with me. I wanted to get this done, but I've been a little freaked out about going into the bar alone. Ghosts, I guess."

"Memory ghosts or the real thing?" I didn't expect an answer, so I went on. "I hope you don't mind that I brought Emma. She's a sweetie, but no one knows that and she looks intimidating."

"I get it. I carry mace with me in my jacket pocket. Just in case." She took her keys out and unlocked the door. "And to answer your question, there are so many memories here. But I've never seen a real live ghost. If there are such things at all. I know your neighbor believes she talks to spirits, but no one in my life has ever come back to tell me anything. Even when Grandma's silver disappeared."

"You don't expect a visit from Chip when we go inside?" I followed her into the foyer area where an old pay phone still hung, as well as menus and pictures from the building's past. I took several photos as soon as Chris turned on the lights. Something might be a clue. You never knew.

"Chip wouldn't dare come back. He knows I'm not only grieving losing him but also mad as hell. We were doing good. Why would he get himself involved in something that got him killed?" Chris straightened a picture of her and Chip in front of the bar many years ago. "We'd just come back from our first wedding reception in this picture. I guess it wasn't romantic, but we both knew that keeping the bar open and making money was more important than going off to Hawaii or Mexico. If we even could have afforded it."

"Do you mind if I measure these rooms?" I pulled out my tape measure, notebook, and pen. "I'm going to take pictures of each room too. Just in case someone missed something."

Tears sprang to Chris's eyes as she smiled at me. "If it will help find Chip's killer, go ahead. You have a history of finding killers since you moved here."

"I've just been lucky." I tried to deflect the comment. Greg would hate hearing that I was getting credit for his police work. Even if sometimes it was true. "Let's get this done and get out of here. It's a little creepy."

Chris laughed as she turned on more lights. "I guess if you're not used to being in here, it can be a little spooky. I've always thought of it as charming and historical. Chip lived upstairs. Did you know that?"

I shook my head as I drew a picture of the front room, measuring the area. Then I wrote the feet and inches on the picture. Later, I'd put it all together into a blueprint that hopefully would match the one at the records room in city hall. Unless there wasn't one there. I planned on seeing Amy right after I left work and before driving into Bakerstown. "I didn't know that. Did you live there when you were married?"

"Until we bought a place out by the Castle. It's little, but Chip gave it to me in the first divorce. He moved back in here. It was just easier with him running the bar." She was taking pictures of the liquor stock and making notes on missing items.

I moved into the larger bar area. It didn't have much room. Mostly a few tables and the large wooden bar where Chris now stood. I drew the shape and then quickly took the measurements. "There's only one more room on this level?"

Chris nodded and pointed to the door to my left. "I'm not going in there. At least not tonight. I'll finish up this listing and wait for you out here if it takes a while."

"I'll be out as soon as I can." I smiled at her, but she'd already turned her back, working on the inventory.

Chip's office was one part storage room, one part office, and one part workout room. He had a weight machine and dumbbells. The wall was covered with mirrors. If there was a trap door, it probably wasn't there. I took pictures of it all, then started on the measurements. Seeing my mirror self watching me freaked me out a little, but I was determined to get this done.

A cold nose poked me in the back as I was bending over and I let out a muffled scream. Emma poked me again to see what was wrong. I sat down on the weight bench and rubbed her head. "We're almost done here, then we'll go to the bookstore and see if Aunt Beth needs to be escorted home."

Emma sat and wagged her tail on the dusty floor. I finished my measurements and then took pictures of the room. Nothing stood out. I went to the back door, unlocked it, and opened it to the alley behind the buildings. Just like on my side of the street. A dumpster was on the left side of the door and a small table and chairs with an ash tray on the other. A place for Chip and Chris to sit and smoke. Maybe talk about the future. It was just all so sad.

I shut and relocked the door after taking pictures of the outside area. Then I was done. Until I could see the building blueprints and compare them to my own measurements.

I turned off the lights and closed the door. Chris wasn't in the bar area, so I headed outside. I turned off what lights I could find, but Chris would need to come back in and finish the job. When I found her, she was smoking again.

She looked up and I saw she'd been crying.

"Sorry, I can't find all the light switches." I sat on another bench.

She brushed the tears off her face. "I was completely and foolishly in love with him. From the first day I met him until that Saturday night when he died. He always had my heart."

I didn't know what to say, so I just nodded.

"I'll get the lights and we'll be out of here." Chris smiled as she paused by the door. "Thank you for doing this with me tonight. I know you had your own reasons for coming, but I'm not sure I could have done this without you being here."

As Emma and I waited for Chris to come back, I heard voices across the street. Beth was leaving the bookstore with someone. I glanced at my watch, not expecting it to be that late, but it was five after nine. Beth laughed as they headed down the street. And as they stepped into a light pool from the streetlight, I saw who was making her laugh. Dominic Reedy was carrying her tote bag in one hand and had a Coffee, Books, and More coffee cup in the other.

This wasn't good at all.

CHAPTER 16

Since Beth didn't see me standing outside the bar, I waited for Chris to finish closing the bar and locking the door before I walked with her to her car in the town parking lot.

"At least Chip's gone and we don't have to worry about his spirit," I said as we paused at the entrance to the parking lot. Inwardly, I groaned. That was probably what every grieving woman wanted to hear. Or at least in the top ten, along with "Thank goodness he went quick and didn't suffer." Why did we say these things?

"You've been hanging out with Esmeralda too long. Chip would never hang around, even if there was a way to become a ghost. He didn't believe in looking back, only forward. One of the things I loved about him."

We said our goodbyes, and as I passed by Lille's again, Gunter still sat on his bike. He watched me stroll past. He didn't seem all that approachable, so I let it be. Just before I got home, I ran into Dom on his way back to town.

"Oh, Jill, we thought you might be asleep." He glanced around but we were alone. "Beth didn't want to disturb you."

"Dom, what are you doing?"

The directness of my question stopped him from walking past. "What do you mean?"

"Beth is engaged to Greg's brother. You're involved with Lille. She's leaving on Monday. Do you want to kick over this bucket of bees?" I crossed my arms and Emma sat at attention, watching both of us.

"I'm not doing anything. Beth and I enjoy talking to each other." He sighed and dropped his head. "I'm sorry. You're right. I am attracted to her. She's smart and pretty. Not that Lille isn't, but she's not interested in books or going back to school…"

I felt bad for the guy. "Beth doesn't even live here."

"She wants to, live here, I mean."

"Everyone wants to live in vacation land but some days you just have to put aside childish things." This wasn't my business, but I cared for Beth and didn't want her to get hurt. Even though she said she wasn't attracted to South Cove's bad boy, I was happily married and I could see the attraction.

A smile crossed his face. "She told me the same thing tonight. I promise that I will no longer seek out opportunities to be hanging around your soon-to-be sister-in-law and your friend. Take care of her, please."

"You better make sure that Lille knows this was all on you and not her. If you get me kicked out of the diner, I'll have to find somewhere new to eat and it won't be at your bar and grill." I matched his smile. I was concerned about my privileges at Diamond Lille's. Well, that and Beth's well-being. But Beth got to go home. I got to clean their mess up, if Lille would even let me try.

"This will not affect anything, I promise." He started to walk away, but then I called him back.

"Dude, if I was paying someone to be my bodyguard, I wouldn't leave him sitting in the parking lot while I went walking around South Cove."

"What?" Dom asked, then realizing what I'd said, clarified his question. "Where is Gunter?"

"In Lille's parking lot, smoking. Isn't that where you left him?" Now I felt like I'd ratted on someone in class.

Dom shook his head. "I told him to take the evening off. That I'd be okay without him."

"He didn't listen, I guess." I jerked my head toward town. "Because I saw him parked in the back of the lot. In the dark."

"Good night, Mrs. King." Dom nodded his head and started jogging up the hill. I hated people who could do that and arrive without breathing so hard that people thought they were dying.

Beth was on the front porch when Emma and I arrived. She glanced toward town, then back at me. "Out for a walk?"

"Not exactly. I met Chris at the bar. I've got measurements and pictures of the entire first floor. I'm going to put everything together and see if I can find original blueprints either with Amy or at the library tomorrow. I'm hoping Amy has them so I don't have to drive to Bakerstown again." I leaned on the handrail on the steps. "I think there might be a secret room somewhere. Do you want to look at the pictures? It's pretty creepy without people inside."

"Oh, I thought..." She paused, then decided to say it. "I thought Jim sent you after me. To walk me home."

I shook my head. "Nope. I was investigating. I had thought about seeing if you were ready to go, but I saw you walking home. You're playing with fire."

"I'm just talking." Beth stood and went inside. As I followed her, she paused at the stairs and added, "I'm sorry I misunderstood your intentions tonight."

I turned on the television. "I'm watching cooking shows for a while if you want to join."

"I'm tired and I need to call Jim." Beth didn't look happy about the pending call. "And write down some notes from what Dom told me tonight. I'll see you in the morning. I'm working an afternoon shift, right?"

"If you still want to. Did you meet Andrew?" I muted the television. Emma snuggled up next to me and watched Beth on the stairs.

"He's nice. Very put together. He reminds me of my first boyfriend. He knows exactly how his life is going to turn out." Beth smiled at the memory.

"It's going to be a rude awakening when the first thing blows up in his face. But he's solid and smart." I turned back to the television and found my show before I silently added what I was thinking, *And a warm body.*

That wasn't why I'd hired Andrew and I didn't think of him that way, but deep down, I kind of did. Until I got to know someone who worked for me, there was a distance I kept from them. I didn't want to get emotionally invested until I knew they were staying. I guess I was a lot like Lille in that manner. I just didn't have my staff wear someone else's name tag until they proved themselves worthy.

Tilly had kind of broken that pattern since she needed the job as much as the store needed her. If not more. But if she'd left the first week or two? I would have been gutted after finding out her background. Heck, I still missed Sasha and she'd been gone over four years. She'd graduated and gotten a great job in the city.

Time moved too quickly in our lives. I didn't want to regret anything. Like how Chris was regretting the time that she and Chip had missed. The problem with relationships is that both people have to be on the same page at the same time for it to work. Jim needed to learn that quickly to keep Beth. She wouldn't be in a holding pattern for long.

Greg woke me up when he arrived home later that night. He picked up the empty quart of ice cream and spoon off my lap where I was lying on the couch. I was pretty sure I'd finished it before falling asleep, but Emma had that guilty look on her face, so I wasn't positive. And the container looked too clean.

"Hey, go to bed. I'll let Emma out," Greg said as he turned off the television. He was pretty good at multitasking since he found me like this a lot.

"Have you looked at Chip's finances? Did he have some hidden income?" I stood and folded the small blanket I kept on the couch for chilly nights.

"If it's hidden, how would I find it?" Greg asked as he went into the kitchen to let Emma out.

I paused on the stairwell. I looked out the transom window on the front and saw Esmeralda's house. What had she said that morning? "You're kind of a super sleuth when it comes to things like this. Did you have a surprising day?"

He threw away the container and put the spoon in the dishwasher. Then he added soap and started it. "No more than normal. Why? Did you?"

"Kind of. I hired a new barista. Andrew. He's Evie's friend's son."

"Twice removed?" Greg asked.

I was tired. The phrase didn't seem to mean anything. "What?"

"Go to bed. I'm staying home tomorrow morning and walking you to work. I'm missing my girl." He laughed as Emma barked from the back porch. She must have heard his wording. "I didn't mean you, but I'm missing you as well, Miss Emma."

Smiling at my guy and my dog, I headed upstairs and got ready for bed. If neither of us had run into the surprise that the spirits had told our local fortune-teller was coming, had we gotten past the test or was it still in the wind? "Maybe a surprise suspect will show up tomorrow and confess to killing Chip."

"And monkeys will fly," Greg said as he and Emma came into the bedroom. He dug in the laundry basket and separated out his uniform shirts. "I'm going to start these now and put them in the dryer when I get up. Hopefully, one will be done before I have to go to the station."

"I could wash those for you." I climbed into bed, ignoring the book sitting on my nightstand. Maybe I'd have time to read tomorrow morning.

"Old habit. I asked Sherry to wash them once and I had to buy all new shirts since she put a piece of her red lingerie in the batch with them. Everything was pink." He found the last shirt and paused by the doorway. "And yes, I know you're not Sherry. I can wash my shirts, though."

I curled under the sheets, a smile on my lips. I knew it wasn't a comparison, but this one time, something Sherry had done hadn't come back to bite me. In fact, it was saving me some time.

* * *

I smelled bacon as I came downstairs. Bacon and maple? Or was that blueberry? Beth, Greg, and Emma were all downstairs and in the kitchen before me. Emma was drooling as Greg fried bacon, and from what I could smell, Beth had something in the oven. No wonder Jim didn't want her to work. She was an amazing cook.

"Good morning, family." I headed straight to the coffeepot. "Greg, did you put your shirts in the dryer?"

He chuckled as he put a plate of bacon and eggs down in front of me. "Hours ago, but thanks for the reminder. I'm just waiting to finish breakfast before I get dressed. The last time I made bacon, Toby complained that he was starving all day."

"He's always starving." I dug into my breakfast. "What are you doing this morning, Beth? I don't want to mention your leaving, but have you been on the beach lately?"

"Every day. I put it as one of my three must-dos in my planner. I'll go as soon as you leave for work. I should have asked before, but you don't mind me taking Emma with me, do you? She knows I don't run, so she just kind of hangs out with me as we walk."

"I bet she's loving it." I reached down and gave Emma a bite of my bacon. I wasn't above bribing my dog to remember who she loved more. "I might be driving to Bakerstown today if you want to go with me."

"I'm off at three if you can wait." Beth opened her planner. "I need to take some books back to the library and I'd love to spend a few hours researching this new cult that Dom's sister was in."

Greg sat down at the table and opened a muffin. The basket on the counter was full of them. He and Beth must have already eaten the protein part of breakfast since he'd cleaned up the pans after he gave me my plate. "What have you found out so far? I asked Esmeralda to do a deep dive and see if there's anything that connects Chip to the cult or Dom's sister."

Beth looked up sharply. "Because?"

"Because Dom is still a person of interest and revenge is a dish often served cold." Greg smiled. "These are good. Thanks."

She smiled back at him. "Well, if this was revenge for Dom's sister, the dish is frozen, not cold. But whatever. You do you. And if you want, you can take some of these muffins to the station. I think I made too many for just us."

"You're sweet, thanks." He didn't stand. Instead he turned his attention to me. "While Beth is researching cults for her book, you'll be doing what?"

"Helping her?" I smiled and felt my lips stretch over my teeth.

"Try again?" Greg pointed out that I'd said I was going before Beth agreed to come.

I opened my notebook and pulled out my phone. "Josh gave me some books on South Cove history to read. I found out that before Chip bought the bar, it had been a speakeasy and a brothel. There were rumors of hidden rooms to hide the bootlegged whiskey. Chris was there last night to see what it would take to open the bar again and asked me to come along. It was emotional for her. So I tagged along and measured the rooms and took pictures. I just need to find an original blueprint to compare the measurements. I think there might be something to the rumors."

He looked at my pictures and my drawings. "Fine. Go ahead."

"Thank you for your permission, but I wasn't asking for it." I closed the notebook and put it away.

"Jill, you never do. Oh, you asked about the cold case murder at the bar before Chip bought it. Apparently, the girlfriend did kill the guy. He was cheating on her. The case was closed, but she committed suicide soon after and the chief at the time didn't want to upset the girl's family. So he took it to the judge and the other case was closed with the note she'd left. Maybe they didn't file all the paperwork to get the dismissal filed."

"That's sad. I know it's only two deaths, but that building might be holding on to the negative energy now." I tried to remember what I'd heard or read about clearing a building. "Maybe we need to sage it? Can you ask Esmeralda?"

"Okay, Miss New Age. Beth, can you keep her from doing anything stupid before you leave? I know it will be hard, but it's only until Monday when you drive off to the airport. Then I'll take over the responsibility." He stood and put about half of the muffins in a bag. "And thanks for the muffins. I've got to get to work."

"Hey, you're making it sound like you're the boss of me," I complained as he walked past me and into the laundry room to get a clean shirt. He'd have them all hanging up on the rack in the room, waiting.

"Brothers. They're cut from the same cloth," Beth commented as she refilled her coffee.

Neither one of them answered me. Greg tapped his watch and reminded me that he was walking me to work.

At the bookstore, I was almost through serving the commuter line their coffees when a twenty-something woman came into the shop. Her long black hair was all braided, each having a little bead at the end that made noise as she walked. A yellow romper and blue neon tennis shoes completed the outfit. No one was going to miss this woman on the street or in a crowded store. She stood out. *Book shopping*, I thought as she went straight to the new releases and touched every book on the shelf. She waited for the last coffee customer to be served before coming up to the counter with one book.

"How can I help you?" I nodded to the book. "I read that last month and loved it."

"Good recommendation." She smiled as she set the book down. "I'm Zara Madison. My aunt said you were looking for help. So I'm here to help. Do employees get a discount? I'll probably just spend my entire salary on books, but it would be so worth it."

I loved her energy. "Let's have something to drink and we can talk about if you're a match. You have good taste in books. What can I make you?"

"Chai, iced." She picked up one of the bookmarks that Deek had designed for the store. "This is good work. Did Auntie Evie do it? I didn't realize she had graphic design skills like this."

I handed her the tea and then grabbed my coffee. I nodded to the table next to the counter. All the commuters had just bought and left. We were alone for a while. "Actually, no, another employee, Deek, designed those."

She tucked the bookmark into the book and left it on the counter. "Oh, the writer? That's unusual for someone to have talent in visual arts and wordsmithing."

"Deek's unusual, that's for certain. Tell me about you."

By the time Beth came to work, I had hired another bookseller. Zara was going to school part-time but hadn't settled on a major yet. She'd spent a few years traveling through Europe after high school, so I knew she and Judith would find some common topics. I liked her. She was starting training on

Saturday since she had classes on Monday, Wednesday, and Friday. Between her and Andrew, I should almost have a full-time barista. If they wanted that many hours.

I told Beth I'd meet her at three at the house and we could eat dinner in Bakerstown since Greg had already mentioned he'd be working late. So first thing was to see if Amy had a blueprint for Chip's Bar and maybe time for lunch. I headed over to City Hall.

She had just gotten off the phone when I came through the door to the mayor's office. "I am so glad you showed up today."

"Oh? Problems?" I glanced toward the mayor's office. Muffled voices came through the closed door. Loud muffled voices.

"Aren't there always? I swear, those two fight like this is a boxing ring, not a government building. Anyway, did you come to get me for lunch or are you just popping in?" Amy had her hand on the door sign that said *Be Back Soon*, with a moveable clock on the bottom.

"I need to ask a favor, then we can do lunch." I stepped closer to the desk. "Chip's place, the building, not the bar, does it have any blueprints?"

She took the file off the top of her desk in a wire basket. "Greg's already been here. He asked for a copy. But the problem is the only blueprint is from the bathroom remodel in 1990. There are no original blueprints here on file. He said you'd get me a copy if you found something this afternoon." She studied my face as I looked at the blueprints.

I assumed they'd match up with what I'd measured, except I hadn't measured the bathrooms last night and I should have. She handed me a folder with a copy of the print inside. "Thanks. This is helpful."

She put the original folder in a desk drawer. "Why did he tell me you'd get a copy of the original prints?"

I rolled my eyes. "Because I'm going to the library in Bakerstown today to research the building. I can't believe he used my information to check your files."

"Isn't that good though? At least he's using your work and not ignoring it." Amy grabbed her purse and rerouted her phone to the police station. She hit the intercom. "Esmeralda? I'm running to lunch. I'll be back in an hour."

"Tell Jill I said hi," was the response.

I rubbed my face. Everyone knows my business before I even do anything. "I don't know why Greg worries. He has spies all over to keep me in line."

"Or he knows you too well." Amy hung up the sign and locked the door. "Let's get out of here before Marvin or Tina open the door with something else for me to do."

CHAPTER 17

Lille seated us as soon as we walked in the door. "Where's your little friend? Maybe she wants to know more about Dom's family tragedy."

"Beth is working, and she's almost my sister-in-law," I said, hoping to remind Lille that she was engaged. "We're heading over to the library later today to get more information about this cult. You know she's writing a book, right? And she's leaving on Monday."

Lille's eyes flickered a bit when I said Beth was leaving on Monday. Whatever Lille thought was going on, at least the problem would be ended when Beth got on that plane.

"I didn't realize Dom's sister was in a cult." I softened my voice a little since Lille was still standing there. "I bet when the New Hope group moved here it must have been hard on him."

"And if you'd known, you would have looked at Dom for Kane's murder too. Is that what you're saying?" Lille challenged my connection attempt, slapping the menus on the table.

"No, I just meant it must have been hard for him and his family to have them open shop here." I stood my ground. I was trying to be nice, but if Lille couldn't hear my words, there was nothing I could do.

Instead of responding, she nodded. "He was a mess when New Hope first moved here. I'm sure it was hard on his mom, too. Carrie will take your order."

I watched as Lille went back to the hostess stand, then turned away before she could see me watching. That was almost the most civilized conversation we'd ever had.

"She's warming up to you, I see," Amy snickered behind her menu. "Soon, you two will be best friends and braiding each other's hair while you talk about boys."

"I don't think we'll ever be friends, but I'd like to stop fearing being banned from eating Tiny's food forever." I set my menu down. Since Beth and I were eating out tonight, I was going to get Tiny's fried chicken salad. It had probably as many calories as the fish-and-chips, but at least it had some vegetables to make it seem a little more healthy.

Carrie came over and took our order. And for the second time that Amy and I ate together, she ordered something healthy. Baked fish and broccoli with a side salad and just water. I was having iced tea. I wasn't that upset that I needed a milkshake.

Carrie left and I studied my friend. "What's up with you?"

She dropped her gaze and moved her fork from one side of the table to the other. "Nothing. Why?"

"Just that you've been acting weird. And, come to think of it, you didn't have coffee at the business-to-business meeting. Are you pregnant?" My eyes widened as I said the words. "Or sick? Tell me you're not sick. You haven't been surfing in forever, either."

Amy narrowed her eyes. "How do you know that?"

"When you're out surfing on the weekend, you come in on Monday or Tuesday and have a tan. Besides, you always brag about how amazing the surf is. I know Deek hasn't gone lately. He's pale and gaining some weight from being at his desk all the time." I stopped talking and waited for Amy to say something.

Finally, after Carrie dropped off our drinks, Amy leaned forward. "Just between us, Justin and I are trying to get pregnant. I'm not right now. But the books say if you're healthy going in, you have a better chance to have a healthy baby. So we've been working out at home and saving money, just in case I need some time off when the baby comes."

I should have known that my intense friend and her equally intense husband would have an intense plan for creating their family. "I'm so happy for you."

"Don't be happy yet. It's been six months since I've been off the pill and no baby yet. Maybe I missed my fertile years." Amy grimaced as she sipped her water.

"I'd blame him first," I said as Carrie set my salad in front of me. "Carrie, this looks amazing. Please tell Tiny he's a god."

"Not in this lifetime. The guy already has a big enough head. Dom's been trying to get him to run his kitchen too." She sat Amy's lunch in front of her. "I don't see you guys out as much lately."

"The holidays." Amy waved the statement away. "Jill's too busy with the bookstore now that her aunt has turned cruising into a lifestyle."

Carrie shook her head. "That's not the reason, but whatever. Hey, Jill, Chris told me to say thanks for coming with her last night. She didn't think she could have done it alone. I don't know how she thinks she can run the bar."

After Carrie left, Amy waved at me with her fork. "What's Carrie talking about you and Chris? I was kidding about you replacing me as your best friend. Although Beth's auditioning for the part, I think. When is she going back to Nebraska again?"

I chuckled. "Beth is leaving on Monday. Chris just needed someone to go with her when she went to the bar to figure out what she needed to do to reopen."

"Seriously? She thinks Greg's just going to let her reopen?" She looked up from her meal. "Oops. Forget I said that."

"Please don't tell me that she moved up on Greg's suspect list. The woman's a wreck." I carefully stacked all the bits of salad, lettuce, tomato, cheese, and chicken on my fork to make it a full bite. When Amy didn't answer, I looked up and saw her biting her lip. "What?"

"I can't tell you anything I see on the copy machine or what I overhear. I already got in trouble with the mayor about letting something out. I like my job." She put her fork down. "Look, I love you and would step in front of a speeding train for you, almost. But Justin and I are trying to make a life here. If I lose my job, I don't know if we could keep the house. I need to be more discreet about Greg's cases. Especially with you."

I set my fork down. I hadn't realized that Amy was getting pressure from anyone about letting me see things. "And Greg approved the blueprints before I even asked."

She nodded. "He's got a tight hold on information for this case. Why do you think Toby hasn't been around? There are too many connections here. The district attorney even questioned your involvement in the tournament."

"I was a suspect? Because I helped set up the charity event?" Now I was floored. What was Greg thinking?

"Not for long. The guy's new and wants to be known for being tough on crime. I think he's running for governor soon. Which has the mayor all up in arms since that's his and Tina's eventual goal. So like I said, access to information has been tight." She picked up her fork and ate a piece of broccoli. "I'll tell you one thing though. Greg was on this guy's butt as soon as he brought up your name. He read him the riot act and the guy just folded like a bad hand in cards. Esmeralda told me that after the meeting."

"If he's going to point a finger at everyone who was involved in the event, most of the full-time residents of South Cove were there. This is stupid." I wanted to call Greg and yell at him, but it wasn't his fault. I'd put myself in this guy's line of sight by always trying to solve the murder before Greg did. Who did I think I was? Nancy Drew?

"I'm sorry I put you in this position." I smiled at Amy, who looked like she was going to have a coronary. "Let's talk about something else. How's the house remodeling going?"

After lunch with Amy, I ran the beach with Emma. It was chilly and she'd already been walking with Beth, but my head needed clearing. I didn't want to get Amy in trouble, especially not cause her to lose her job. But we'd been able to talk about everything for years. Now, she hadn't even told me that she and Justin were trying for a family. And she was fearful of being fired because of me. Amy was my best friend. If we couldn't talk to each other, then what was the point?

I went home and worked on the bills. If I was going to be depressed, I might as well do something productive.

The door opened at 3:10 and Beth came in chatting. "I adore Zara and Andrew. How in the world did you find two people who were so perfect of a fit for the bookstore?"

"I have good employees who have good contacts." I was on the couch, watching an old romantic comedy Christmas movie that always perked up my mood. Today, even the movie wasn't working. "I don't know if I'm up to going to Bakerstown today. Maybe I should just sit this investigation out."

Beth frowned and went to sit by me. She moved the bowl of red and green M&Ms out of my lap and pushed my hair out of my eyes. I still had my running clothes on, except for the sneakers, which were in the middle of the living room floor where I'd kicked them off. "What are you talking about? You live for these investigations. And you're good at seeing past what Greg sees through his law enforcement filter. Besides, you love it."

I couldn't help it, I started crying. "Amy's been threatened with her job if she leaked information. Toby's avoiding me. And Greg was looking at me as a suspect."

"One, I don't think the last one is true at all. And two, you saw Toby at Thanksgiving. Three, I agree that Amy is in a hard position. She has to deal with confidential information all the time. Besides, she never really tells you things, does she? Isn't it more that she confirms what you know? Or that she lets you look at files that are open under the Public Information Act? Besides, you're not out there publishing what you learn or suspect like your friend Darla." Beth wiped my face with a clean tissue. "I thought you were stronger than this. You've been the one holding me up when I thought I needed to give up my career for love. Now you crumble over one lunch?"

I laughed and grabbed another tissue. "You're right. Greg wasn't looking at me, the district attorney brought up my name since the store was sponsoring the dart tournament. Greg shut him down, fast."

"As he should. He's your husband, yes, but he's not stupid." She turned the movie off. "So tell me what Amy actually said?"

After I walked Beth through my lunch, I realized I was reacting more to the idea that Amy and Justin were planning a family. Something she hadn't mentioned. Was it because she didn't think I wanted kids? Or did she just want this to be between them? "I feel like an idiot."

"I've felt like one for a few months now, ever since I told Jim about my amazing job offer with the next degree. I didn't understand how we could have gotten on not only two different pages, but I think we're in two different libraries in two different countries. Okay, he's probably reading a magazine at a ball game and I'm in a library." Beth nodded as I smiled. "There you are. Let's go get our work done. I'm dying to know if there is a secret room in the bar building. I wonder what could be hidden inside."

"Whatever it was, I'm certain that the item or items was why Chip was killed. According to Doc Ames, Chip bled out. The killer didn't shoot him or cut his throat. He died because he was tortured. Maybe the killer thought Chris would come looking for Chip. Or even that Chris was upstairs in the apartment. She said they'd been trying again." I saw Beth's smile widen. I was starting to feel more myself. "You got me talking about the murder again on purpose, didn't you?"

"Maybe. But I like this Jill much better when she's trying to help someone else rather than worry about not being first to know something about a friend." Beth stood. "I need to clean up. I smell like coffee and cookies. It's not a bad smell, but it makes me want to eat all the time. I don't know how you work there."

"The books keep me company." I stood and glanced at my running clothes. And honestly, I did snack all the time. "I'll be ready in a few minutes. Thanks for pulling me out of my funk."

"No problem. I feel like I still owe you a few pep talks after this visit." Beth hurried upstairs and I let Emma out to run a little before we left. Then I followed Beth upstairs to change. I had microfilm to review.

* * *

After coming up empty-handed after a few hours of searching, I was waiting for Beth to come downstairs so we could go to dinner. Mary Ann waved me over to her research desk. "Your friend is diving deep into local religious sects and cults. I just printed off a list of online libraries that list more recent articles. Did she come with you?"

"She's just finishing up some notes upstairs, then we're heading over to Rascal's Seafood for dinner. How have you been?" Mary Ann helped me with several projects when I was working on my MBA.

"Good. We're busy all the time. The school needs to hire another librarian, but they keep saying we can have more interns. Who don't show up since it's unpaid work and they get invited to a party down the hall." She opened a book and scanned it back into the system. "So I'm doing outdoor drop box check-ins most days. I guess you don't have that problem at the bookstore since you don't get returns."

"Not usually. But I feel your pain on hiring. I just had to reassess and shuffle staff assignments and hire two more part-time employees. One of my main guys is releasing his first book next year. Either he's going to be busy because it's probably freaking great, or he'll be too depressed to work if it doesn't sell."

"That's Deek Kerr, right? He was a regular around here until you offered him work and a place to live. Make sure you send over his release party info. A lot of us would love to come and support him." She checked in another book. "And we'll buy a copy or two for the library. I've got a shelf of books written by our graduates near the entrance."

"He'd love that." I adjusted my backpack. Beth still wasn't down. "Hey, do you know of anywhere that might have an old blueprint of a South Cove building built in 1922?"

She set the book down and reached into a file on her desk. She pulled out a flyer and handed it to me. "If anyone has it, it will be this place. California history research and development. It's funded by the state. We send all our old material there if it has anything to do with California history."

I scanned the page. It had a website and an email address for specific research questions. "This is great."

"Are you ready?" Beth asked, now standing at my side.

I nodded and tucked the page into my tote. I could research it tonight when we got home.

"Sure. But first, Mary Ann has a parting gift for you." I let the two of them talk. As we were walking out of the library, I paused. "Are you coming back before you leave?"

"I'll probably write here for the next three days while you work. I find I get so much more done here than at the house. Emma keeps falling asleep under the desk and then she makes me tired." Beth held the door open. "Besides, there's just something about being on a college campus that makes it seem like anything's possible. I think that's why I'm so excited to start in January."

"So you're taking the offer?" We headed to the visitors' parking lot where I'd left the Jeep.

Beth glanced around the still-green quad area. Not a lot of students were here because of the holiday break, but the few who were out were reading or chatting. "I believe I am. I'm just going to hope that God gives Jim the insight he needs to understand my calling."

"You will be amazing." I unlocked the doors and started the engine, turning on the heater to full blast. Other people might not find the temperatures cold here, but I loved my days at seventy, seventy-five at best. Unless I was tanning on the beach. "Let's go eat."

By the time we got home, Greg was there, waiting. Emma was sitting outside with him and there was evidence of a steak being grilled along with a baked potato in the oven.

"I didn't think you were coming home for dinner," I said after Beth had excused herself to go work upstairs in her room and call Jim. "We could have made dinner here."

"I know how to cook." He looked up at the stairs where Beth had disappeared. "Is she okay?"

"She's resigned to the fact that Jim's going to be Jim. And she's taking the job offer. We're going to have a doctor in the family if your brother isn't an idiot." I grabbed a bottle of water from the fridge. "Do you want to go out to the porch and talk?"

"Sure. I have something I need to say, anyway." He grabbed a water and we, along with Emma, went outside on the back porch. The sun had already set but the color was still hanging around. Greg turned on the back porch light as we came out.

"Am I a pain?" I decided to start with the obvious. "Do I make your job hard?"

He sat next to me on the swing and put his arm around me after putting the water on a side table. "Every day of my life. And I love it. Amy told me you were upset about the talk she got about confidential materials, but that mostly came from Marvin. And it wasn't about you. Marvin's worried that someone, ahem, Amy will leak campaign information to his rivals. Of course, they always change since Marvin never really commits to running for anything else besides South Cove mayor."

"I wasn't as worried about that as the fact that she kept something personal from me. But I think she felt like it needed to stay between her and Justin. I realized I keep our stuff a little close to the chest too. I know you have an image to uphold in South Cove."

He squeezed me. "I can take care of my image. And no, I don't like you investigating but, Jill, you have a knack. And if you weren't ninety-five percent devoted to your bookstore, I'd suggest you go to the academy. But that's not you."

"You're lucky it's not. How on earth would we stay married if we also worked together? I need alone time or I'd never get anything read."

CHAPTER 18

Friday morning, my commuters kept me busy pouring coffee until long after nine, so I didn't have time to check out the website that Mary Ann had given me. Andrew showed up at ten and I worked with him, setting him up for the day, before returning to my couch with my laptop.

And of course, the agency or library stated that they had a blueprint but didn't have a scanned copy online. Then a popup asked me if I wanted to donate time to get the backlog of materials scanned and available for use.

It wasn't my cup of tea, but the headquarters of the place was only a few miles up the road, so I sent an email with the volunteer information to my staff. Not that I needed to lose anyone, but if they were looking for a chance to give back, this might work for the techier of them.

"My friend works there," Andrew said behind me, pointing at my screen. "He's getting his graduate degree in history and has an internship with them."

"I'm looking for a blueprint for an older South Cove building. What's the best way for me to go about getting a copy of it? It's not on their website. Can you ask him?"

"Sure, hold on." He pulled his phone out of his khakis and texted a message. The response came back quickly. "Huh. He says if you come today, he's got some free time and he can help you search. Otherwise, sending an email request will get you an answer in a week or two. They prioritize people over emails."

"Great. What's his name? I can be there by one." I had already checked directions in Google Maps, so as long as I left here on time, I should be able to make the appointment I'd just made.

"His name is Jamal and he'll meet you in front of the building. I guess the old stuff they haven't scanned as a digital record is all filed by room. South Cove has its own room. He told me that our town has a lot of interesting stuff. Did you know there used to be a mission here?" He looked up as someone walked into the bookstore. "I'll get this and let you know if I have questions."

From Beth and Deek's report on Andrew's first day, I didn't think he'd have any questions at all. Evie was thrilled I'd hired both of her referrals. And she'd be even more thrilled if they stayed ninety days since I would give her a bonus for each hire. Getting solid referrals kept me from having to do much if any work on hiring.

I slipped the flyer Mary Ann had given me into my notebook and took that and my laptop to the counter, tucking them into my tote. Then I grabbed the end-of-shift clipboard and started my to-do list. I wanted to be ready to leave on time since meeting up with Andrew's friend seemed like the fastest way to get the information.

As I cleaned, I listened to Andrew chat with the customers. He was funny without being crass and attentive without watching over everyone's shoulders. I thought he'd do very well. And if he didn't, I'd make Evie fire him.

Beth worked this evening and she'd told me she'd be at the library this morning, so when I got home from work, I let Emma out and grabbed my keys for the Jeep. I wished I could take Emma, but I knew she wouldn't be allowed inside, and even though it wasn't hot, I didn't like leaving her in the car for long. And who knew how long this project would take? It was better to be safe than sorry. I turned on the television so she would have some noise and then got in my Jeep to head out to the historical library.

The weather was perfect for watching the waves while I drove. Luckily it wasn't too far for me to get distracted.

When I got there, a tall young Black man sat on the steps, waiting. He looked like he worked out. Not your typical library rat. He wore dress pants and a button-down shirt. "Are you Jamal?"

"You must be Jill King. I've been in your shop several times, but it's usually nights when Andrew's godmother or your blond surfer dude with dreadlocks is there. I don't think we've ever met." He held out his hand.

I shook his hand and looked around. "This is amazing. I'm not sure I knew it existed."

"The original library started in Sacramento. We took over the coastal area about ten years ago when Sacramento cried uncle on all the historical documents it was being given. So now there are three libraries. Northern, inland, and our coastal building. We handle from San Francisco down. I bet both San Francisco and LA will have their own buildings within ten years. There's just too much history happening here for us not to grow." He paused the history lesson as he held the door open for me and we went inside. "If you need a jacket, let me know. We have the temperature low to keep the materials safe. All the South Cove stuff is in this room down the hall."

I followed him to a room where there were boxes of materials lining the walls. Several bookcases were sparsely filled with either books or boxes. He led me to a set of drawers that weren't more than four inches tall. He slapped the top of the cabinet. "All the blueprints should be in here unless they haven't been unboxed yet. We separate them by year. Do you know what year your building was built?"

"In 1922," I said as I scanned the labels. "Here's 1900–1930, fingers crossed."

I pulled open the drawer to see three blueprints. The bank, the library, and a building I knew had been torn down when they built City Hall. "It's not here."

"I would have been shocked if it was." Jamal smiled at me. "Don't freak out. We've got a lot of stuff to look through. You take all the drawers from 1800 forward and I'll start unboxing over there. I thought I saw some boxes labeled tax records."

I knelt on the floor and pulled out the first drawer. Empty. Same with the second, and third. If there ever was a picture of what a wild goose chase looked like, it would be me, on the floor looking through empty or almost empty drawers.

Two hours later, I'd gone through all the drawers and Jamal had unpacked five boxes. Neither one of us had been successful in finding the building's blueprints.

He held out a notepad. "Write down your name and phone number and exactly what building we're looking for the blueprints for." He hadn't found any blueprints during his search but he had found some old menus from a restaurant in South Cove in the fifties.

I took the paper and wrote my information on it, even though I figured I was at a complete dead end. "Thanks, Jamal. I appreciate everything you did."

"Andrew says he's working for you. He's a great guy. A little buttoned up, but a good guy. We bonded in undergrad. We lived on the same floor in the dorms. I'm glad he's finding his path." He took back the notebook and pen and walked me out to the front door. "Come any time. We love having visitors."

Which I knew was a complete lie since he'd walked me to the room and escorted me out using his passkey for every door. The security here was tight. At least Greg couldn't say I was putting myself in danger, sitting in a locked library digging through historic documents.

As I drove home, I wondered if Josh knew about this treasure trove of history. I would stop in tomorrow and return his books and tell him about the document library. Beth was still out when I got home, so Emma and I ran on the beach.

After that, I texted Greg to see if he was coming home for dinner. *Maybe*, was the response. When I texted Beth, I was surprised to get an answer. She kept her phone off, so she must have been in the car with the phone plugged in.

I'm meeting someone for coffee, then going directly to the bookstore. I had a big lunch.

Her response seemed normal, but I wondered who she was meeting for coffee. Hopefully Sadie or a fellow student. There was only one person who could be an issue. Dom. But as Greg liked to say all the time, at least to me, not my circus, not my monkeys.

Unless Lille took it out on me.

I would be alone for dinner. Greg's *maybe* usually turned into a *no*, so I needed a plan. The fridge was empty. I could drive into Bakerstown to get groceries, or I could leave that chore until Sunday. I picked up the phone and placed a to-go order at Diamond Lille's. This way, at least I'd have Emma to keep me company. And we could walk there and back. I got her leash, tucked my wallet and Josh's books into my backpack, and headed into town. After I got back, I'd curl up with the book Deek had assigned me for the Staff Recommends part of the newsletter and see if I could get far enough to write something for his upcoming newsletter.

First stop, the bookstore, just to check in.

Deek and Judith were there, as well as a few customers scattered about. They must have had a rush earlier, because both of them were in the dining room cleaning when I came inside. Deek saw me first. "Jill, what's going on? Did Beth bail on her shift?"

"No, I'm just checking in." I stayed near the doorway, hoping Emma wouldn't bother anyone. I could have come in the back and left her in the office, but I wanted to make this visit quick. "How did Andrew do?"

Judith moved her bin to the next table, spraying and wiping down the last one as she talked. "He did great again today. He's curious and thinks ahead. And he's got a wide variety of reading habits. I think he'll be a real asset."

Deek nodded. "I'm beginning to worry about my job. You hired two people in two days who should be amazing and blend in with the crew."

"I have to keep you around. You know where too many bodies are buried." I smiled and because of the shocked look on a customer's face, I added, "Figuratively, that is."

"Did you need something?" Deek moved closer. "Judith's about to leave, but if you need to talk to one of us, I can ask her to stay."

"I was just checking in, so I'm out of here." I pulled on Emma's leash. "Have a great shift with Beth. She's enjoying playing barista."

"She can work with me anytime." Deek held the door open for a customer and then followed him up toward the counter. "Coffee or books tonight?"

I wasn't needed. On one hand, it kind of felt good, but then again, I felt empty. I knew too well how Deek felt about being easy to replace.

Our next stop was Antiques by Thomas. Mandy was at the front desk and came around to see Emma as we walked inside.

"Is Josh around?" I asked.

Mandy looked up at me as she rubbed Emma's back. "I sent him out to an estate sale. He's been driving me crazy all day."

"Oh?" Honestly, being around Josh for just a few hours drove me crazy too, but Mandy had married the guy.

"Yeah, he's all upset that the new jeweler has ghosted him. She said she had some connections in used jewelry and now she won't even answer the phone when he calls. The woman called late on a Saturday night a few weeks ago. I got to his phone first and reminded her that he was married. She hasn't talked to him since."

"You picked up her call?" I was trying not to laugh.

She stood and rolled her eyes. "I was up reading. Josh crashed as soon as we got home from the dart tournament. He's such a lightweight. Anyway, his phone was in the living room, so I picked it up, thinking it might be an emergency with family."

"But it wasn't," I guessed.

She leaned against the checkout desk. It was an old bar from some restaurant that got torn down a few years ago. "No. It was that Matty chick asking for Josh. When I told her he was asleep, she said he'd promised to help her move something. At one o'clock in the morning? I told her I wasn't waking him and she should go to bed and sleep off whatever she was on. Because she was tripping if she thought my husband was leaving our house in the middle of the night to go help her."

"I can't believe she even called at that time." I dug the books out of my tote as we were talking. "What nerve."

"I know. Then she went off saying he'd promised and to tell him she wasn't supporting him anymore at your business meetings. That he'd just lost his only ally." Mandy waved at some customers who were just leaving the shop. After they were outside, she continued. "I don't know what power she thought she had over my husband, but I told Josh the next day, if he talked to her again, I was going to move back home to the farm."

"Do you think they were…"

Mandy interrupted my question. "No way. Josh wouldn't cheat on me. He would help someone he thought was a friend but who was using him. I don't know what she needed help with in the middle of the night, but he didn't need to be involved in the caper. Now the contact number she gave him for the jewelry has been disconnected. I don't think they ever had any antiques, but he still believes in her. He only calls when he's in the room with me, and the woman won't pick up his calls. He'd told one of his customers he might have some items coming into the shop. Now, he knows she was using him."

"I'm sorry. I heard her make fun of him with some friends at the beach. I didn't want to tell him she wasn't a good person. Not a lot of people get Josh." I nodded to the books. "Hey, tell him thanks for loaning me the books and to call me. I found a new historical document library he might be interested in. They have all kinds of stuff about South Cove. And you know Josh loves his South Cove history."

"I'll tell him. Thanks for being Josh's friend. He speaks highly of you. One of these days we're going to have to get the four of us together for dinner, like we talked about before." Mandy turned to the desk as the phone rang. "Sorry, I'm running the shop solo today. Thanks for listening to me complain."

"Believe me, I would be thinking the same thing." Except Greg did answer his phone and leave in the middle of the night. Because it was his job. It wasn't Josh's. As I walked to Diamond Lille's I wondered what Matty had wanted from Josh. Was it just to keep him on the line? Some girls were like that. They wanted what wasn't available. And Josh did have a wedding ring.

When I got to the restaurant, Carrie was playing hostess along with having her section. "Sorry, Jill, Emma can't come inside."

I had opened the door, but we were still standing outside. "Hi, Carrie. Just picking up a to-go order. I paid on the website."

"Oh, hold on, I just saw one being bagged up." Carrie left her post as a couple came up behind me.

"Go on in, I'm waiting for a takeout order," I said as they queued up behind me.

"I didn't realize they did takeout," the man said as he nodded to Emma. "Is she going to bite me?"

"Not unless you're mean to her." I smiled at the woman who was now offering the back of her hand for Emma to sniff.

"She's a beautiful girl, that's what she is," the woman cooed to Emma. When Carrie came back, she stood and walked into the foyer area. She pulled her husband inside, grabbing his suit jacket with her hand. "Your dog is so well mannered. I wish I could train Brad as well."

"Hey now, I resent that remark." He kissed her on the head.

Carrie handed me the bag as she reached the door. "I'll be right with you guys. Jill, here you go. I hope you enjoy your dinner. I think Tiny tucked something extra in there for Greg and Emma."

"I'm not sure when Greg's coming home," I said.

Carrie shrugged. "I'm sure it will reheat well."

As the door closed behind her, I thought I saw Matty in the diner with a man. It wasn't Josh or I would have tied Emma up, asked Carrie to hold my food, and dragged him out of there myself. The guy in the booth was bald. Josh still had hair.

Another crisis avoided. I don't know, maybe I get too involved in my friends' lives, but neither Mandy nor Josh needed someone playing with their young marriage. If he messed this one up, he might not find anyone else who'd put up with his oddities.

I headed home. Emma closely watched the bag that held the food just in case I did something stupid like falling or leaving it behind. My dog liked food.

As I was passing by Matty's closed jewelry shop, I realized something that Mandy had said. Matty had called Josh on the night Chip had been killed. Had she wanted him to help her finish him off?

I looked down at Emma, who was now watching me since I'd stopped walking. "Sorry girl, I'm seeing zebras instead of horses." I didn't like Matty, but there was no evidence saying that she'd killed South Cove's grumpiest bartender. Or that she'd even known him. All I knew was she was messing with my friend Josh.

That was enough to justify my dislike.

Maybe more than enough.

CHAPTER 19

When I got home—well, while I ate, I'm not a savage—I did some computer research on Matty Leaven. I texted Amy and asked if she would pull her business file for me on Monday. As head of the business council, I had access to everyone's business applications. Mostly to give me the information to look for marketing opportunities among different businesses in town. Whatever the reason, it also gave me information on our new residents. Like Matty.

I'd have to wait until Monday to see what evils the woman had hidden in her file, but I'd find them. And maybe accidentally leave a copy of my notes on Mandy's notebook. Or in her hand. I didn't want Josh to throw the paper away. Playing cupid for a married couple was hard.

Besides, Beth would be gone on Monday and I'd need a new hobby.

There wasn't much on the internet about our newest business owner. She'd moved to South Cove from Los Angeles, where her shop had been robbed too many times. She had talked to the local paper, okay, Darla, and said she was tired of big city life. So she'd moved to South Cove after the last insurance check cleared and opened a new shop.

I called Darla. When she answered, the noise in the background told me she was at the winery. Probably bartending. "Sorry, I forgot you were at work."

"Not all of us can be done with work by noon," Darla said. "What can I do for you? Do you need takeout?"

I glanced guiltily at the almost empty basket of fish-and-chips on my coffee table. I should order from the winery more often. "Not tonight. Do you remember your interview with Matty Leaven when she moved here? Was there anything weird about it?"

I heard the interest in her voice as soon as she asked, "Why? Is she a suspect?"

Darla had gotten the wrong idea. "No, not with the murder. Sorry, I was working on something else."

Laughter erupted from the other end of the line. "I wish you could tie her to the murder. Of all of our fellow business owners, that woman is the grumpiest. I swear, she's worse than Josh. Although together, they are a pair."

So others had seen the connection too. "Anyway, I'll let you go back to work. I'm working my normal shift tomorrow if you think of anything by then."

"Sure, like I'm going to be up and coherent at six in the morning." Darla hung up.

I put away the computer and turned on the television. I finished my meal and then cleaned up the mess. Tiny had sent Greg a quart of his famous Irish stew and a dog bone for Emma. I gave her the bone and put Greg's stew in the fridge.

And suddenly, it hit me—what made me the maddest about Matty's interference with Josh and Mandy. In South Cove, we were a family. We looked out for one another. We didn't talk bad about someone behind their back. And if we did, it was because we cared. Not to make fun of them. Matty had broken the South Cove family code.

And she was ticking me off.

Beth came home at nine and she'd brought home two of Sadie's Christmas tree cookies. "Any Christmas movies on?"

"I could find one." I opened the menu on the television and narrowed it down to movies. "What are you looking for? Touching or funny?"

"Funny, I think. I'm going to cry enough on Monday when I fly away from you and your magical kingdom." She nodded toward the kitchen. "Do you still have cocoa?"

"And marshmallows. I'll find the movie. You make the drinks." I found *Elf* and cued it up to play as soon as she came back into the living room. Emma was sniffing the cookies, so I moved Beth's purse. A note fell out with Dom's name and a number. He'd written on the page, *Call me anytime.* I didn't move the note.

When she came back from the kitchen, she put the cups on the coasters I'd laid out and tucked the note back in her purse. "It's not what you think."

"It doesn't matter what I think, but if Jim finds that note, I know what he's going to think." I leaned back and changed the subject. *Not my circus*, I repeated in my head. "How was work? Did you get time with Andrew at all?"

"He was gone by the time I got there. Deek is amazing. I can see why Evie likes him so much."

"Likes, likes? Or just likes?" I held the remote.

"I'm not getting involved in that one. Evie can tell you herself if she decides to." Beth laughed and shook her head. "Changing the subject, did you know that the jewelry store where we found the patch is still closed? That robbery must have freaked out the owner. Or is it just open on the weekends?"

"Really?" I wondered if Mandy had talked to the owner about personal boundaries with her husband. "I hadn't noticed. I thought I saw her at the diner earlier tonight."

"I was going to stop in on the way to the bookstore this afternoon to do some shopping but the door was locked and the windows still empty. You would think they'd try to rescue the holiday shopping season, even with the robbery. You have so many people coming in and buying books or gift cards for stocking stuffers. Deek's great at upselling a little treat for the buyer too." Beth stirred her hot chocolate with a candy cane she'd added to the cup. She saw me watching. "I didn't ask if you liked peppermint. I drink mine this way from November first until way after the New Year."

"It's fine. I didn't realize I had any candy canes."

Beth laughed. "You didn't but you do now."

"Thanks. Now, let's watch the movie. We could have Friday night watch parties from now to Christmas if you want. We could text each other." I started the movie but as Buddy made his way to the magical world of New York, I thought about Evie and Deek. Could they be a match? I always thought of Deek as young and irresponsible. Evie was divorced and world-weary. Or she had been when I hired her.

Maybe she was ready for a real relationship now. *Circus, monkeys*, I reminded myself. Besides, not everyone wanted to be part of a happy couple. And not all couples were happy. I settled into the movie to start believing in the magic of the Christmas season again. I wished it was just as easy as singing loud for everyone to hear. Matty needed a group to gather in front of her house and sing. Maybe she was South Cove's very own Scrooge.

Beth's observation about the store's closure gave me the perfect excuse to go see Matty. If she was okay, then I'd tell her to leave Josh alone. If she was upset, maybe I'd be a little nicer. Maybe.

* * *

Walking to work the next morning, I slowed down in front of the jewelry store. It looked the same as it did when Beth and I had noticed it closed. I pulled out my phone and texted Esmeralda, asking if Matty had put in an out-of-town notice with the police station. Greg had implemented the process so if someone was gone, the patrol officers could keep a closer eye on the property, just in case.

Now I questioned if it had been Matty at the restaurant. I'd only seen her back and I'd been worried about her being there with Josh.

That done, I hurried into the bookstore and started my day. Around ten, Darla came in, looking like she hadn't slept much. I hurried to pour her a coffee. She folded herself onto a stool and took the cup. I started to say good morning, but she held up her hand for me to stop talking, so I waited.

After she'd drunk half the cup, she set it down and looked at me. "What exactly did you want to know last night?"

"Was there anything weird you noticed about Matty Leaven during your welcome-to-South-Cove interview with her last year?"

Darla finished her coffee and handed me the cup for a refill. As I set it back down, she took out her notebook and looked at some prior entries.

"You have last year's interview notes in your current notebook?"

She sipped her coffee. "No, I pulled out the notebook this morning before I came over since you mentioned Matty on the phone."

"Oh, sorry." I refilled my cup and came around to sit by her. There were no customers in the shop anyway.

She finished reading her notes and then tapped her pen on the page. "There was one thing. She'd just gotten robbed for a fifth time in her building. She said she hoped things would settle down when she moved here. Her insurance had threatened to cancel her policy unless she moved out of the neighborhood where she had the shop."

"Seems reasonable. If the neighborhood is dangerous, why stay?" I didn't understand what Darla was getting at. She tapped her pen on the page again.

"She was robbed five times before even considering a move. She sells some high-end stuff. Why did she even open a high-end jewelry store in a bad neighborhood? And once she realized it, why did it take four more robberies for her to move? I would have been out of there after the first one. Honestly, I would have done my research and not opened there in the first place." Darla sipped her coffee at a calmer pace now. "I dug around and realized I had a friend who lived in an apartment on that same street. She said that the place wasn't a bad neighborhood. That no one else besides Matty's shop was getting robbed. The police thought it was an inside job."

"She faked the robberies?"

Darla shrugged. "Or knew someone she could pay to rob her store. She collected the insurance money, then she probably sold the pieces reported as missing to someone on the black market."

"Her store here was robbed on Thanksgiving night." Darla probably already knew that. "She gets robbed, and a few days later, Chip dies from what appeared to be torture. Can it just be a coincidence?"

"Do pigeons like statues because they admire the person behind the work? No, it's not a coincidence. Have you told Greg about this?" Darla looked at me like I had two heads.

I stirred my coffee, still thinking about Matty and Josh. Had she asked him to help get the jewelry back from her robbery partner in crime? Just as I was about to say something, Evie came into the store, followed by Andrew and Zara.

"Hey, boss lady. I'm going to supervise as these two fly solo this afternoon. Tell your sister-in-law we don't need her tonight. Deek and I have it covered. But if I don't see her before she leaves, she needs to know she rocked it." Evie pointed the two new baristas to the counter. "Go wash up and get ready to start your shift. Your bosses are watching your every move."

Evie came and stood by Darla and me. "So what's going on here? Solving the world's problems using scented markers?"

"You're kind of nosy. You know that, right?" Darla finished her coffee. "I need to go and try to write up something about the murder for next week's edition. I was hoping you'd have information about that, not some insurance fraud."

"Insurance fraud is a real thing," Evie added to the conversation. "In class last year, my professor went over tooth and nail on what was and wasn't stealing from your employer. He even had a timeline that listed the amount of insurance claims filed per year. It's no wonder our insurance rates keep going up."

"Thank you, Professor Evie," Darla teased. "Maybe you should give a presentation at the next business meeting."

"I was just—" Evie realized Darla was teasing her. "What? Too much information for this early in the morning?"

Darla was already walking out and didn't even look back as she waved. I laughed as my phone beeped. Amy was at work and had the information I'd asked for. "Are you serious about not needing me for the rest of my shift?"

"I'm putting them both through a trial by fire. How else will we know if they can do a shift on their own?" Evie groaned when Beth came into the bookstore. "And I forgot to call you. Unless you need the money, we don't need you to work today or tomorrow."

"I was working to stay busy and help out, not for the money. Jill and I can do some Christmas shopping, or I could just work on my book," Beth added as she looked over at me. My face must have been reacting to the idea of shopping. Not my favorite activity.

"I'm heading over to see Amy now, then we can shop here or go to Bakerstown or wherever. I'm your personal tour guide until you take off on Monday." I was glad that we'd have a couple of days together. Beth and I had been so busy the last few days that we hadn't talked about what she was going to do when she went back to Nebraska. I knew she was taking the job, but what about Jim?

"Okay, let me just grab a book for the flight and I'll be ready." Beth disappeared into the bookshelves as I took off my apron.

"Thanks for taking over the training, Evie."

"No problem. I have a vested interest in seeing them succeed since I recommended them. I don't want you to think I hang out with flakes." She took the end-of-shift clipboard off the counter. "We'll take care of this too."

"I'm beginning to think I'm not needed here," I teased. Kind of. First Deek was making me feel like he had it all under control. Now Evie was showing the same maturity with the job.

"That will never happen. None of us like working the early shift and you've developed a huge customer base who like their coffee at the crack of dawn." She glanced over at Beth, who was deciding between two books. "She fits into the team. Too bad she lives in Nebraska."

"Believe me, I've thought the same thing several times since I met her." I took the book that Beth tried to hand to Evie to buy and gave it back to Beth. "Put that on my account. It's my little thank-you for stepping in when we were swamped."

"It wasn't a problem at all," Beth protested, but then she put the book in her tote. "Thank you."

"Let's go see what Amy has before she leaves for the day. She said she was only working until noon." I made sure one more time that Evie was set and didn't need me. Then we headed outside to the sunny day.

Beth stopped to admire the Christmas display in front of City Hall. "This is beautiful at night because of the lights, but during the day, it's hard to get into the Christmas spirit when so many people are wearing shorts."

"Not a winter wonderland." I reached out and turned over the *Santa Is In* sign to its *Santa Went Back to the North Pole* side. The man playing Santa only did weekend appearances until the last week before Christmas, and then he was here through New Year's. Except for Christmas Day. South Cove would be a ghost town that day, except for the beach, if it was nice. "Are you from Nebraska?"

"Oh, no. I grew up in Oregon. Probably why the New Hope cult drew me in as a study case. I went to college in Omaha and never left. Yet, that is." She lifted her face to the sun. "If Jim and I break up, I may just come here to work after I finish this degree. Of course, it's all going to hinge on who's willing to hire me."

"A professor with cult knowledge should be a slam dunk here in California. The whole country thinks we're wacka-doodles here anyway." I held open the door. "We're filled with surfers and people who use alternative medicine instead of going to normal doctors."

"Are you trying to sell South Cove to Beth or warn her away?" Amy stood and came around her desk to greet us. "We're also big on being outdoors and living healthy. And we get more sunny days than Omaha. I can look it up if you want. There's a website that can compare the weather of two cities. Hold on and I can tell you what the temperature is in Omaha."

"It's a balmy thirty-two with snow expected this evening." Beth held her phone up. "I have the weather app. I'm not thinking about moving. Yet."

"But I keep tempting her," I added. "So did you find Matty's business application?"

CHAPTER 20

Amy handed me an envelope. I opened it and pulled out a copy of Matty's business application. Amy summarized the report as I read the details. "She's moved around a lot. And when she leaves a place, it's always, in her words, a bad neighborhood. I hoped that she'd reconsider moving to South Cove, because I knew as soon as she left, she'd be badmouthing everyone. One of her references even told me good luck when I asked if he'd recommend her to join our community. He said she was disruptive and just not very nice."

"I can't believe she got approved to open her shop." Beth stood near Amy's desk. "When you leave one troubled environment for another, the one thing you take with you is you."

"It was a close vote, but I guess she's friends with Tina, the mayor's wife, so she was approved. Besides, we look more at your ability to finance and upkeep your business. And whether you're going to be too much competition for the other stores. No one sold fine jewelry here before she moved into town." Amy filled us in on the way the council made their decisions.

"She was a pain in her last community and she's a pain now." I wasn't going to betray Mandy's revelation to me but Amy's information made me like Matty even less. Nothing I'd heard this morning was evidence that she'd killed Chip but I wasn't about to trust her with anything important in the next business council meeting. "Thanks for this. It helps for me to know a little more about our business council members."

As we walked out, I knew I couldn't just kick her out of the business council, but the next time she snarked off, I was going to give her a warning.

Then I was going to write a formal complaint to the city council. Bill Sullivan, who ran South Cove Bed and Breakfast with his wife, Mary, was my liaison and he'd keep the reports confidential. Once I had issued enough of the warnings and filed the paperwork, I could disinvite her to meetings. She'd get the minutes but wouldn't be allowed to come in person and bring down the group. It was a painful process, at least for me, but I thought it was about time to deal with this Negative Nancy.

I'd never even thought of disinviting Josh from the council because, with all his complaining, he wanted to make South Cove better. Matty just wanted to stir up trouble.

"Do you want to grab lunch in town or wherever we're going?" Beth asked, breaking into my mental planning.

"Your choice. Where do you want to go?" We window-shopped for a few minutes as we planned our day. "There are some places that won't be open tomorrow."

"What about the Christmas craft fair in Bakerstown? I'll see if I can find anything for my family. It can't be too big since I'm shipping everything."

"I just need to make a stop at the jewelry store. I'm a little worried that Matty hasn't reopened." I was mostly curious and hopeful that she was thinking about moving again. Especially after Mandy had stopped whatever Matty had going on with Josh.

"Honestly, I am too. I talked to someone at the bookstore who was looking for a piece of jewelry for a Christmas gift and I immediately thought of Matty's shop. I can't believe she's missing all these impulse shopping days right after Thanksgiving. Everyone's freaking out, thinking they waited too long to get the perfect gift."

I was half listening to Beth as we approached Matty's shop. I looked in the window. The lights were off and mail had been piling up under the mail slot in the door. I tried the door, locked. Then I knocked. "Matty? Are you in there? Are you okay?"

I thought I'd heard something, but when I called out again, nothing. I called the dispatch line and got Esmeralda. "Hey, real quick, did Matty Leaven put in a vacation notice?"

"Hold on a second, Jill, I was just looking that up. It's been crazy here." Esmeralda put me on hold for about a minute. When she came back, I could tell the news wasn't good from her tone. "I went back to last month's book, just in case someone had written it in wrong, but no, there's no vacation notice. Do I need to send Toby out?"

"Beth and I are going to look around. I'll let you know."

"Call me when you leave the property even if you don't find anything. I've got a bad feeling." Esmeralda cut off the call and I tucked my phone into my pocket.

Beth met my gaze. "Everything okay?"

"Not really. She's not on vacation. Or at least she didn't report it. She could have not known to call in. Let's walk around and find out if we can see into any of these windows." I went left and Beth went right. We both kept calling out Matty's name.

When I got to the back door, it was locked but had a window in the door. I looked into the back room and saw a woman lying on the floor. Blood pooled around her, turning her blond hair red.

I saw Beth coming around the building. "Call 911. Tell Esmeralda to send Toby and an ambulance. I found Matty."

We heard the sirens almost immediately. Toby showed up in his police car. Beth stayed in the front to wait for the EMTs and the ambulance. Since they were located on the highway rather than in town, they had a few more miles to drive to get here. Toby followed me to the back door. "She's in there."

"Matty? Can you hear me?" Toby yelled through the locked door. A groan answered him. We looked at each other, then Toby moved me away from the door. "Close your eyes. I'm breaking this window to get inside."

I stepped away from the doorway and turned my face toward the backyard. The building used to be a house that Matty converted into her business. She lived upstairs. Had she fallen down some stairs I couldn't see through the door? Or had someone done that to her?

Questions that I couldn't answer. I thought of Josh and the phone call. Had she been down here since then? But no, Mandy had said she'd answered it. If Matty had been hurt then, all she had to do was call 911. Or tell Mandy.

"Ma'am, where's the victim?" A tall, young man in an emergency service uniform was at my side.

"She's in there, with Officer Killian." I pointed to the door. "Tell Toby that Beth and I are leaving. We're going to Bakerstown. I'll have my cell."

"Maybe you should hang around and talk to the police officer," the second guy who was following with a gurney said as I walked by.

"They know how to find me." I grabbed Beth's arm and led her away from the backyard and toward our house. A crowd had already gathered around the sidewalk and we had to push our way out of the mess.

After we got through and before the hill dipped to the house, Beth turned around. "Maybe we should go back."

"Beth, Greg's the police chief. If he needs us, he'll call. Right now, we need to let them do their jobs." There wasn't anything we could do or say to change what happened to Matty.

Beth resumed walking toward the house. When we reached the front porch, she sank into one of the porch chairs. "Do you think she's alive? How many times have I walked past her store and maybe she was lying back there, dying?"

I went inside and got a bottle of water and took it out to her. "One, I heard a groan when Toby called her name. Two, we don't know when this happened. It could have been this morning. And three, you don't have X-ray vision or the power to talk to ghosts, do you? If she dies, Esmeralda will hear her from the other side."

Beth started giggling, then slapped a hand over her mouth. "It's not funny and yet I can't stop laughing."

"You might be in shock. Do you still want to go to Bakerstown?" I glanced at my phone, but so far, no message from Greg telling me to either come down to the station or stay home. Which was a good sign that Matty was still alive.

"Do you think it's okay? They won't arrest us for leaving the scene, right?"

"We didn't do anything but find her." My phone beeped and I read the message from Greg aloud. "Matty's at the hospital. She's heading into surgery. It was a head injury. They don't know what happened, so we're free to go shopping. He won't be home for dinner."

Beth stood and headed inside. "I need to freshen up and change clothes. I'll be down in a few minutes."

I let Emma out, checked my fridge, and added items to the shopping list. Since we were going to be in town, I wanted to stop at the grocery store before we came home. That way, tomorrow we could just hang out without doing chores. Beth needed a day with nothing scheduled. In January, her life was going to be filled with to-do lists. A thought hit me and I called the bookstore and talked to Evie. She promised to set what I'd requested aside, ready for me to pick up in the office.

I grabbed my planner and checked one person off my gift-buying list. She'd just get her present early. Most of my presents came from my shop.

People needed books. Even when they didn't know that they did.

On the way to Bakerstown, Beth turned down the music and turned to me. "Do you feel lonely?"

"Right now?" I joked, but I knew what she was asking. "I'm kidding. I suspect you're talking about Greg and his missing dinner during investigations."

Beth nodded but waited for me to answer her question.

I glimpsed the Pacific on my left as I drove. "Honestly? Sometimes, yes. But it fades. When he's in the middle of an investigation, sometimes it feels like I'm single again. But with chores for two."

I paused for a minute, searching for what I was trying to say. "I like having time alone. Emma's always with me. I've got the bookstore to run and my books to read. And I've got friends and some family. So yes, at times I feel lonely, but if I stay in that mood, it's my fault for not reaching out to someone to meet me for dinner. Or figuring out something else. Like Carrie's book club. After the wedding and finishing my MBA, I found that I had a lot of free time. Of course, it was during an investigation. So we built the book club. Our lives are always changing and expanding. If I choose to stay stagnant and unhappy, that's my fault."

"You're a wise woman." Beth smiled at me.

"I've just had to adjust more often than others. Especially when I left the job I'd wanted all my life to start something new." I tapped the steering wheel as I thought. "Maybe it's just my personality. I like to change more than the average person."

"One of the classes I'm teaching this year is on learning your personality. We'll be taking a bunch of personality tests, then we'll compare them. I'm hoping to take the materials further and try to pin down the most likely personality type to be swayed by a cult. And the one most likely to become a leader. It should make an interesting book someday." Beth stared out of the window thinking about her work.

"You are a complete nerd. There is no way you can let Jim stop you from doing this. He just needs to get with the program." I smiled as we turned off toward the craft fair. "And if he doesn't get it? He's not worthy of you."

"I wouldn't say that," Beth demurred the compliment.

"I would." I parked the car on the field next to the community center holding the fair. "You should own who you are. Greg's even given up on complaining about my keeper bookshelves. Although he did take over my office. I'm much more of a couch and laptop person than sitting at a desk.

I'm glad the room is being used. Jim needs to see the entire you. Do you talk to him about things like this personality class?"

"No, I haven't." Beth didn't elaborate.

I looked over at her as we walked toward the fair. "Maybe you should. If he ignores you, at least you can say you tried."

"He's going to freak out when I get home and make a list of what we're going to do before the wedding. But I'm not going to back down." Beth's phone rang. She checked the ID and put it back in her purse.

"Expecting a call?"

Beth shook her head. "It can wait. Come on, I need help figuring out what to buy for Amanda. I bet you already have all your gifts bought and wrapped."

"Hardly." I followed her into the madness that was a Christmas craft show.

Three hours later, we were back in the Jeep with bags filled with Christmas joy and a lot of candy. I now had to stop at the craft store to buy some sort of Christmas-themed containers for all the small gifts and treats I'd bought for the staff. "Now all I want to do is eat chocolate."

Beth took a big whiff of the sweet smell that filled the car's insides. "We should spend the day tomorrow making Christmas cookies. And peppermint cocoa. We can buy jars at the craft store and that can be my addition to the barista boxes. They were all so nice to me."

"You were a warm body to help the store when Toby disappeared and Deek freaked out." I laughed at the look on her face. "Fine, they were nice to you. Hold on and I'll get directions to the craft store. I also want to stop at the grocery store. Do you need anything from there?"

"Probably." Beth pulled out a small notepad. "I'll start making a list while you figure out where we're going."

Her phone buzzed again. She looked at the message, then asked, "What's the craft store we're going to?"

"Bakerstown Crafts and Yarn. Why?" I put the car in gear and headed out of the parking lot.

She texted something, then put her phone away. "Don't freak but Dom's meeting us there. He needs to show me something."

I turned onto the street and headed into town.

"You're not going to say anything?" Beth didn't look up from her list-making.

I shook my head. "I've said this before. Not my circus or my monkeys. I'm just going to be grumpy when Lille kicks me out of the diner for knowing you."

"She's not going to kick you out of the diner." Beth grinned as she snuck a look at me. "I promise."

When we pulled into the parking lot, Dom was waiting for us. He leaned against his motorcycle like a bad boy on Sunday waiting for the preacher's daughter outside the church in a movie. I could see the attraction. I wanted to climb on back and ride away into the sunset with him. Okay, not actually, but he looked good as he pushed his hair back and stood as we pulled up.

We got out of the Jeep and I looked at Beth. "I'll see you inside."

She walked over and he took something out of his jacket to show her. I pretended not to watch while I got my purse out and locked the doors. We didn't want the bags of puffy quilted Santas and chocolate fudge to get stolen.

Finally, I could stall no more, so I went into the store and got a cart. I don't know how I would explain this to Greg and heaven help me if Jim found out. But Beth was an adult. She could talk to whomever she wanted to talk to. Even someone who looked like one of the dark romance book boyfriends that my customers were always drooling over.

I, obviously, went for a more clean-cut version of the alpha male. Too many *Law & Order* shows as a teenager, although I'd always thought I'd go for the lawyer type. I smiled as I considered several options for the staff's gift containers.

I texted my aunt and asked if she wanted to put a small something in the gift box/stocking. I got a quick text back.

From her answer, she and Harrold must have just returned from their cruise. She told me it was a great idea and she'd already picked up charms for the staff at the last port. I texted her that we had two more baristas, and then put my phone away. I didn't want her to call and start questioning my hiring, even though she didn't technically work at the shop anymore. She would call this "consulting," whether I wanted her opinion or not.

Beth handed me a small jar. "This should hold enough cocoa mix for ten cups, depending on how strong they like it."

"You snuck up on me." I nodded at the jar. "We should get some ribbon to wrap around it and stickers so you can name it: Beth's Candy Cane Cocoa. Or something like that. Too bad your name's not Candy."

"Whatever. I would make a horrible Candy." Beth grabbed a box of the jars and counted them out. Then she picked out a plaid Christmas ribbon. "What container are you choosing?"

"This one. Aunt Jackie's putting a little something in the staff boxes too." It was killing me, so I asked, "Why did Dom need to see you?"

She shook her head. "It's a secret and I told him I wouldn't tell."

"You know you shouldn't keep secrets with dark and dangerous men you meet on the street. It's not safe," I deadpanned.

Beth started giggling and then broke out into full laughter. "I'm going to miss you so much."

"FaceTime. I swear, it's almost like being there." I filled my cart with the chosen boxes that looked like Christmas presents and then met Beth's gaze. "I'm going to miss you too."

CHAPTER 21

We were almost back in South Cove when I realized something. "Beth, did Dom say where Gunter was at?"

"Gunter?" She turned down the Christmas carols on the station she'd found. Christmas twenty-four seven.

"His bodyguard? The guy he couldn't even go to a book club without?"

Beth blinked and said, "Huh."

"What's huh?" A pit was forming in the bottom of my stomach. This was important but I didn't know why or how.

"Come to think of it, I haven't seen Gunter in days. He was waiting for Dom in Lille's parking lot that night Dom walked me home from working at the bookstore. And since then, Dom's been around, but no Gunter. Maybe Dom thought he couldn't keep a secret."

"What secret?"

"Oh no. You're not tricking me into telling you," Beth said, but she looked worried. She got out her phone. "I'm going to ask Dom where he's been. And before you say anything, I should be able to tell you what's going on sometime tomorrow."

"After the bombing happens?"

Beth looked up from her text. "What bombing?"

"Just a joke." I turned off the highway onto the road to South Cove and my house. "Maybe not funny but you're being so secretive."

Beth just smiled. "Tomorrow."

We dragged all the packages inside and then sat at the table. "Do we want to work on these tonight? Or just do everything tomorrow?"

"Why don't you set up your staff gifts in the office, then we'll add to each one. I'll start getting the cocoa mix ready to put into the jars."

"And tomorrow we'll make cookies?" I rolled my head back. "Maybe we should have started this on Monday."

"We'll be fine." Beth picked up her buzzing phone. "Okay, to answer your Gunter question, Dom doesn't know where he is. He took off a couple of days ago and hasn't checked in. Dom says he doesn't need a bodyguard anyway."

"Weird. The guy was all freaked out about Dom's safety, then he just rabbits?" I picked up my phone and called Greg. "Did you take Dom off your suspect list?"

"Did Lille corner you at the diner and ask?"

I laughed. "No, but we ate in Bakerstown. Has she been hounding you?" I mouthed the word *Lille* to Beth and she rolled her eyes.

"Not since noon. Why did you ask about Dom?"

I heard the other unasked question as well. *Why are you asking me about my investigation?*

"His bodyguard has disappeared. Gunter."

There was no response on the other end of the line.

"Greg? Are you still there?"

"Sorry, I just pulled up the interview from Dom, but I don't think anyone interviewed Gunter. He was at the dart tournament, wasn't he?"

"A lot of people were there, but yes, Gunter came with Dom and a few of the guys. He brought a date. I was surprised. How's Matty?" Emma wanted out, so I opened the door and went out on the porch to talk.

"Oh no. The quick conversation switch trick isn't going to trip me up today. Although her store's robbery is a Bakerstown issue, since they were covering." He paused and then added, "I just got off the phone with the hospital. She's out of surgery and doing okay, I guess. Not awake yet."

"Greg, was it an accident?"

This time the pause was longer. "I can't prove it yet, but I don't believe it was an accident. She's still out, so I'm debating on driving to Bakerstown tonight to talk to her or waiting until the morning. What are you two doing tonight? Are you home?"

"We are home," I said and went on to tell him our plans for the next couple of days.

He chuckled. "I like having Beth around. I don't have to worry about you during the day while I'm working."

"Thanks, but you don't have to worry anyway." I pointed out the flaw in his theory.

"Honey, I've been worried about you since the day we met so many years ago," he said, but then he sighed. "I get it. You're a big girl. I can't help but worry because I know how you fall into these things."

"I'll admit, some of the situations have been a little scary. Nothing to worry about here. Like I said, Beth and I are setting up a mini Santa's workshop here for tomorrow. I'm going to miss having her around." I paused, looking inside the kitchen. Beth was mixing up the cocoa and sugar. "Is Dom still on your suspect list? He and Beth have gotten close this trip."

"Great. That's going to please my brother. I can just hear the lecture now about me not protecting her from a known malcontent."

I giggled. "That's not the word I'd use to describe Dom, but it does fit Jim's vocabulary. Anyway, she told me something big was happening and I should know everything tomorrow."

"That sounds ominous."

"I know, right?"

Beth looked up and saw me watching her through the screen door. She waved.

"Look, I've got to go. Take care of yourself, please. I'd hate to have Christmas ruined forever if something happened to you."

"You'd hate that. I'll try not to be inconsiderate and get myself killed around a major holiday. Hopefully, it will be a boring day in June if it occurs." Greg chuckled. "If you find out what's happening, would you call me? I don't want to be clueless here."

"June is a lovely month. Why would you want to spoil it for me?" I smiled, even though I knew he couldn't see me. "Talk to you soon?"

"I'll touch base in the morning at the latest."

We said goodbye and Emma and I went back into the kitchen. She'd been sitting at the open screen door and sniffing for the last few minutes. I had a feeling she was going to be in dog heaven for the next day or so, at least until her Aunt Beth left for the airport.

My phone rang as soon as I tried to set it down. It was Carrie. "Hey, what's going on?"

"Just checking in to see if Beth will be here for book club, or if she'll be home to Zoom in with Amanda," Carrie asked. "I'm making treats, so I'm getting a roll call. I can't reach Gunter but Dom's in for Monday. He's so nice. I don't think I've heard him say this many words since he started dating Lille. She kept him outside of the diner."

"Yes, Dom is very nice." I smiled at Beth and she had the grace to blush. "How long have he and Lille been dating?"

"Four years now? I think it's getting serious, at least that's what the rumors are saying. I can't see anyone marrying Lille. She has a heart of stone, that one."

"Maybe not for Dom." I covered the mouthpiece and asked, "Will you be available for book club?"

Beth shook her head. "Probably not. I think Jim and I will be having dinner, but if I happen to be alone that night, I'll attend. Have Carrie send me the Zoom link."

I relayed the message. "So why the treats? Early Christmas baking?"

"No, we're celebrating Chris getting off the hook for Chip's murder. She let a friend's sister and her husband stay at her place and they were up talking with this sister until late. Joanie, the friend, is dating a jerk and everyone including Chris and her sister is worried. Joanie's sister didn't get the message that Greg was trying to reach her until yesterday. She dropped her phone while they were traveling back home outside San Diego. Then she had to order a new one. Cell phones are a pain." Carrie summed it up. "Okay, so one more invite for Zoom and one less to consume the treats. See you Monday."

I hung up and started washing the jars Beth had sitting out on the table. "Chris is off the hook. She was with us all night at the dart tournament and Chip was still alive when we all left. Then she had a friend's sister alibi her today. Carrie's making treats for book club."

"I'm sorry I'm going to miss out." Beth grabbed a clean jar and started drying. "You all are a tightly knit community. I'm going to miss that when I get home."

"You and Jim have the church." I washed another jar.

Beth shrugged. "Maybe. I'm beginning to think that my pastor isn't on my side and he's got a vested interest in me staying at my secretary job."

"You were too good at it." I smiled as I finished washing the last jar.

"Whatever. But today and tomorrow are all about Christmas, family, and friends. I hope Greg can be here for dinner because I'm cooking." Beth counted the washed jars.

"I'll let him know in the morning." I let the water out of the sink and dried my hands on a towel. "If we're baking all day, are you sure you want to make dinner too? We could go out to that seafood place you like."

Beth hit me with the towel she'd been using. "Stop tempting me. I want to cook to thank you for letting me stay for an extra couple of weeks. You didn't have to let me crash here."

"You're family," I said. "Now let's get those packages done for the staff. I still want to watch a cooking show before I crash for the night."

* * *

I didn't dream of sugar plums, candy canes, or even Santa's reindeer that night, but I wish I would have. It would have been better dreams than the ones I had with poor Chip tied to his chair, begging for his life. When I finally climbed out of bed, I wasn't in the mood for the Christmas carols and making too many cookies. But I figured if I drank enough coffee, I could get there.

Besides, I heard Greg's laughter downstairs and realized I was the only one still in bed. I hurried downstairs to see a pancake flying in the air.

Emma was watching too, probably hoping that Greg would miss the pan. No one looked at me as I came into the kitchen. "Good morning, family. I see breakfast is well on the way?"

"I think you just pretend to sleep in so you don't have to cook." Greg set the pan back on the stove and pulled me into a hug. "Did you sleep well?"

"Not really, but thanks for asking." I kissed him and headed straight for the cup of coffee Beth had just poured me. "Oh, Carrie said you cleared Chris of killing Chip. Thanks. I know it was weighing on her."

"I didn't clear her because she was upset. She has an alibi. She couldn't have done it." He put the last pancake on the top of my plate, drizzled it with warm maple syrup, and set it in front of me at the table. "Now eat before you start getting grumpy."

I'd argue with him, but not eating did make me moody.

"So if Chris and Dom are off your list, who's still on it?" Beth asked, sipping coffee. Since Greg had turned off the stove, I assumed they'd both already eaten.

"Who said Dom was off the list?" His eyes twinkled and I could see he was messing with her.

"Lille," Beth shot back. "Because she said if you put her boyfriend in jail she was going to close the restaurant."

"She's not closing the restaurant, but yes, Dom has been cleared." He turned to me. "Your uncle came forward and told me he had a late-night visitor at the Train Station the night Chip was killed. He said Dom stayed until three that morning when your aunt came down and broke up the boys' club. He said they had some things to discuss."

"What would Dom be chatting with Uncle Harrold until three in the morning for? Is Harrold becoming an investor in his new bar and grill?"

"Not that I know about." Greg glanced over at Beth.

She shook her head. "I'm not talking. And you can't make me, copper."

After that, Greg left to go to the station. He often worked seven days a week, especially when there was an active investigation. I felt blessed that he had been able to take Thanksgiving off completely. Of course, that had wound up being an issue on its own with Matty's robbery.

Beth and I were discussing what cookies to make when a knock on the door interrupted our conversation. I went to the door and Andrew stood there, a package under his arm. "Hey, sorry to bother you on a Sunday, but Jamal said you were looking for this. They made a copy for you. They have such amazing toys there at the library."

I took the cylinder from him. Was this a copy of the original blueprints? "Thanks, Andrew. Are you working this morning?"

"Yes, I have a shift with Evie. She claims she's going to put us on a shift alone next week. I hope she's kidding." Andrew waved and skipped down the stairs. "See you later."

I closed the door and locked it. The kitchen table was covered with baking supplies. My office desk had partially completed Christmas presents on it and the coffee table was too small. "I'm running upstairs for a minute," I called out to Beth.

I went into my bedroom and closed the door. I didn't need Emma jumping in the middle of this and tearing the blueprints. I knew it was just a copy, but I wanted to see if my intuition was right.

As I scanned the blueprint, I compared it to the pictures I'd taken the other day when I was in the building with Chris. It didn't take long, but as soon as I saw it, I couldn't believe I hadn't noticed it before.

A built-in door in a bookcase. It was cracked open. I wonder if Chip had tried to hide in there when the killer came.

As I studied the picture, I spotted something else. A patch under the doorway. A jacket patch. Usually, these were all sewn together so tightly that they wouldn't come off. But this club had changed a lot in the last few years. Stopping activities, ending allegiances, and even removing patches. They'd been taken off to indicate the loyalty had also been broken. But when you remove one, it affects the others close to the separated patch. And the killer had lost two in the last few days. One here at the murder scene. And one in front of a jewelry store where he'd picked up the so-called stolen merchandise to take to Chip to hold. At least that was my theory.

Had Chip threatened to renege on their deal? Or had the killer decided that he didn't need help to fence the jewelry and wanted it all back? Or had Matty tried to double-cross him? Was this the favor she'd needed from Josh? To help her get her property from Chip while she threw steel tips at him to get him to talk?

I needed to talk to Josh. And then I'd go see Greg. Right now, all I had was suspicions and questions. I had a feeling that Josh could paint a little more between the lines. At least enough for Greg to bring in the killer for probable cause.

Besides, I needed to pick up Beth's Christmas present before she left tomorrow. That way, she'd have something to do on the plane ride home. For an excuse to go into town, it was pretty good.

CHAPTER 22

After getting the first batch of cookies ready to bake, I told Beth I needed to run to the bookstore (truth) to check in with Evie about next week's schedule (lie.) Okay, maybe not really a lie, but a misdirection. The reason I was going to the bookstore was a surprise. So it was a Christmas lie, which didn't count. I hoped Santa used the same logic pattern. I just didn't mention the other stops. I'd be in South Cove, not wandering the countryside looking for killers.

I tried not to play back the conversation where Greg said he liked having Beth here because it kept me out of trouble. I decided to take Emma, giving me one more excuse for leaving. The dog needed a walk.

As we passed by Lille's, I saw that Dom and his friends, the gang, were there, as well as Uncle Harrold. I could see Dom and Uncle Harrold through the windows. The motorcycles lined up against the back brick wall where the parking lot ended. I'd pop my head inside, but I had Emma, and Lille hated me. So I kept walking.

Dom and Uncle Harrold. That was a strange combination.

If Uncle Harrold wasn't honest as the day was long, I'd question it. But he didn't even lie to Aunt Jackie if an outfit wasn't quite her style. He'd tell her. I never questioned my aunt's clothes or motives. I didn't want to be on her bad side. We were out at a restaurant having dinner one night when Harrold told her if she didn't want the truth, she shouldn't ask him. I had about choked on a glass of wine when he said that. My aunt handed me a napkin and just said, "Wipe your face, dear. And close your mouth. You're going to attract flies."

Her way of saying, "Stay out of it."

What had Dom and Harrold been talking about so late at night?

That was a question for another day. I kept walking and we passed by Matty's still-closed shop. I wondered if Greg had talked to her yet. I wouldn't want to be on Greg's bad side, and even though she'd been attacked or fallen in her shop, he wouldn't take it easy on her.

I groaned as I realized Greg was probably in Bakerstown and not at the station. He'd ask why I didn't wait and give the blueprints to him tonight at dinner. Emma nudged me and I started walking again. The dog needed a walk and I had something to drop off and pick up.

When we got to the station, Greg was out like I'd expected. Esmeralda took the blueprints and pictures, gave Emma a treat, and went back to answering the phone. Sunday morning dispatch must be busy.

I saw Chris's car at Chip's Bar. It was still early enough that she could have a car on the street, but time was ticking, so I left her alone and headed to the bookstore.

Emma and I came into the front and Andrew hurried over. "Can you have a dog in here?"

"Sometimes. My dog, always. Can you get a bag that Evie left for me in the back?" I asked as Andrew focused on Emma.

"I've got it." Evie came out of the back with a bright red gift bag. "Hey, I wanted to tell you we're doing a trial Monday opening tomorrow—ten to three. If we get enough shoppers, I've got commitments from staff to work the shift until Christmas, when we'll go back to being closed. Thoughts? I'm overstepping, right? Do you hate me?"

"Why would I hate you?" I took the bag and looked around. The bookstore was busy and several people sat in the dining room, drinking coffee and reading. It was the image of a perfect Sunday morning. At least in my head. "I've got to go. See you on Tuesday."

Andrew was already back at the counter, washing his hands after petting Emma. He waved as we left. For the second time that week, I felt like my baby birds had all flown the nest. The store was doing well without me. Maybe I needed another hobby.

I'd talk to Beth when I got home. Maybe she would have some ideas. First up, I needed to ask Josh exactly what Matty had asked him to help with. I found him in the store, sweeping. "Okay if Emma comes in?"

"Sure, she's a good dog. Not like some of the ones people bring in. I caught one chewing on a leg of a dining room set I'd just bought from an estate sale." He put the broom away. "Mandy said she told you she put her foot down with Matty. Now I hear she was attacked in her store. Something's wrong with that woman."

I tried to hide the smile. I agreed. Something was really wrong with Matty. "Josh, what did she want you to do that night she called? Do you know?"

"I wasn't going to go anyway. She'd told me she needed help with a situation. Someone talked her into robbing her store to help her get through this season. She's been having money issues. She told me that the only person hurt would have been the insurance company, but whoever she was working with had lied to her and was keeping her jewelry. She wanted me to talk him into giving it back." Josh sighed. "I should have called Greg, but all I knew was what Matty told me. And I stepped away from her then. There was no way I would be involved in something like this."

"Did she say who was helping her?" I thought I knew the answer, and so when Josh told me the name, I wasn't surprised.

"She's not a nice person. I talked to her after she and Mandy got into it and she was horrible to me, calling me names and such. I guess I'm just not a good judge of character." He adjusted a stack of papers on the desk.

"You chose Mandy. That was a good decision," I reminded him. A text came over my phone. Beth was ready to start the next batch of cookies, and if I didn't get home quickly, she was going to make sugar cookies that I would be responsible for decorating alone. I smiled as I let her know I was on my way back. "Thanks for talking to me this morning, Josh. Did Mandy tell you about the document library?"

I shouldn't have opened that discussion. Five minutes later, I finally left the antique store to head home. It was almost nine and Chris's car was still on the street. The mayor had told Greg to tow any car that still was left on the street, so instead of heading straight home, I went over to Chip's Bar. The front door was open, but I knocked and called out, "Chris? You need to move your car."

I heard voices in the back. Then an upset Chris hurried out of the office and into the bar area. It looked like she'd been thrown through the open door. "Sorry, I'll be out of here in just a minute. I'm taking stock of the liquor bottles to see if we can reopen next week."

It was a great reason to be there, except Chris had already done an inventory last week. I was there. She brushed tears away from her face.

"You look upset. Maybe you should do this another day. You shouldn't just push away the grief." I tried to wave her toward me. Someone had to be in the back. In the room where I'd found the secret entrance on the blueprints that I'd left for Greg.

"I'm fine. I've got to get back to my normal life sometime, right? I'd invite you in for a drink but you can't bring that dog inside." A noise sounded behind her. "Look, just leave me alone. I'll move my car in a minute."

She disappeared into the back and I left the bar. I didn't pick up my phone. I was worried that whoever was in the bar with Chris might see me calling for help and do something stupid. Instead, once I was out of the line of sight, I called out to Emma. "Should we see if your Daddy's back from Bakerstown yet?"

If I was being watched, maybe this would give me a good excuse that wouldn't get Chris shot.

I headed into the station, locking the door behind me. Then I sank into a chair near Esmeralda's desk.

"Jill, what's wrong?" She came around and sat next to me.

I looked up into my friend's face. "I think Gunter is holding Chris hostage as he looks for Chip's secret room."

I sounded like a lunatic, but instead of continuing to question me, Esmeralda stood and called out to Toby as she picked up the phone. "I need you in here, now."

It took Greg less than ten minutes to arrive, and by that time, Toby had assembled all the deputies in town. They were dressed in riot gear, which included helmets and bulletproof vests. Greg had told them to get ready but wait for him.

I'd called Beth and told her to stay in the house with the doors locked. And that I'd be late getting back. There was no way I was walking home during this mess. Not with a murder suspect in town. Greg had sent officers to block off the street and Esmeralda was calling every business in town letting them know it was a total shutdown.

Hopefully, this would be over before the Sunday holiday shoppers arrived. Darla had already tried to call me twice after she got the call from Esmeralda.

Greg rubbed Emma's head and kissed me on the cheek when he came inside. "Show me the blueprints."

As I did, he and Toby talked about the best access points. They were going to storm the bar. My heart sank as I heard them talking. "Greg? Is this the best answer? Can't we wait for him to leave?"

He took me in his arms before getting in his protective gear. "I'm afraid we'd risk losing Chris if we wait. Have a little faith. Beth knows to stay inside?"

I nodded, holding up my phone. "I called her. And Darla would like to talk to you."

He chuckled. "Figures. It's always about the story, right?"

"That's our Darla." I touched his cheek. "Be careful, okay?"

"How do you know it's Gunter? Did you see him?"

I shook my head. "Josh told me. Matty's involved too. Some sort of insurance scam. I guess it's not her first time, either."

"I talked to Matty and she said she fell. When I asked how, and then pointed out the flaws in her story, she pretended to fall asleep. I heard from the guard that's posted on her room that she tried to leave right after I left. I had this covered. You didn't need to get involved." He looked up as Toby came back into the room.

"We're ready," Toby said as he rubbed Emma's head.

"We'll talk later." Greg stood and headed out the door with Toby. "Oh, and Jill?"

"Yes?"

"Can you and Emma hang around and keep Esmeralda company until we get back?" His eyes twinkled as he asked.

"I swear, I wasn't investigating. I went to the shop to get Beth's Christmas present so I could give it to her and then I talked to Josh."

"And?" Greg paused at the door.

"And then I popped my head in to keep Chris's car from being towed. I was being a good business council manager."

"Keep telling yourself that. Oh, and don't call Darla back, please." He nodded toward the door, and they all headed out of the station and toward the bar.

Esmeralda came with a cup of coffee and a bowl of water for Emma. "And now we wait."

I nodded, but inside I was freaking out. I wasn't good at waiting.

CHAPTER 23

It seemed like forever, but it was less than an hour before I heard the all-clear on Esmeralda's radio. She stood up from where she'd been sitting with me and headed to the phones to let the officers who were blocking eager shoppers know it was okay to let people in. Then she started calling the stores.

Santa and his elves had been waiting with us at the station and with a "ho, ho, ho," he left the lobby after giving me a candy cane and Emma a dog treat. Santa told me, "Your actions today give you an upgraded spot on the nice list, so don't mess it up next year."

Esmeralda rolled her eyes as we watched him leave. I guess the fortune-teller didn't believe in the big guy in the red suit. Then she went back to making her calls. I called Beth and told her what had happened and that everything was fine. I'd be home soon.

Just as I hung up, Toby and another officer brought Gunter into the station, directly to the back into a small jail cell. He'd get transferred to the county facility in Bakerstown soon. Greg and Chris came in next and she ran to me.

"Thank goodness you understood what I was trying to say. You know Emma's always allowed in the bar. I was just trying not to upset him. He said I should know where Chip's secret room was if we were so close. I kept telling him I didn't know." Chris was talking really fast and had a pack of cigarettes in her hand that she kept opening and closing again. "I guess I can't smoke in here?"

Esmeralda shook her head, and Chris tucked the cigarettes back into her purse. "Gunter was always so nice. I didn't even question why he came into the bar. I thought he was worried about me. I'm an idiot."

"You're not an idiot. I know about the secret room. I've been looking for the original blueprints, and finally, the document library sent them over this morning. So I dropped them off with Greg along with a picture of a patch that got caught in the door when Gunter wasn't looking. I guess Chip never let Gunter see where he was storing the stolen goods?"

"Gunter said he stayed in the bar area that night and any other time he'd visited the bar. He claimed he'd never been in Chip's office where you found the patch. We think he went into the office during the dart tournament, hoping that confusion would cover his tracks, but he couldn't find the secret room. When Chip saw him coming out of the office, he must have checked to see if the jewelry was still there. Then Gunter came back," Greg explained. "Some of it is conjecture since Gunter's not talking. As soon as we found the patches, Dom didn't want to talk about it, but Lille brought in his jacket to show that Dom's patches were still there. She made him confirm her statement that Gunter was the only club member who would have had that patch."

"So Lille scares other people too." I smiled as Toby came back into the room. "Can I go home now?"

"As long as you take Emma with you," Greg said as he asked Toby to take Chris into an interview room to get her statement. "Text me when you're home or I'll call Beth to make sure you got there."

"I don't need a babysitter." I stood and Emma came with me to the door.

"You had one and snuck out on her." Greg came over and kissed me. "Be safe, okay?"

As I was walking down the street to go home, I saw Dom and Lille coming up toward me. To my surprise, Lille stopped me.

"Are you okay?"

I blinked and nodded. "Chris was at the bar with Gunter, not me. Emma and I just peeked our heads inside to remind Chris to move her car. That's when I realized she was in trouble. We went straight to the station and locked the door after I got inside. I'm glad he made his move early rather than when all these people were around."

We moved to the side as people streamed up the sidewalk from the car parking lot the city had set up.

Dom looked around. "No matter what, Christmas shopping must go on."

"The money from this season keeps us alive on the slow days. Evie's opening the shop tomorrow to see if we get seasonal customers." I was rambling, but I glanced at my watch. Greg would be concerned if I didn't text soon, but I thought I had a few more minutes. "Anyway, I'm glad Greg found Chip's killer. I'm sorry it was your friend."

Dom stepped closer to Lille before he spoke. I wasn't even sure he realized what he was doing. "I considered Gunter more than just a friend. He was my brother. I thought he was on board with our move to respectability, but he must have been working on this scam for years. He and Matty were close. He knew her before she moved here."

Lille rubbed his arm with her left hand and something sparkled on her ring finger.

"Wait, what's that?" I asked as my eyes widened. "Are you two engaged?"

Lille narrowed her eyes as she glared at me. "What? Did you think you and your friends were the only ones who could find a man?"

Dom chuckled and held out Lille's hand. "Lille, be nice. It's a beauty, isn't it? I had to get your uncle's approval, first, but then I surprised her this morning after taking a ride up the coast to this beautiful spot overlooking the ocean. We're getting married." He kissed her cheek.

"Congratulations. The ring is beautiful and I wish you both all the best." I did hope that this was Lille's soul mate. Maybe Dom would make her nicer. Marriage had worked for Josh. Finding the love of a good man or woman could change someone. Even Jim was a little nicer.

"Please thank Beth for helping me pick out the ring. She translated all the clues this one gave me over the years." Dom squeezed Lille and she giggled. "It has my mom's old stones in the setting as well as a new one, just for my Lilly flower."

Lille giggled again. The world must have shifted. I felt Emma lean against my leg, so I assumed I was awake. "I'll let her know."

Now, I understood why Dom and Beth talked so much. Yes, they were talking about his sister and the effect of the cult on the family structure, but he was also planning this surprise.

The surprise that Beth had warned me about had arrived. Lille was getting married. I wondered if the theme would be black goth or Halloween. Somehow, I didn't see her in a white princess wedding gown. But maybe a silky white gown that accentuated all her curves and assets. I didn't know why

I was thinking about Lille's wedding dress. I probably wouldn't be invited to the ceremony anyway.

"I better go. Greg's expecting a call when I get home. He's a little overprotective."

Dom smiled and nodded at me as we started to leave. "I understand his feelings."

I tried not to hear Lille giggle again. The first one had nearly put me into catatonic shock. As we hurried home, I hoped that the happy couple would stay that way. Dom seemed nice, even with his sordid past. Had Lille finally found her bad boy with a heart of gold?

When I got home, I let Emma off the leash and she ran to the water dish in the kitchen. I could hear Beth chatting with someone on the phone.

She smiled as I came into the kitchen. "She's here, do you want to talk to her?"

"I was talking to Dom and Lille and they told me the good news." I didn't wait to let her hear Greg's response. I grabbed a bottle of water and sat down at the table, putting Beth's gift on the table.

"Oh, he popped the question?" Beth did a little joy jump. The girl was all about the good news. "Sorry, Greg, I've got to go. Cookies to bake and all."

She sat next to me. "Isn't the ring the most stunning thing you've ever seen? I went with him to pick out the setting. I hope she loves it."

"She seemed happy. Sorry I questioned your motives with Dom." I moved the gift bag toward her. "This is to help you stay on track in January when you go back to school."

Beth opened the bag and pulled out a planner and a goal-setting book that Deek had loved. "This is amazing. I usually use a cheap planner I can get at the dollar store. This has stickers and everything."

"If you're going to be a professor, you need a good planner for all your appointments and wise thoughts." I drank more water as I watched her page through the planner. "Make sure you put my birthday in there. I don't want you to miss it."

She went to her purse and grabbed a purple pen. "Okay, give me your birthday and Greg's. I already know Amanda's."

After she played with the planner for a bit, she put it in the living room and then washed her hands. "I'm glad you're back. It's time to make peanut butter kisses."

And just like that, we were back in Christmas mode. I turned up the carols on the radio and we spent the afternoon covered in sugar and flour. By the time Greg came in the door, the kitchen was clean, and the ham was baked along with a batch of scalloped potatoes. A pumpkin pie sat on the counter, cooling. The house smelled like the holidays.

We sat down around the table as a mini family. As Beth prayed over the food and our lives, I silently added to the prayer that Jim would figure out that this woman was already part of our family. All he had to do was accept her for who she was. Even Lille had found her soul mate. Jim just had to open his eyes and unharden his heart.

Just before Beth said amen, I also said a prayer for Chris and Chip. Their happily ever after hadn't happened, but hopefully, Chris would find someone else. Or at least find something that made her happy.

Life was too short for anyone to be miserable.

CHAPTER 24

Beth left South Cove Monday morning with her planner in her backpack and a promise to check in on Tuesday night for book club. I had the day free, but the house seemed empty, so I bagged up some cookies and headed into town to drop off the product of our Christmas cookie mania with my friends. First up, City Hall and Amy, then I'd pop into the station.

Amy was at the desk when I came in and her eyes brightened when she saw the bag. She waved me over to her desk and glanced around the empty room. "Thanks for these. I'm starving and I'm late."

"For a meeting?" I was confused. The mayor's office was dark and there wasn't anyone in the conference room.

"No. I'm late." She waited until her meaning hit me. "Now, you can't tell anyone. Justin says we should wait until I get through the first trimester, but I bought a kit on the way to work, and it's positive."

"You're pregnant?" I hugged her.

"Yes, but I bought two kits, so really, don't say anything. I'm going to do it again tonight with Justin and he wants to be the first to know."

I laughed. "Then why did you tell me?"

"Because you've been there long before Justin, and if something goes wrong, you'll be there after too. We're best friends. And the first test was a little light. I might just be late. I'll call if it goes the other way tonight."

"So, a baby?" I counted months. "An August baby?"

"Of course. I'll be huge during summer and not able to surf. The baby bump is going to throw off my balance on the board. Justin and I planned a trip to Bali for New Year's. You and Greg should come along. White beaches, blue water. If that test is right, it might be our last couples' trip for a while."

"But you'll have a baby and a family." I hugged her again. "I'm excited for your journey, even if it doesn't start today. It's going to happen soon."

I told her I'd ask Greg about the trip, but I didn't think we'd be going. We had used a lot of his time off for our honeymoon in January. I moved through the halls and came out by the water fountain and the bathrooms and into the station.

Esmeralda was cleaning the coffee station in the lobby. "Greg's in Bakerstown. Initial arraignment for Gunter. He'll be gone all day."

"I came to drop off cookies for you. Beth and I went crazy yesterday." I handed her a couple of bags of cookies. "And one for the guys. You know they'll eat all yours if you don't hide these."

Esmeralda stared at me, then took the bags. "Next summer is going to be different, but it will be wonderful. Change isn't always bad."

"Okay." I tried not to meet her eyes. If Esmeralda could read my mind and know that Amy was pregnant, I was going to be in trouble with my friend. "That's nice."

She laughed and went to her desk where she set down the cookies. "I can keep a secret too, Jill."

I paused before leaving the station. "You didn't call from New Orleans. I thought you were going to call."

"You seemed to have the situation in hand." She smiled. "I didn't say it was a big choice. But you supported your friend, even when you didn't know what was happening. Beth's lucky to be part of your family."

I hurried out of the station before she could tell me more about my future. I liked to be surprised by what was coming. Okay, that wasn't true. I was the kid who unwrapped and peeked at Christmas gifts. I knew where my mom stashed things as soon as she bought them.

Maybe this was the choice I was supposed to be making. Learning to live with the change happening around me.

Amy was having a baby. I knew it in my bones, and with Esmeralda's confirmation, I looked forward to welcoming a new member to our South Cove clan. Even though Justin and Amy had bought a house in a nearby town, they'd always be part of the family here.

I hoped Beth would soon be joining the King tribe. And Beth and Jim's upcoming wedding was another reason I wouldn't be on the beach with Amy at the beginning of the new year. But that was okay. I had three more stops to make, then I was heading home.

Time to make the house look like Christmas. I corrected myself as I crossed the street to Antiques by Thomas. Time to make our home look like Christmas. I might even run to Bakerstown and pick up a family of Christmas gnomes for the living room. I just hoped Emma wouldn't eat them.

Acknowledgments

When we were looking for a place to build our forever home, one of the advantages of Tennessee, at least to my husband, was the distance from the coast and hurricanes. Helene proved him wrong. As I wrote about Christmas in California, I was thinking about flooding and mud and the loss of too many homes and lives. Now as I'm editing this book, I'm thinking about the LA fires. 2024 was a bad year.

South Cove is always a gentle respite from the real world, at least for me as I write. I hope reading about Jill and her extended friends and family group gives you the same peace of mind. Good is out there, you just have to recognize it. I wish I had a Beth in my life. We could all use one.

As always, thanks to my editor, Michaela Hamilton, and the rest of the Kensington crew, for her understanding as the deadline for this book floated past me. And thanks to my agent for her support.

Recipe

Ribbon Cookies

I have an old cookbook that my mom bought when I was in FHA (Future Homemakers of America). We were selling them to fund a trip to the national convention in Seattle. I think…it's been a while. Anyway, the price sticker is still on the *Homemade Cookies Cookbook* – $2.99. In the back is a faded handwritten recipe for what I call my signature cookies. Ribbon cookies. The original recipe was for pinwheels but making them in ribbons is a lot easier. And they still taste amazing.

Enjoy,
Lynn

Ribbon Cookies
Mix together in a bowl the dry ingredients.
2 ½ cups flour
¾ tsp baking powder
½ tsp salt

In a mixer bowl, cream the following:
2/3 cup butter
1 cup sugar
2 large eggs, one at time
1 tsp vanilla

Add the flour mixture and beat until well combined.
Separate out half of the dough.
Melt 1 tbsp butter, then stir in 3 tbsp of cocoa. Add this mixture to one half of the dough.
Now you have dark and light batter. Alternately press them into a bread loaf pan that you've covered the insides of with butter. Refrigerate for at least 30 minutes. Cut out even slices of cookie and bake on a baking sheet covered with parchment paper in a 375-degree oven for 10–12 minutes.

Are you over the moon about Lynn Cahoon?
Don't miss the first book in her new series!
Turn the page to enjoy the opening chapter of *An Amateur Sleuth's Guide to Murder*, a Bainbridge Island mystery from Kensington Publishing Corp.

CHAPTER 1

What doesn't kill you counts as work experience.

Meg Gates studied her empty apartment through bleary eyes. It was her and Watson. She sank into the papasan wicker chair after moving the empty wine bottle from last night next to the other one on the floor. Meg had kept a case of Queen Anne White from the shipment that was supposed to be used to toast the happy couple at her wedding reception in two days. Instead, her father had scheduled an appreciation party for his Stephen Gates Accounting clients. He'd taken the wine, the reception location, and her caterer and charged them to his company credit card. Now her wedding failure could be a tax deduction for his company rather than another hit to his bottom line, like when she'd left college to work for that startup. As her father always reminded her, since they weren't related to *that* Gates, they had to make sure the lemons turned into lemonade. Or, more likely, imitation lemon-flavored water.

As Meg sat staring at the Space Needle, drinking water and trying to get rid of her hangover headache, she realized she was now a three-time loser. She'd failed at college, work, and now love. But who was counting? Besides her, her family, and everyone she knew in the greater Seattle area?

Last night she'd sat in this same chair, listening to John Legend and Bruno and any other artist with a sad song she could find on her phone. She'd never figured out how to pair her phone to Romain's pricy Bluetooth stereo, which was tucked on a bookshelf in the living room. All his belongings were here, surrounding her. Waiting for Romain and Rachel to return from their Italian vacation, which was supposed to be her honeymoon. Romain Evans had been her fiancé. A few weeks before the wedding, he'd changed. He'd been distant. Cold. She'd thought it had been pre-wedding jitters. It hadn't been.

Rachel had been a bridesmaid and a sorority sister. What she hadn't been was a true friend.

Mutual friends had whispered to her that Romain was moving into Rachel's condo down by the sound. She hoped he tripped and fell off the dock. Maybe he could drown, too. But that seemed unlikely. Tripping on the way to happiness was more Meg's style.

Several times last night, Meg had considered throwing the sleek black stereo over the side of the balcony, but it had seemed like too much work to commit to the failed relationship. Besides, at the time, she still hadn't finished the task at hand, drinking the wine in her glass.

By the end of the night, or maybe sometime this morning, she had been playing Barry Manilow, Joni Mitchell, and the Carpenters, her mom's favorites. As the music played, Meg spent the time cutting her designer wedding dress into pieces that matched her shattered heart. The lights from the Space Needle sparkled in the window and kept her company while she destroyed the dress. Worse, she vaguely remembered possibly making a few Facebook Live posts during the night.

Her eyes felt dry from all the tears and probably also the wine. Looking at the pile of chopped white lace on the floor by her chair didn't make her feel better. She loved the dress. Destroying it was symbolic of what Romain's betrayal had done to her soul.

Meg had been called dramatic before.

Today, she reminded herself, was the start of a new chapter. Twenty-six wasn't too late to start over. Again. Or at least she hoped it wasn't. She might be single, unemployed, and sans degree, but there had to be real jobs out there for someone like her. She was alive, young, and though not vibrant this morning, she could fake it.

To tide her over, her mom had hired her to work evenings at Island Books, the family bookstore on Bainbridge Island. Meg figured it was her mom's way of keeping her out of trouble as her heart healed. Today was moving day. Moving home. One more indicator that her life was in the toilet. At least she wasn't moving back in with her mother. Instead, Aunt Melody and Uncle Troy had let her have the apartment over the garage. She groaned and leaned back into the chair, closing her eyes. Maybe she could put moving off until next week. The hangover should be gone by then. Or at least the wine would be.

Waiting meant she'd run the risk of seeing Romain. And probably Rachel. She didn't know if she could stop herself from throwing things at them or, worse, projectile vomiting like in that old movie. Today was as good as any day to run home with her tail between her legs.

Watson, her tan cocker mix rescue, jumped onto her lap and licked her face. He must have read her mind about the dog analogy. Watson liked sleeping in, so if he was awake, it was time to take him outside for a walk.

"You know I'm destroyed, right? Heartbroken and worthless." She stared into his deep brown eyes as he whined his request. "If you want to be a Seattle dog, you should break free of your leash and run as far away from me as possible. Go toward the Queen Anne neighborhood. Maybe someone rich will adopt you."

Watson patted her chest. He didn't care about her heart; he needed to go out. She pushed him off her lap and finished the water in one gulp. Then she grabbed Watson's neon blue leash. It matched his collar and his bed. Watson's dog accessories were stylish and expensive.

"Don't wear these out, buddy. For the next year or so, we're only buying essentials."

Watson stood at the door and whined again. He wasn't impressed with her cost-cutting ideas.

"Fine. I'm hurrying." Meg checked to make sure she had her keys. No one was around to come to save her if she locked herself out except for the building's super, who usually slept until noon. She had people coming at ten to move her back home. And she hadn't paid this month's rent yet. She'd let Romain deal with that.

Home. She'd planned on this apartment being her and Romain's home until they got pregnant. Then they would move out of the city and closer to his job in Bellevue. They'd buy a cute cottage with a fenced yard for Watson and the new baby. She'd become a tradwife with a side hustle, some sort of craft that would sell like hotcakes online. They'd be a perfect little family. She'd even make homemade baby food. She'd be the yoga mom who wore crazy-colored jumpsuits and Birks, except on date nights, when she would shimmer in designer dresses and heels, having magically dropped the baby weight. Romain would never even look at another woman, he'd be so in love with her.

So that fantasy had a few holes. Romain hadn't even made it to the wedding night.

Watson did his business, and she cleaned up, using a biodegradable bag. Just like a good dog mom. She'd done everything right. So why was she being punished?

"Wishes and horses," she said as she found a trash can on the street and deposited the bag. A homeless man leaning against the building glared at her. Her pity party was over. It was time for a new life and a new song. She sang out quietly, "What doesn't kill you makes you stronger."

Thank God for Kelly Clarkson's anthems.

When she turned the corner toward the apartment building—*Not home*, she corrected herself—she saw her moving crew. Her mom, Felicia Gates; Aunt Melody; and Natasha Jones all stood by her mom's bookmobile van. Someone was yelling at her brother, Steve, whom everyone called Junior. His head stuck out the window of his Ram truck as he tried to parallel park on the street. Dalton Hamilton, Junior's best friend, motioned him back near the curb. Mom's van was parked in Romain's spot, since his BMW was at the airport.

"Felicia, she's across the street with Watson." Her aunt poked her mom and pointed at Meg. She called out, "Meg, we're here, darling. Don't you worry anymore. We'll have you back on the island and home in no time."

Meg smiled, hoping she didn't look as bad as she felt. She should have jumped in the shower, but it had felt like too much.

Bainbridge Island was a thirty-five-minute ferry ride away from Seattle in distance and more than fifty years behind the city in lifestyle. Residents and tourists hiked and had picnics in the forests that covered most of the island. Lately, large tracts were being sold with a single house built in the middle of the wooded land. Or on the waterside of the property. Houses that longtime residents like her parents and aunt and uncle could never imagine owning.

In Seattle, Meg had lived in an apartment building where no one knew her name, including the super. She loved that freedom. Now she was moving back to the island to the apartment over her aunt Melody's garage. An apartment where her bedroom window overlooked the backyard and her every move could be watched.

Natasha Jones met her halfway as she and Watson crossed the street, and handed her a large coffee. "You look horrible. I should have come over last night."

"Then both of us would be hungover, and we'd have one less bottle of wine to move." Meg hugged her friend.

"One? I'm disappointed that you think so poorly of my ability to comfort drink." Natasha squeezed her back. "Are you sure about moving back? It's a big step."

Meg nodded, looking around the neighborhood she'd called home for the past five years. She loved it here, but she couldn't afford the apartment on her own. Not since the startup she'd worked at had shut down. She had applied for a job at Romain's workplace, but she'd put off her interview until after she returned from her honeymoon in Italy. Now, that career step was totally out of the question. "It's a big step backward, you mean."

"Not even close. Seattle's not good enough for you." Natasha put her arm around her as they finished crossing the street.

Natasha had been Meg's best friend since they'd found they had matching Malibu Barbie dolls in preschool. Natasha had warned Meg that Rachel was a player, but Meg hadn't imagined that her sorority sister would go after Romain when she'd asked her to be a bridesmaid. Or that he'd jump on the offer. Until the day she'd gotten Romain's phone call from the gate at Sea-Tac, before he and Rachel boarded their rescheduled flight. She pushed away the memory and smiled at Natasha. "Thanks for coming. I hope you haven't started the wedding cake yet. I'll pay you for it if you have started. We can feed it to the ducks in the park."

"Cake isn't good for ducks. Besides, I called the couple I'd turned down last week and sold it to them. She thought your design was beautiful." Natasha owned her bakery, A Taste of Magic, on Bainbridge Island. She catered to the tourists who liked having fancy cupcakes to eat along with her coffee while they walked through the small town's streets. For the past year, she'd also been making wedding cakes. "I have a check for your deposit refund in my purse."

"I hope the cake doesn't bring them bad luck." Meg unlocked the door to the lobby, and the group followed her into the elevator. Finally, she unlocked the door to her apartment. As they entered, they stood around behind Meg, staring at the chaos.

Last through the door was Dalton, who'd been her big brother's best friend since he'd arrived on the island. Before passing through the doorway, he hugged her. His arms felt safe, making her want to lay her head on his chest. After an hour or two in that position, she'd be fine. She reconsidered, since it was probably not the best look for a jilted, brokenhearted fiancée.

"He wasn't good enough for you, anyway." Dalton stepped back, breaking contact. Then he punched her in the arm. "Welcome back to the boonies, Magpie."

Dalton was the only one who ever called her that. Typically, she found it annoying, but today she was so grateful for the extra help, he could call her anything. "Come on in, brat, and help me move my meager belongings home."

She pointed out the furniture she was taking, including her grandmother's china cabinet, her desk, and the papasan chair she'd bought in college. The rest of the furniture was Romain's. He hadn't liked her mishmash of yard sale furniture finds, so she'd sold most of it when they moved in together. She handed Junior a pile of blankets to protect the furniture. Especially the china cabinet. Then he and Dalton started moving the larger items into the truck.

"Mom, will you and Aunt Melody pack up the kitchen?" Meg didn't even look up as she told them the few things not to box up. The kitchen had been Meg's domain. Right now, she was on autopilot, and if she stopped to think, the tears would start to flow. Again. Biting her lip, she refrained from crying. Not in front of her family. "All the dishes, silverware, glasses, pots, and pans. And all the appliances except the Keurig on the counter. It's all mine."

Natasha went into the living room and started boxing up Meg's complete series of Nancy Drew, Trixie Belden, and the Hardy Boys titles. "I'm assuming *all* the books are yours?"

"Exactly. I should have realized that before saying I'd marry the guy. You can't trust a man who doesn't read." Trying not to run, Meg headed to the bedroom to pack her clothes. At least in here she didn't have to worry about someone seeing her crying. She taped up a box for her shoes, but most of her clothes fit into her three suitcases. She needed to remember to check the coat closet. She had a North Face puffer in there that she'd paid too much for to leave. As she emptied her side of the closet, she froze.

Romain's new tuxedo hung by his suits. She ran her left hand over the smooth fabric, imagining him standing there, watching her. The engagement ring on her finger still sparkled even as pain dulled her senses. She could keep it. Wasn't the rule if she didn't break the engagement, she got the ring? She took off the ring, studying the marquise-cut diamond and platinum setting. He'd picked out the perfect ring. He just wasn't the perfect man.

Meg tucked the ring into the breast pocket of the tuxedo. Romain had bought his tuxedo. He'd shuddered when she'd suggested getting a rental for the day to save money. *Someday when he puts this suit on, he'll find the ring.*

Meg imagined the moment when he pulled it out and realized he'd made a horrible mistake. He'd try to call her, but Meg wouldn't answer. Romain was dead to her. Just like her fantasy of a perfect life.

She ran her hand across the top shelf to ensure she hadn't missed anything. Her fingers brushed a bundle. She pulled it down and realized it was a money clip with five hundred dollars in it. Romain's cash stash. Their just-in-case money. She'd contributed to what used to be their fund. He'd probably forgotten to take it on vacation with him.

"You should take the money. It will help pay for your moving expenses." Dalton stood at the doorway, watching her consider the cash. He walked inside and stood next to her. "He owes you at least that."

Meg fanned out the money. "He does, but I'm not taking all of it." She peeled off a hundred-dollar bill and tucked it and the money clip into the tux pocket with the ring. Then she handed two hundred to Dalton. "Share this with Junior for your time and gas money."

Dalton stood close enough that she could smell the aftershave he'd used since he'd been a teenager. Musky and woody at the same time. Like he'd stepped out of the forest on his way to build a log cabin.

"Meg, I'm sorry about this. But he wasn't the guy for you." Dalton pushed a lock of hair back away from her eyes. "You deserve so much more."

A cough made her jump.

"Hey, Meg." Natasha stood at the doorway, watching them. "Your mom wants to know what you're doing with the wedding gifts."

"I'll come and sort them. I'll be responsible for sending back the ones from my relatives and friends, but the others, Romain's going to have to deal with." She stepped away from Dalton, clearing her head of his forest smell. She had work to do. "I'll need another box."

Meg returned to the living room and saw her mom sitting on the papasan chair, putting all the lace pieces of her wedding dress into a garment bag. "Mom, leave that."

Mom searched the floor for the last few pieces of lace. "I'm not letting you throw this out. You paid too much for it. Maybe we can save it."

Meg picked lace off Watson's fur and put it with the rest of the dress. "I don't think even a miracle could save this. I was furious last night. I'm glad the dress distracted me."

Aunt Melody snorted. "Felicia has always believed in a patron saint of lost causes."

Ignoring her sister, Mom zipped up the bag and headed to the front door to take the pieces of the dress downstairs to the van. Meg watched her go, knowing that she couldn't say anything to change her mind and reeling from her mom's guilt trip that still hung in the room over destroying the expensive dress.

It didn't take long to sort and pack the wedding gifts, so after cleaning out the pantry and boxing up what she could save from the fridge, Meg looked around the apartment. She stepped out on the balcony to retrieve her fern, which was somehow still alive, and paused to take in the view. "I'm going to miss you, Space Needle," she declared as Natasha joined her on the balcony.

"Bainbridge Island has views, too. Including the Space Needle and the rest of the skyline. We can walk to the dock every time you want to see it." Natasha hugged her. "Come on. If we're done here, the guys want to catch the next ferry home."

* * *

When they got settled on the ferry, Meg went up to the observation deck to get a cup of coffee and to keep Watson happy. She found a rear-facing seat at the stern and watched the city disappear into the distance. She would be living less than an hour away, but it might as well be across the world. They'd gone outside to sit, and the spray from the fog stung her face as she fought the tears. She'd cried enough over Romain's betrayal, but now she realized, it wasn't the man she was grieving. It was her life.

She was desperately searching for a silver lining in all this. Then it came to her. The book she'd been talking about writing since she was in high school. A real-life guide to solving mysteries. Not how to be a private investigator. But instructions for a normal person like her—a way for all people who wanted to crack cold cases or figure out who trashed the park by using a well-proven method. Or at least it had worked when they were in high school. Her mood started to lift, but then she had a thought.

She hadn't even seen the signs of her fiancé's betrayal. She felt a wave of depression overwhelm her again.

A man's angry voice brought her out of her anguish.

"The woman doesn't know what she wants or what she has, for that matter. Don't worry about the advance. She'll be grateful for even the part we tell her about," the man continued, his tone even harsher as he stood by the rail near Meg, his back to her and Seattle.

What a jerk. Meg scooted closer on the bench as she wiped the tears from her face. Mom had always said the best way to get over something was to get involved in something else. Maybe she could help the woman this man was trying to cheat. Unless he wasn't going to Bainbridge to meet with her. He could be talking about someone somewhere else. Maybe she had her mom's love of hopeless causes, as well.

"I brought you hot chocolate to warm you up," Dalton said, suddenly appearing on the deck. He held out the cup. She turned toward him and saw the man give them both a dirty look. Like she'd been trying to listen in on his conversation. Well, she had, but he was the one who'd interrupted her pity party.

"Thanks," she said as she watched the man go back inside the passenger cabin. She took the cup but didn't take a drink. Hot chocolate was always too hot when you first got it. She'd learned that lesson years ago. Still, the warm cup felt good in her cold hands. It was late May, but warm weather typically didn't arrive in Seattle until late June. Being outside on the ferry only made it colder.

"Do you know him?" Dalton followed her gaze.

Meg shook her head. "No. I overheard part of his conversation. He's not a nice guy."

"I got that feeling from him, too. It's funny how you know sometimes." Dalton leaned on the railing, watching Seattle disappear. "Look, Magpie, Bainbridge isn't that bad. And who says it's forever? You'll be back on your feet sooner than you think."

Meg sipped her still-too-hot hot chocolate, not sure what to say. She could tell him that she felt broken. That she needed a whole new life. A new purpose. In other words, she could open up and let him into her head. But Dalton was only trying to be nice. He wasn't offering a free counseling session. "You're right, of course. But it feels like a step back. At least I'll be employed again."

"I heard you're going to be working at the bookstore." He moved to stand closer to her, his back to Seattle, breaking her view of what she was leaving behind.

It didn't occur to her until later that he might have moved to that spot on purpose.

"I'll be manning Island Books from three to ten Thursday through Saturday and sometimes on Wednesday and Sunday. It's too bad I'm not a writer. I bet I'd get a lot of work done." She stopped trying to watch Seattle disappear. Bainbridge was her new life. Not there. "Thanks to Aunt Melody, I also got a second gig. I'll be working as an author's assistant for Lilly Aster."

"L. C. Aster, the mystery author? I just finished reading her last book." Dalton looked impressed. "Her summer home is beautiful. I helped my uncle with the flooring when it was being built."

"Well, if there's anything I do know, it's how to solve a mystery. My name might not be Nancy, and this isn't River Heights, but I think I can be useful to Ms. Aster. Besides, it will get me inside that house. I'm looking forward to seeing it. I wonder what my first assignment will be. Researching what it's like to be a spy with the CIA or maybe tracking down jewelry heists that haven't been solved?" Meg had imagined several different topics her first assignment could involve, and she'd also envisioned having coffee with the author as they discussed their favorite books.

"I haven't seen that look on your face since you solved the mystery of who was spiking Coach Bailey's energy drink. Did you ever tell him it was the cheerleader adviser?" Dalton glanced around her at the upcoming dock. "Hold that thought. We need to get back in the vehicles. We're almost at Bainbridge." Dalton worked on the ferry, so he knew all the whistles and noises.

The announcement came after they were already on the stairs. She followed Dalton down to the vehicle level and climbed into her car. Watson sat in the front, with the rest of the space in the Honda Civic taken up by plants and boxes. While she waited for her turn to drive onto the island, she thought about working for Ms. Aster. Maybe this was the start of her new life. She'd joked about writing at the bookstore, but maybe she'd try her hand at a guidebook about solving mysteries as an amateur.

She might have missed all the signs between Romain and Rachel. But that had been her heart talking. She knew she could do this investigation thing. And after some time working with the famous *New York Times* best-selling author, she'd have even more tools and maybe some experience.

Now all she had to do was convince Uncle Troy, the town's police chief, to let her help investigate the next murder on Bainbridge Island. Unless the dead guy was Romain. Because if her ex-fiancé ever showed his face again on the island, she'd be at the top of the suspect list. With good reason.

Meg Gates is no loser. She stared into the rearview mirror and rephrased her badly phrased affirmation. "Meg Gates, that's me, is on the way to being Bainbridge Island's top consultant for murder investigations."

The woman in the mirror didn't look convinced. Maybe she'd start small, like trying to find a missing clock.

It worked for Nancy.

About the Author

Photo by Angela Brewer Armstrong at Todd Studios

Lynn Cahoon is an award-winning, *New York Times* and *USA Today* bestselling author of cozy mysteries including the Kitchen Witch Mysteries, the Cat Latimer Mysteries, the Tourist Trap Mysteries, the Farm-to-Fork Mysteries, the Survivors' Book Club Mysteries, and the Bainbridge Island Mysteries. She is a member of Sisters in Crime, Mystery Writers of America, and International Thriller Writers, and her books have sold more than a million copies. Originally from Idaho, she grew up living the small-town life she now loves to feature in her novels. She now lives with her husband and two fur babies in a small historic town in Eastern Tennessee and can be found online at LynnCahoon.com.

- An Amateur Sleuth's Guide to Murder — Lynn Cahoon
- Seven Secret Spellcasters — Lynn Cahoon
- Six Stunning Sirens — Lynn Cahoon
- Dying to Read — Lynn Cahoon
- Vows of Murder — Lynn Cahoon
- Olive You to Death — Lynn Cahoon

Kensington Publishing Corp.
Joyce Kaplan
900 Third Avenue, 26th Floor
US-NY, 10022
US
jkaplan@kensingtonbooks.com
212-407-1515

The authorized representative in the EU for product safety and compliance is

eucomply OÜ
Marko Novkovic
Pärnu mnt 139b-14
ECZ, 11317
EE
https://www.eucompliancepartner.com
hello@eucompliancepartner.com
+372 536 865 02

ISBN: 9781516111770
Release ID: 153060870